She wasn't aware of when he took her in his arms. Jeannie only knew that she had been racked by this terrible anguish, suffering alone as always, then suddenly she wasn't alone anymore. Paul was there, encouraging her to accept his strength.

"Parents are damn vulnerable," Paul said, breaking the silence.

It was an odd moment of true giving, of two-way understanding in which one doesn't see or think.

Both Jeannie and Paul experienced only the sensation of each other, drawn together and alone no longer....

Dear Reader,

It is our pleasure to bring you a new experience in reading that goes beyond category writing. The settings of **Harlequin American Romances** give a sense of place and culture that is uniquely American, and the characters are warm and believable. The stories are of "today" and have been chosen to give variety within the vast scope of romance fiction.

Sharon McCaffree enjoys writing stories in which the characters are mature adults. She feels, as we do, that romance and marriage go hand in hand and get better with age. We know that you will enjoy *Now and Forever.*

From the early days of Harlequin, our primary concern has been to bring you novels of the highest quality. **Harlequin American Romances** are no exception. Enjoy!

Vivian Stephens

Vivian Stephens
Editorial Director
Harlequin American Romances
919 Third Avenue,
New York, N.Y. 10022

Now and Forever

SHARON McCAFFREE

Harlequin Books

TORONTO • NEW YORK • LOS ANGELES • LONDON
AMSTERDAM • PARIS • SYDNEY • HAMBURG
STOCKHOLM • ATHENS • TOKYO • MILAN

Published April 1983

First printing February 1983

ISBN 0-373-16004-6

Printed in Canada

Chapter One

The telephone would not stop ringing.

Jeannie Rasmussen stirred restlessly, her night-clothes sticky in the muggy heat, her sleeping body instinctively protesting that the slight breath of air coming in from the window was unseasonably hot for this time of morning. She tried to focus on the clock barely visible in the predawn glow. Surely not four thirty?

Despite the absurdity of the hour, the phone shrieked for attention.

"Oh, all right," she groaned, her hand awkwardly slapping around the bedside table trying to find the receiver in the dark.

Groggily she wondered why Dad or Mother Rasmussen had not answered the extension in their room, because they always complained that her duty calls from the hospital awakened them.

The hospital!

In a flash Jeannie was out of bed, throwing off her nightgown and reaching automatically for the stack of clothing she always placed nearby before she went to sleep.

But the clothes were not there.

Nothing was in its right place!

Even after turning on the dim bedside lamp, she was still unable to find the strident phone. Disoriented, she paused, naked, momentarily puzzled by the strangeness of the bedroom arrangement until her dulled con-

sciousness finally recognized that she was *not* in the
Rasmussens' Hawaiian cottage that had been her home
for the past twelve years. She was in her St. Louis apartment. Remembering that fact pleased her so much that
it did not occur to her to be alarmed by the early call.

"You'd think after three months I'd be used to my
own apartment," she fumed as she draped her discarded nightgown sarong-style around her and walked
down the short hall to her noisy kitchen phone. It was a
wonder the din hadn't wakened Bruce.

"Hello?" A yawn interfered with her intention to
identify herself.

"Mrs. Rasmussen, is that you?" The intense voice
didn't even wait for an answer. "This is Jill Craig.
Mother just called—Billy's taken sick and it sounds like
appendicitis. I hate to bother you but I remembered
you said you're to have today off."

"That's all right," Jeannie soothed drowsily, the
nurse in her automatically attempting to calm the
caller. One of her most necessary duties as head of
the Honolulu pediatrics intensive care unit had always
been to reassure frantic parents. She could transmit
confidence without even thinking. But it would be nice
to go back to sleep. She could almost do it standing
right there at the wall—just close her eyes, relax a little.

"We're driving to the farm right away. If you could
just show Mr. Raymond around the apartment? His
wife won't be coming with him, but I'll leave a note for
him to give her." The woman's nervous voice seemed
to drone on hypnotically. Glancing into the darkened
living room, Jeannie could make out the shape of the
couch and lamp she had so recently purchased—she
and the bank. And beyond it in the dining nook, her
lovely table and three chairs. The furnishings were a bit
sparse. But with just herself and her son, they did not
need much to start out. And she could gradually add
more.

Her lips curved in a self-satisfied smile. So she was

not still dependent on the domineering Rasmussens. She had escaped!

The thought that at last she was building a private life for herself and her son excited her.

"... he'll be able to contact me." The woman's pause indicated she was expecting an answer.

"I see," Jeannie lied politely, actually shaking her head in her attempt to clear her foggy thoughts.

"Thank you so much," the woman sobbed.

Jeannie frowned guiltily. "Now explain again about this Raymond... what did you say his last name is?"

The phone was silent.

"Hello? Mrs.... ah, Craig?"

Jeannie couldn't accept it. Surely the woman had not actually hung up?

Insane!

She stared into the receiver like a comic-strip character expecting some answer to come flowing visually out.

"Hello. Hello?"

"Mom?" A sleepy voice called out from the other bedroom.

"It's all right, son," she answered softly, cradling the receiver before she hurried back to her room to pull the nightgown on properly and add a robe. But her modesty was unnecessary. When she entered Bruce's small room, he was again sleeping peacefully.

Noting that his pajama shirt was wet with sweat, she reluctantly closed his window, deciding that trying to depend on evening breezes was not going to be a satisfactory way to cut down on her utility bills; Missouri just did not cool off enough on August evenings.

She closed her own window and turned on the central air conditioning before finally settling uneasily on the edge of her bed to puzzle out the strange call. In the humid stillness of her room though, it was difficult to think. She laid her robe aside, hoping that the air conditioning would do its job soon. The woman had mentioned appendicitis. Could she have been a neighbor, perhaps, needing a nurse? The idea did not seem probable because in the three months since Jeannie had moved in she had simply not had time to get acquainted with her neighbors. And since she did not wear a uniform to work, she doubted that many people seeing her come and go would guess her profession.

Of course she had talked occasionally with that one couple across the hall. The man always spoke in a worried tone, rushing his words as if he had only a few moments to spare before hurrying to another job interview. He had been laid off so long from the Chrysler plant that he had sent his hungry children back to his parents' farm. But he and his wife remained in town, picking up odd bits of work while they tried to sublease their apartment.

Craig! That was the man's name. And they had given her their extra key in case any prospective tenants stopped by while they were away. They were desperate to get out of their lease commitment.

"There goes my day off," Jeannie moaned, realizing that Mrs. Craig must have made an open appointment to show the place to that Raymond person, and was expecting Jeannie to fill in for her. And it would have been her first day off in six weeks! Frustrated and disappointed, she sank down against the warm sheets.

She needed more sleep; she had stayed up much too late the night before. But it was difficult to relax. She kept thinking of all the things she had hoped to do: eating a picnic lunch in the park while she heard the free symphony concert at the outdoor bowl, browsing at the library, shopping for a new blouse. It would be just her luck that the man would come too late for her to do any of those. And she had worked so hard scrubbing her kitchen and vacuuming the apartment the night before, just so she could get out for the day.

Feeling slightly martyred, she was tempted to go ahead with her plans anyway. But almost as soon as the idea occurred to her, she knew she would never do it. She had been through too many financial problems herself to let down another troubled parent.

"Damn, damn, damn!" Jeannie tossed about restlessly, ashamed of her selfish thoughts. Normally she took the world one day at a time and expected little. But since her control over her life was so new and precious, she found this demand on her personal time unsettling.

For some while she lay thinking of the man named Raymond, hoping he would come early and take the apartment so she could get the pitiful Craig family off her conscience. Not until the few brief moments before exhaustion finally claimed her did the hazy hope enter her mind that he might even be a neighbor she and Bruce would like.

HE WILL NEVER WANT TO RENT IT, Jeannie thought when she caught sight of the stranger.

From her kitchen window she watched the tanned, black-haired man stroll slowly up the long sidewalk from the front parking lot, seemingly in no hurry as he examined the building in front of him. The late afternoon sunlight glistened off his hair and Jeannie wondered if the highlights were actually gray. He moved as if he were a young man, but then, in this day of physical fitness one could not always predict age by appearance alone.

"I should have known he'd be that way, taking his time about things." In exasperation she glanced back around her kitchen where the stack of letters, a pile of crisp ironing, and her freshly polished shoes indicated the numerous postponable tasks she had done, just to fill time while waiting for him to arrive. Absentmindedly she sloshed her rubber-gloved hands in the laundry she was doing as she watched him stroll about the yard. The anger and frustration she had felt toward him as the day dragged on had finally given way to fatigue, and she was beyond being upset with the man.

But her waiting around all day did seem rather pointless. She could tell at a glance he was definitely an unlikely candidate for the Craigs' apartment.

As he continued to look around, she was amazed that the 100° temperatures did not hasten him inside. The asphalt blacktop in the parking lot behind him was blistering and buckling, sending out waves of heat that shimmered in visible distortions. She could hardly understand his continued interest in his surroundings. From the look of his tailored trousers and the gleaming white shirt he wore unbuttoned at the collar, she guessed that he had left an equally well-fitting suit jacket in his car—undoubtedly his air-conditioned car. It was not likely that a man who dressed so elegantly would be interested in their humble apartments.

The complex was situated in a raw, new area of west St. Louis County, and was populated mainly by young couples just getting started in life. Each building was stubbornly alike, housing eight families in a two-story structure whose center concrete stairwell had been left partially open to the elements. Calling the roofed, iron-railed area a breezeway hardly disguised its obvious money-saving purpose. But Jeannie liked the openness because it drew the sunlight and fresh air a little closer. She could never get too much of nature, even in cold weather.

The place suited her. It was more reasonable than most two-bedroom apartments she had priced, and unlike most urban complexes, it had some lawn around it. The builders had cleared out all the trees except a wooded hillside behind Jeannie's building; but despite the rawness, the area was nice for young children. She felt her son could have room to stretch those growing legs of his, and even shout with joy once in a while without disturbing neighbors too much.

But she doubted that the handsome man who was giving the area such scrutiny needed those options.

As Jeannie followed his line of vision to the rock

sculptures decorating their circle drive, she had to admit that the sight was not pleasing. The elaborate plantings that the management had put in without installing a backup watering system, had long since withered away in the summer heat. Even the freshly sodded lawn had browned out. The only sign of life in the whole area was the patch of red and white petunias Jeannie planted and watered herself.

Between the heat and the dismal external appearance of the complex, she was amazed that he did not make a snap judgment condemning the place and leave. She liked a man who had patience enough to search out the right home for his family. She tried to think of what positive points he should know about. There was the woods, of course. And she could explain about the lawn. Everyone said that bluegrass bounced back, beautiful and green, once the first cooling autumn rains came.

As the man moved out of sight to enter the building, she quickly set her washing into the second basin to rinse. Not wanting to keep him waiting, she planned to run a comb through her hair and pull on her sandals. But just enough soap had slipped over the cuffs of the rubber gloves to create a suction, and she was still tugging unsuccessfully at them when the doorbell rang. There was no point in rushing to answer it because her hands would be too slippery to turn the knob. After a few more unsuccessful tugs she resorted to surgical techniques, peeling the cuffs downward, snapping them off wrongside out. They could be sorted out later.

As she hurriedly padded barefoot across her carpet she thought she could hear footsteps crunching away from her door and so gave up any idea she had of improving her appearance. She would never forgive herself if she let him get away.

"I'm sorry, I was covered with soap." She called out the apology even as she was swinging open the door.

The man's back was to her as he was walking away. He

paused, then turned around tentatively, as if he did not know what to expect. He was of medium height, a fit, solid man in his forties if she were any judge of age— even more out of place than Jeannie in this area of very young couples. Her welcoming smile was warm, as it occurred to her for the first time how nice it might be to have people nearer her own maturity next door.

"I didn't mean to keep you waiting so long." Her low-pitched voice was formally polite. "Can I help you?" As she eased her T-shirt into a smoother line around the waistband of her shorts, she wished that she had run to freshen up the moment she had noticed that elegant man outside. She would hardly make the best impression for the neighborhood.

He walked slowly back toward her, his expression puzzled, and Jeannie decided on closer scrutiny that he was too craggy and muscular to be called elegant. And it was gray peppering his temples. But despite the privileged aura set by his well-chosen clothes, he looked extremely competent, just from the way he moved, in the alertness of his eyes, in the no-nonsense way his large hands gripped the scrap of paper at which he was looking.

"Are you"—his lips quirked briefly as he assessed her with equal frankness—"the widow in Two C?"

"Mrs. Craig didn't say that?" Jeannie glanced down at his note.

"Oh, but she did." He held up the message he had just untaped from the Craigs' door. It was brief:

Mr. Raymond:
    Family Problem. Widow across hall in 2C will show you apt. Have left details on kitchen counter. Call us collect.

Mrs. Craig.

"'The widow in 2C'. How ignominious. My son will never let me live that down." Self-consciously she ran a hand through her short brown hair, which, although set the previous evening, had drooped into soft waves. "I can see I'm going to have to work to improve my image."

"Actually I was rather relieved when I saw you," the man admitted. "When you said you were covered with soap, I didn't know what to expect." His glance roved quickly over her, taking in her shapely legs and bare feet, the full curves of her figure softly molded by her casual clothes.

"I see what you mean." Jeannie suddenly felt a little flustered, wishing even more forcefully that she had dressed more appropriately for meeting a stranger.

Apparently realizing he had inadvertently made her uncomfortable, he was suddenly all business as he thrust out his hand. "I'm Paul Raymond."

"And I'm Jeannie Rasmussen." Her hand seemed engulfed in his huge grasp. She felt how heavily callused his palms were, noticed the blunt fingers and trimmed nails—he had working hands with powerful wrists. In fact his whole body appeared so powerful that, even though he was of average size, he gave the aura of filling her doorway. She shuddered a little in nervous reaction as he released her fingers.

"I guess this temperature is a shock, coming out of air conditioning." He misinterpreted her reaction.

"You must be so hot," she said hurriedly. "I'll get the key so you can cool off in the Craigs' apartment."

She was back quickly.

"Do you and your wife have teen-aged children?" she asked conversationally as she led him across the breezeway. "My son gave me strict instructions this morning that I was only to rent this place to old people like myself who had teen-agers." She laughed softly at the memory.

"Your boy is a teen-ager?"

"No, twelve. But he feels quite grown-up."

"Too young to see his mother realistically, though."

He studied her intently. "I would hardly classify a woman in the fullest bloom of life as old."

The comment was so surprising that she momentarily fumbled the key in the lock.

"Well, you know how children can be. ..."

"Don't I just." His voice was amused. "In answer to your question, yes. Both my children are teen-agers. They think I'm a dinosaur."

She laughed. "Bruce would be delighted to have some children his own age here, even if their father is a dinosaur. That's been the only drawback of this place for us. Most of the couples here are extremely young. Once the Craigs move out, the only other children in our building will be two babies downstairs."

She had got the lock to turn and pushed the door open, but he appeared in no hurry to go inside.

"The Craigs are the people wanting to sublease?" he asked.

"Yes, in fact 'desperate' would be a more accurate description. He's been out of work for months and things are so bad they've sent their children to his parents." She glanced through the doorway. "It looks as if they've carried most of their furniture into the living room, ready to move."

As she led the way inside, muggy heat even more blistering than that in the breezeway engulfed them.

"It's going to be awful in here," she gasped the apology. "They've shut off the air conditioning."

"It shouldn't take me long anyway."

She watched him pick his way around the mess of furniture. The cluttered appearance was so horrible that she felt some encouraging explanation was necessary.

"The room isn't as small as it looks with all this stuff in here. I can show you my living room later if you want to see how the apartment would appear normally."

He didn't answer as he worked a path into the kitchen. Even it was piled high with boxes, so he paused only long enough to glance at the appliances and take the note Mrs. Craig had left for his wife.

Jeannie was encouraged that he did take longer examining the three bedrooms. They were quite small, because they were carved out of the same amount of space that housed her two bedrooms. So there was little she could extol about them. As she stood in the hall waiting for him, she noticed him study each one intently, seeming to measure them spatially in his mind, as if deciding how his furniture might fit in.

"The bathroom is a nice size." She opened the door near her to prove her point and was relieved that at least it was not littered with furnishings.

"She mentions in this note" — he was glancing at the paper as he came out of the smallest bedroom — "that there is something wrong with the tub. Do you know what it is?"

"No, the one in my apartment works perfectly." Jeannie slid back the shower curtain and looked at the faucets and drain. They appeared all right. And there was no accumulation of rust to indicate constant dripping. Puzzled, she carefully turned the nozzle control from shower back to the tub fill. "Maybe there's not enough water pressure on this side of the building."

It happened so fast. She couldn't have prevented it.

He was standing in the doorway, wiping the sweat off his forehead, watching her check things. And she was leaning over the tub to turn on the cold water. They both listened to the more-than-usual pause while no water came out, and she was about to say that inadequate pressure must be the problem, when the forceful blast from the overhead nozzle hit her full in the face.

She could feel the iciness soaking her body as she slid inexorably backward into the tub. It was as if everything were happening in slow motion. She could sense the tile wall coming roughly toward her and flung up a hand to protect her head. But the hurtful contact never came. Somehow Paul Raymond had almost instantaneously crossed the room and dragged her up into his arms. As he was breaking the force of her fall, the water momentarily enveloped them both, then he had regained his balance and pulled her to her feet. Or more accurately, he had pulled himself to his feet. Jeannie was draped against his chest, unable to find firm footing.

"I don't believe this," she moaned in apology, aware that she was dripping all over his shirtfront and that his head and shoulders had become soaked when he grabbed her. She was a short woman, and she stretched with her toes, wondering where the floor was, until he gently lowered her enough that she could stand. For moments longer he held her loosely, giving her a chance to regain her equilibrium. When Jeannie could move away, she was mortified, and it showed.

"At least we know what's wrong with the tub." He, on the other hand, appeared unbothered as he bent to turn off the water, which was still splattering out against his pants leg. "They have installed the shower handle backward."

"I've got you all wet," Jeannie stated the obvious.

"Actually, in this heat it feels pretty good. I'm tempted to jump back in."

Jeannie wondered how he could possibly be that calm and polite. Surely he must be offended by her soaked appearance, if not his own. She could feel her shocked nipples hardening, thrusting against the clammy shirt. Hazy, horrifying recollections flitted across her mind of a TV feature she had seen about some tavern's Miss Icy T-Shirt Contest. The smiling girls had allowed ice water to be poured on them, and then paraded before the cameras, while the men voted on— She could not help groaning aloud.

"I'm going to have to change clothes," she mumbled as she slipped past Paul Raymond. She resisted the urge to fold her arms across her stimulated breasts, thinking such anguished modesty would only call more attention to her embarrassing situation. She wished she could act as sophisticated as he was doing. "I know you need to look around some more, but—" She tried to conquer the shakiness in her voice.

"You can go ahead and lock up. I've seen enough inside. I can look around outside on my own." She couldn't interpret his expression as his glance took in her erotically hardened bosom, then moved quickly to her face. "But I'd appreciate borrowing a towel if you don't mind me dripping in your breezeway a minute? I'll hang it over the railing when I'm done."

"Of course. I should have thought...."

Hurriedly she led him back to her own apartment and got him the towel, then left him at her doorway sopping up the moisture on his shoulders and hair. Only when she had retreated to her own bathroom did she fold her arms across herself, her face vividly warm.

Once she had calmed down, it did not take long to towel off, spread a quick puff of talcum powder across her body, and change into dry underwear and an orange printed muumuu. But she was still in no hurry to face the prospective tenant again. Half-heartedly she combed her damp, curly hair, grateful that although it never held a style long, at least it dried quickly and half-way attractively.

She studied her reflection in the medicine chest mirror, wondering why Bruce thought thirty-two was so ancient. It had been rather touching, what Paul Raymond had said about a woman her age being in the fullest bloom of life. She wasn't, she thought, all that bad-looking for a mother. Her complexion was fine, a little pale perhaps, but she might have time to get some sun before the weather turned cold. And surely her large brown eyes would not look so tired on a normal day, especially not after she got around to putting on makeup. It was gratifying that her brown mop of hair didn't have a trace of gray; that made Bruce's remark about "old folks like yourself" a little less hurtful.

Bitterly she leaned closer to the mirror, wondering if she had looked as foolish as she felt. She regretted the shower incident. Until that fiasco she had been somewhat hopeful that the apartment would appeal to Paul Raymond. Longingly she thought how ecstatic Bruce would have been if *two* teen-agers had moved in next door. And assuming Mrs. Raymond was as likable as her husband, it would even have been nice for Jeannie. She would enjoy being around adults with whom she had something in common.

Although it seemed likely she had goofed up any interest the man might have had in the apartment, she decided she could at least offer to answer his questions. With one last glance at herself, she shunned applying makeup and went looking for him.

She had halfway expected Paul Raymond to have left. But when she emerged into the breezeway, he was standing with his back to her, looking out at the small lawn with picnic tables and charcoal braziers that abutted the back parking lot. Taking her cue from his relaxed posture, she guessed that he was actually enjoying the view. Beyond the grassy area was the tiny woods Jeannie so liked. That land fell steeply away down a rugged hillside to the highway leading to the apartment complex. Since the slope was unsuitable for building, the contractors had allowed it to escape the voracious bulldozers. Native Missouri oaks, hickories, and maples grew in profusion, almost hiding the hundreds of cracker-box houses that filled the valley below.

"I see you've discovered our woods!" Her voice perceptibly showed her own pleasure in the wild area as she stood beside him. "Does your family enjoy the outdoors? Those woods are beautiful in the early mornings. I've found toads, lizards, squirrels, lots of birds' nests...." Her face glowed as she talked. He was looking at her intently, and she wished she could fathom his thoughts.

"I suspect that my son is rambling down there now,"

he eventually said. "I left him to explore while I checked out the apartment."

His eyes slid over her impersonally. "You look nice and fresh, without any ill effects from that faulty shower. I take it from that outfit that you've been to Hawaii."

"I was a nurse in a Honolulu hospital for years. Muumuus were most women's second uniform!"

"Were you transferred here? You don't often hear of people voluntarily leaving the Hawaiian climate for the midwest."

"That's what everyone says," she laughed. "And after this month I'm inclined to agree with them. But I got a job offer here too good to pass up."

"Oh?"

"I was chief nurse in a children's critical-care ward in Honolulu when some Saint Louis professors came through on a medical tour. Their universities are starting a joint research unit for children's disabilities, and they hired me as nursing administrator of the program."

"You must be good if they would draft you all the way from Hawaii."

"I suppose they needed broad experience, and working in a major pediatrics hospital can certainly give you that." She started to tell him more about her new work, for it was a subject she found endlessly fascinating. But just then Bruce's shout bellowed from below. The interruption was unmistakable and unignorable.

"Hey, mom! We got a flat!" His exuberant voice preceded his lanky body up the stairs.

"Slow down," she urged, wondering how she could have missed hearing his creaking camp bus pulling up the hill. "Was anyone hurt? Did you get the flat on the way home or—"

"Not on the bus. Your car. *You* have a flat."

"But those tires are new!" Jeannie was almost disbelieving.

"Well, it's flat anyway. I saw it as I got off the bus. I met this red-headed kid outside, though, and he said he'd help me change it. But we need the key to your trunk." He didn't even notice Paul Raymond behind her as he bounded into Jeannie's apartment.

"I suspect that the 'red-headed kid' he met is my son." The man joined her at the top of the stairs. "Don't look so worried. Greg has been helping me with cars for years. He'll have no trouble changing the tire."

He had no way of knowing that her concern was not just polite regret at seeking help from strangers, although she felt that too. But she was seriously wondering how she could possibly stretch her month's budget to include another new tire. When Bruce returned and noticed the stranger with her, it was Paul Raymond who solemnly introduced himself and began explaining how to approach the job. They were well down the stairs, talking comfortably together, before Jeannie had recovered herself enough to follow.

"THAT'S WHAT MY SON NEEDS—a role model like Greg. He's loving this."

Jeannie was sitting under the one tree near her parking lot, her sandaled feet stretched in front of her as she watched Greg Raymond meticulously showing Bruce how to change the tire. Paul Raymond was beside her, his arm resting lightly on one knee as he kept an eye on the two boys.

"You know, it's funny how boys imitate their elders," she continued her train of thought. "I noticed how carefully you were instructing Greg on safety procedures, and how he then talked in the same patient way to Bruce. Do you suppose *my* son will be inspired to share any of that same patience with me?"

"I'm afraid boys save their best behavior for their peers." He seemed a little preoccupied as he continued to watch the two put the hubcap back in place, so Jeannie did not feel rude in leaving him alone.

"I think I'll go get them both a Coke. They haven't been able to enjoy this shade like we have." She was on her feet and starting toward the sidewalk when she suddenly recalled that she had intended to show him more of the apartment building. "I really have neglected my duty! Your wife would want you to look at the coin laundry room. And there's a storage closet off the breezeway."

He stood up, but waved aside her offer. "You go ahead. I'll just stroll around down here."

When she returned with the Cokes, Paul Raymond was not around. So she resumed her spot under the tree and half listened to the boys' desultory conversation as they lounged in the shade near her. It amused her how Bruce was trying to stretch out in the same lanky way Greg did, but was still too baby-awkward to achieve the same effect.

When she saw Paul Raymond eventually return to her car and examine the flat tire the boys had placed in her trunk, she thought he looked very hot and tired. It dawned on her that she should have offered him a drink too, perhaps a beer. But because his wife was not along, she hesitated.

"I think this tire can be repaired," he told her as she joined him. "But if you decide to leave that spare on, have the service station men tighten it with an air wrench. Greg is strong, but I'd like to see those bolts tighter for highway stress."

"Thank you, I will." She watched him close the trunk, then decided to compromise with propriety. "Would you like a Coke too?" she offered shyly.

"Not really, it's almost six o'clock. We'll have to be off."

"Six o'clock!" Bruce exclaimed, jumping to his feet. "Gosh, Mom, I forgot to tell you. You're going out to supper tonight at six thirty with Coach Hannah."

"I'm what?"

"Going to supper with Coach Hannah. He's asked

you so many times and you always say you're too tired after work. So today I told him you could go because you had the day off." He looked proud of himself.

"Bruce, you didn't!" Jeannie couldn't hide her dismay.

"I can stay by myself. I'm grown up."

Hearing a masculine chuckle behind her, she flashed Paul Raymond a quelling look.

"I can see you have some further explaining to do with your matchmaking son." He was undaunted by her scowl as he cheerfully handed her the boys' Coke bottles and moved off toward the parking lot.

"But, Mom. You told me the only reason you couldn't go with him was—" Bruce's eyes widened as he tried to figure out why his mother seemed displeased.

"I know what I told you," Jeannie interrupted, aware that an amused Paul Raymond was still listening. "You definitely asked Bill Hannah to take me out tonight?"

"Sure. And he said to tell you six thirty."

There was nothing she could do except go. But she certainly didn't like the idea. "Six thirty is an uncivilized hour," she mumbled unfairly.

"I envy your date," Paul Raymond called out with a grin, almost as if they were old friends. "You're going to be wonderful company tonight."

Belligerently she watched him and Greg climb into a sleek Mercedes sedan.

"Very funny," she snapped back.

"MR. RAYMOND SAID he'd be seeing me," Bruce enthused, his mother's displeasure forgotten as he hurried back to the apartment with her. "That means they'll be moving in soon, doesn't it?"

"No, it's just a polite expression. It doesn't mean anything."

"But do you think they'll move in?" he persisted.

"Greg has a sister too. She's fifteen and a half and can drive. Do you think she has a license?"

"I would guess not; you have to be sixteen to get a license in Missouri." She picked up her towel as she passed the railing where it was draped.

"Greg is fourteen. They're from Arizona, maybe you can get it younger there. Greg says she's a pain in the neck, his sister."

"I'm certain all sisters are pains in the neck to you boys. See how lucky you are not to have one."

"Yeah, but it would be nice to have a brother."

"All you'd do is fight. Now come on, you might pick up this camping stuff you dumped in the breezeway while I get ready."

As she headed into her bedroom she called out, "And Bruce, when you're finished with that, add a few lines to the letter I wrote Grandma and Granddad Rasmussen. I left it out for you on the kitchen table."

"Okay. I'll tell them about our new neighbors."

She closed the door on that optimistic comment. Poor Bruce! She felt certain he was doomed for disappointment. As she thought of Paul Raymond, she felt a little sad—for Bruce, for the Craigs, and, strangely, for herself.

"He didn't even say good-bye...."

Chapter Two

"I promise you, Jeannie, this man isn't going to drag you to bed with him after he takes you home. He's my husband's boss!"

"That makes a difference?" Jeannie's generous mouth tilted as she warily eyed her colleague.

"Of course it makes a difference. He's in his sixties. And besides, I know him."

"You said you knew Harry Whatshisname too."

"You've never forgiven me for Harry?" Dr. Karen Matthews, the psychologist assigned to the disabilities screening unit, perched on the edge of Jeannie's desk and tried to appear contrite. But her quarry looked unconvinced.

Although Jeannie's shy manner won instant friendships—people wanted to protect her—Karen knew that it also masked remarkable capabilities and independence, and that independent spirit was especially activated at the moment. The psychologist could almost measure the resistance running through her friend's thoughts.

"I forgave you, all right," Jeannie responded, "after I'd sewn up the tear in my blouse and called your precious Dick to come and pick up his drunken buddy. But I'm too old for this nonsense, Karen. So no more tricking me into blind dates; I don't trust you."

"Tonight wouldn't really be a date. I just need an even number because we're having Dick's boss over to dinner. He's a widower too."

"I'm not a widower."

"Widow then. Quit nitpicking. Will you come?"

"No. I especially don't trust you when you ask me to make even numbers at dinner. Both times I've fallen for that story there's been an extremely uncomfortable single man there, eyeing me suspiciously."

"Seriously, this time I'm not trying to fix you up. We're long overdue in entertaining Dick's boss. But he's a terrible conversationalist and since Dick's aunt can't come, we need help."

"In that case I am sorry. But I have to go shopping for a new blouse this evening."

"That's the weakest excuse I've ever heard."

"I mean it. I don't have any clothes for when the weather turns cooler. And you Missourians keep promising me this heat will soon pass. I want to take advantage of the two-day sale at Neiman-Marcus, and I wasn't able to get there yesterday, after all."

Karen wondered if further cajoling would do any good. She doubted it. In a pastel sleeveless dress Jeannie looked particularly cool and aloof—almost too aloof. The psychologist found it intriguing that while Jeannie was warm and open with her married friends, she always threw up a protective facade around strangers, particularly single men. Intriguing, because she could hardly still be grieving; her husband had been dead for years.

"It's the fact that she doesn't seem to want men to be interested in her that makes her so attractive..." Dick had commented after the fiasco with his friend Harry. And Karen, while not knowing what quality made women appealing to men, had to agree that Jeannie had a certain...?

Naive voluptuousness. That would be the term to describe her. And... tired.

"You work too hard." Karen abandoned her invitation and bluntly expressed her concern instead. "Did you work again yesterday? I'll bet you've skipped half your days off since you've been here. That's no way for an adult to live."

"No, I didn't work yesterday. Something came up at home." Obviously she intended to end the conversation before it got too personal, for her polite smile prefaced what Karen had come to label as Jeannie's I-like-you-but-stay-out-of-my-life voice. "I'm not going to continue working on my days off much longer. But it's taking me awhile to get used to this new job." She began walking toward the door, leaving Karen with little polite choice but to follow her. "This is different from hospital routine—easier in many ways but still with a lot to learn. And I do have to get this screening done by the end of August so we'll be ready to set up our therapy programs. You're planning to work with our conference group this weekend too, aren't you?"

"Yes, I am, and quit trying to change the subject. Psychologists recognize all those maneuvers, you know. Dick and I worry about you spending so much time alone."

"Karen, it's not so terrible being alone." Her laugh was genuine. "As a matter of fact, after twelve years being dependent on others I love being on my own. You can't imagine what a luxury it is to occasionally do just what Jeannie Rasmussen wants to do."

There was no mistaking the conviction in her voice. In any other person it might have been militant, but in Jeannie it came out almost a sad plea: Get off my back!

"Okay, I give up on you. No more fixing you up," Karen promised, allowing herself to be propelled out the door. "But just remember that after a while all that independence gets old. I'd gotten mighty tired of it by the time I met Dick. It's a lot better to wake up each morning and find your own man filling your bed."

"I've already had a man in my bed. But I'm glad you're happy, Karen," Jeannie laughed softly, unperturbed. "We don't all need the same things, you know."

"The hell we don't. Freud learned that years ago."

Jeannie frowned as she closed the door on that parting remark. Well-meaning as Karen was, she just couldn't seem to understand that the two of them were dealing with life on different levels. And independence was the level Jeannie valued above all others. She'd fought too hard to achieve it. Certainly she could have done without a bargain blouse from Neiman's and gone to Karen's dinner instead. But she felt she had to stop this matchmaking before it got out of hand. If she couldn't maintain control of her own life here, she'd have nothing. Loneliness, she knew, was a small price to pay for independence.

After walking over to the closet to dig out a brown paper bag, Jeannie anxiously checked the clock before realizing that she no longer had to grab lunch on a haphazard basis. It was hard getting used to the luxury of time—no more wolfing your food down in anticipation of a hospital emergency.

But marvelous too!

With a sigh of contentment Jeannie sank down at her desk and began spreading out her lunch. But once that was accomplished she ignored the food and looked critically around her office. Sometimes she just needed to reassure herself that this well-paying, challenging job was really hers. Only seeing the trappings of her small success convinced her.

Jeannie's office was a large one, combining the efficiency of a desk, typewriter, computer, and wall-hung storage units in one corner, with the pleasantry of a plush conference area in the other. A green couch and deep chairs surrounded a colorful area rug, and an expandable wood table was nearby, closed now to its smallest position since no staff meetings were scheduled that week. But one folding oak conference chair was set up in case someone coming into the office needed a place to work.

It had everything Jeannie needed to do her job well, and it was a comfortable environment as well. The only disadvantage to the decor, she reflected as she picked up a large red apple, was that it had no windows. She loved lots of sunlight. The three-story building housing the University Research Center had been designed with the lounges and typing pools around the windows, and the private offices walled into a cluster in the center. Despite being on the second floor, Jeannie had felt as if she were working in a cellar.

Pete Randing, the affable paper salesman who stopped by their building weekly, had eased her irritation by helping her install an artificial window. She had discarded his suggestion of a mural of Waikiki, but when he alternatively suggested a unit with a plant light, she knew she had found her answer.

Foliage plants did very well in her mock window, and occasionally she brought a geranium or begonia from its thriving spot in her sunny kitchen, just to provide a little temporary color.

Everything would be perfect, she thought, ... *my job, my life, if my friends would just accept that I don't mind being alone.*

With my son, of course, she mentally amended. Having a twelve-year-old around was hardly being alone.

Feeling somewhat drained after surviving the battle of wits with Karen Matthews, Jeannie hungrily bit into the apple.

Its juice was delightfully cool so, like a child, she ran her tongue across her lips to catch every delicious droplet. Good fruit was such a delight. After twelve years enjoying the abundance of fresh Hawaiian harvests she had found it difficult to readjust to mainland produce, picked before its time and stored to ripen. But happily the local fall apples were now arriving in the St. Louis markets. Jeannie had bought a huge bag the previous week and it was almost gone, Bruce enjoying the fresh fruit as much as she.

Noisily she ate the remainder of the apple, thinking as she did that it was extremely handy to have a private office; you could crunch with impunity and bother no one.

She had crunched her way through a second apple and had just opened a package of celery when a loud knock on her door only momentarily preceded a huge bear of a man who lumbered cheerily up to her desk.

Oh, no! Not a second scene today, she thought helplessly before managing to mask her displeasure at seeing Pete Randing.

"Hello, darlin', did I catch you at lunch?" He peered at the leavings on her desk, noting the two decimated apple cores and the pile of celery. "Good Lord, what kind of lunch is that? You don't need to be on a diet."

"I'm not on a diet." Jeannie smiled cautiously, trying to conquer her annoyance at the interruption. "I love fresh produce. I was just thinking of you, by the way."

"Fresh produce makes you think of me?" He grinned. "You know I've offered to make an honest woman of you. Marry me and we'll help each other raise our kids."

"Pete, you're absolutely crazy! You propose to everything in skirts."

"You're the only woman I've proposed to in the last six weeks," he denied. "From now on I'm concentrating my wife search; my kids will love you."

"Actually I was thinking how much I enjoy this plant window you helped me set up." Pointedly Jeannie ignored his bantering. She liked Pete. But since she was never fully certain just how serious his cheerful advances were, she was always undecided whether to joke back or get firm. The situation made her distinctly uncomfortable.

"I did do a good job on that window." Pete easily allowed himself to be diverted. "It looks almost real since you put the curtains around it."

"I appreciate your helping me install it." Hungrily she picked up a piece of celery, then, thinking of the noise, changed her mind and put it down. "What did you want?"

"Actually I just stopped by to say hello. I'm taking off early today to check out a vacant apartment."

"I thought you were going to rent the one you saw last week. Didn't the court approve it?"

"Oh, the judge thought it was a great place to raise kids. But when I figured up dollars and cents I realized I couldn't afford it. And my ex-wife won't give up the kids if I cut her alimony. So I'm back to looking for a cheaper three-bedroom place. It's hell to find in a decent neighborhood."

Jeannie nodded sympathetically. She knew the brief anguish she had gone through before coming across her own housing.

"Say, darlin', there wouldn't be an apartment available in your neighborhood, would there?" he asked earnestly. "It's an ideal location."

No, no! Jeannie felt panic-stricken.

"I'm afraid not," she lied uncharacteristically, her stomach churning madly as she tried to convince herself that there was a chance Paul Raymond might decide to take the place. But just remembering the smooth way his tailored trousers clung to his muscular thighs, the sleek luxury of his imported car, she knew it was no-go. Her vocal chords tightened in silent guilt.

"Well, I was just hopeful. If I don't find something soon, I'm afraid my ex will change her mind or the judge will set aside the custody adjustment. I miss those kids so damn much!"

"I'm sorry, Pete," she stammered hesitantly.

"Too bad I couldn't talk my ex into giving me back the house and taking over my room in the boardinghouse in exchange." His joking voice held a note of bitterness.

Jeannie stared at him miserably, the guilt almost oozing out her pores. But she couldn't say anything. She couldn't.

"For chrissakes, I didn't mean to come begging for sympathy." He brightened boyishly. "What about taking an afternoon off next week when I come on my rounds? I've got a friend who has a private swimming pool we could use...."

"I can't, Pete." Her answer was too immediate. She fumbled for an explanation. "We're winding up the screening for the children who will be admitted to this new therapy program and—"

"Some evening, then?"

"Right now I have such a lot to do in the evenings, getting Bruce ready for his new school."

"Maybe after school starts would be better," he agreed thoughtfully. "If I can get an apartment located, I'll be tied up for a while myself, getting my own kids in school. So good, we'll make it later."

"Yes, well..." Jeannie couldn't quite voice the definite refusal she preferred to make. She wondered if guilt were all-transparent.

The thought of her deception about the vacant apartment still troubled her after Pete left. So much so, that she collected the rest of her lunch and tossed it into the wastebasket. Her appetite was gone.

"But dammit," she told herself as she buried her head tiredly in her arms, "I couldn't stand to have him next door. I've been through that sort of thing before. He'd be over all the time on one excuse or another; his kids would get Bruce involved...."

"You've become selfish, Jeannie." Thinking of the Craigs and of Pete, she didn't much like herself. Groaning miserably, she buried her head even deeper on her desk.

"Damn Paul Raymond for not fitting into our corner of the world!"

THE AFTERNOON GOT BETTER. Never one to consider herself a victim in life, Jeannie had given herself a stern lecture and was back at work well before the lunch hour was over. At first it was slow going. But after an orthopedist had stopped by with some X rays for her files, she had managed to get her concentration honed in. His advice on a couple of cases she had been doubtful about helped her get her own professionalism in order. By quitting time she was well satisfied with the stack of completed screening reports she had sent on for processing.

At home that evening she was tired, but it was a good tired, based on accomplishment, not despair. She had even given in to Bruce's suggestion that for once she fix them a late-evening snack.

While she was popping some popcorn, she impulsively set out on the kitchen table a box of photographs she had run across while waiting for Paul Raymond the previous day. That was one accomplishment for the day, she thought ironically. The box of family pictures that she thought she had lost in moving had turned up underneath the shoe polish.

When he was younger, Bruce had loved going through family pictures. And she found he had not changed, for as soon as he roamed into the kitchen to get his popcorn he delightedly settled down to delve into the box.

"I don't remember this one. Was it at Okalu Park?" He stuffed a handful of buttered corn in his mouth before grabbing up a snapshot of himself scrambling up a jungle gym. He must have been about four years old, his happy face covered from ear to ear with grime.

"No, the playground at your nursery school, I think." Jeannie watched him reach for another picture.

"Look, here's my third-grade picnic. That was when Toby and I won the astronaut relay." He thumbed through several pictures clipped together because apparently they were of the same event. She noticed that his greasy fingers were leaving marks on the photographs.

"Oh, Bruce, I shouldn't have gotten those pictures out until we finished the popcorn; we'll ruin them." She handed him a napkin to wipe his sticky fingers.

"But I'll be carfbg..."

"Don't eat with your mouth full." She grinned as she collected the pictures.

"Huh?"

"Don't *talk* with your mouth full, you know what I meant, young man! Here, I'll hold the pictures for you to see while you finish your snack."

Content with that, he leaned back and munched away, sometimes laughing aloud at the views she showed him.

"That's the time you took me to the zoo so early in the morning."

She glanced at the one she had just selected. "Right, the zebras. Remember how much more active the animals were then, than when we usually saw them in late afternoon?"

"Monkeys must like to get up early."

"Unlike you," she teased. "Oh, look, here's that picture of your dad. How did it get in with the zoo things?"

Carefully she eased the ragged picture from the stack. The young face staring sightlessly back at her stirred up few recollections. It had been taken for high school graduation, just a few months before they had been married. And it troubled her that her reaction was so blank.

"Am I going to look like him?"

She remembered the game Bruce used to love to play: "Tell me about my Dad," he would say when they were alone. And she would spin long stories of what she and his father had used to do together, recognizing in his question the small boy's need to put reality behind the father who had died before he was born. But his father's life had been so short that after a while the stories had become repetitious. He seldom asked anymore.

"Mom?"

She forced her thoughts back to his question.

"No, you look more like my side of the family, I think. Your father was blond. But you'll be tall like him. And you have his name, you're a Junior, of course."

"Grandma said I— Oh, I forgot to tell you. Grandma and Grandad Rasmussen called last night."

"Called, from Hawaii?" She felt alarmed, not believing that they would casually go to all that expense.

"What did they want?"

"Just to talk, I guess. Oh, I remember. They wanted to know what we were doing."

She frowned in puzzlement.

"Because it was the day Dad died, you know. I said that you had gone out to supper with Coach Hannah and that I was fixing myself a jelly sandwich...."

My God, no! She was frozen in silent horror, stunned, unhearing. The black memories washed over her in alarming clarity. Memories she had hoped would never recur—the interminable length of the Rasmussens' self-absorbed grief, those ridiculous black armbands they insisted on dragging out every year on the anniversary. And the pitiful tales they began to tell their friends about their son, "the war hero."

Jeannie felt nauseated.

It was like going through it all again—the scenes, their tight-lipped disapproval when she finally put a stop to dragging little Bruce through their annual reincarnation of grief.

"Mom, are you okay?"

She stared at him blindly, beyond tears. She was certain that she was going to be sick.

"Mom?"

His touch on her arm was featherlight.

She smiled brokenly, controlling the nausea and resisting the impulse to embrace him protectively. Wouldn't they ever let him alone, let him grow up to be his own man?

"I was just thinking. I'm sorry, son." She fumbled around with replacing the photographs.

"Do I have to go to bed now?" He thought he had done something wrong.

"It's time," she said gently. "You have to leave early for camp tomorrow since it's the last day." The picture of her husband seemed to be staring at her from the top of the photograph box.

Bruce slowly pushed away from the table, never anxious to give up and go to bed. He would be a night owl someday.

"Son..."

"Yeah?" He turned back eagerly, hoping for a reprieve from his curfew.

"Would you like this picture of your dad to put up with your other photographs?" She visualized the mirror over his dresser lined with smiling faces of favorite friends.

"Sure." Agreeably he reached for it—more, she thought, to please her than from any interest of his own.

But a boy should know what his father looked like.

"I'll put it up next to my canoeing partner. Jimmy Hale gave me his school picture last week—he's under my St. Louis Cardinals bubble gum card."

She smiled spontaneously at that, the nausea miraculously gone. She had been terrified of the effect on Bruce of the Rasmussens' annual pilgrimage to the shrine of Death. But apparently he was better insulated than she.

For a moment he looked like a man. "Are you sure you're all right, Mom?"

I'm not sure of anything anymore.

"I'm fine, Bruce."

"I love you."

"Now I know I'm all right." She smiled lovingly at him. "Good night."

Chapter Three

"Did you notice how significantly this girl's school-work improved during the quarter she took daily swimming lessons?" Jeannie passed a file across the table.

"Her parents had noticed the improvement," Karen Matthews recalled as she studied the file. "They came in for a conference with me. We discussed any changes at home that might have accounted for her progress but we couldn't come up with a thing. However the swimming wasn't discussed."

"It just makes me wonder...." Jeannie took the file back and studied it thoughtfully. Karen watched her with interest, since during the months they had been working together she had developed great respect for Jeannie's judgment.

"As a matter of fact," Karen added, "I included that girl in the screening only because her parents have been pushing the school for help. Her doctors and counselors say that since she has no major behavior problems and her symptoms are mild, they feel there is no present cause for concern."

"But her parents have five older children; they should have a good feel for what is normal behavior," Jeannie pointed out. "So if they worry about her day-dreaming, her frequent irritability and short attention span, I'd be inclined to listen to them. I have a gut feeling we could help this girl now without waiting the year or so it will take to collect the data we need for most of our participants."

"But the doctors haven't found anything."

"I know that, but some doctors treat children only slightly worse than she with rigid physical conditioning such as we recommend for a hyperactive child, or one with cerebral palsy. In similar cases I've seen," Jeannie went on, "the doctors varied widely in their diagnoses of what was wrong, but the amazing thing was that they all noted behavioral and academic improvement after instituting regular gross motor exercise."

"So you think we could help her even if we don't know what's wrong?"

"If she were my child, I'd think it worth a try to return her to daily swimming and get her into our testing program. I think the center doctors would approve that recommendation."

"Then I'll authorize her inclusion," Karen agreed, taking a form from her briefcase.

They finished the remaining two files in a few minutes.

"And that's it!" Karen exulted, glancing at her watch. "We've finished the screening by six o'clock. Not an early start on the Labor Day weekend, but—"

"Six o'clock!" Jeannie moaned. "And I still have several errands to run. Will it foul up your plans if Bruce and I don't get over to your party until eight or so?"

"That will be fine. Dick's sister is always late anyway. I'm just glad you've agreed to come. I promise it will be just family there, no eligible men. Don't forget your swimsuits. As hot as it is we'll probably be swimming after dark."

"Bruce is looking forward to meeting Dick's nephews. I wish we had children his age around our neighborhood."

"That couple with the son you liked didn't take the apartment across the hall?"

"I guess not. No one has moved in and it's been over a week since the Craigs left with the rest of their things."

"If you don't watch out, your conscience is going to get the better of you," Karen warned. "You're not going to tell Pete Randing about that vacancy, are you?"

"I feel that I ought to," Jeannie admitted dejectedly as they finished putting away their papers. "I know what it's like to struggle to keep your family together. I feel sorry for Pete and the Craigs."

"But Pete Randing next door? Jeannie, you know that would be a disaster. He's so anxious to get remarried he wouldn't give you a moment's peace. And since you haven't wanted to date any of the men I introduced you to, I doubt—"

"I've been going out with a man named Bill Hannah," she objected. "He's Bruce's camp coach. The three of us will probably do something this holiday."

They had started to leave, but Jeannie turned back to her library shelves, selecting a large reference book, before she rejoined Karen at the door.

"It doesn't look as if you're planning a fun weekend if you're taking work home," Karen pointed out.

"This isn't work exactly. I'm trying to sort out a problem of my own and I can't find much helpful literature." She looked up as if an idea had suddenly occurred to her. "Say, Karen, have you always just worked with kids? I mean, do you know much about older people's hang-ups—parents, for instance?"

"Dating problems for single parents?"

Jeannie laughed out loud despite the concern on her face. "You have a matchmaker fixation! No. I'm trying to figure out my in-laws." She bent over to lock the door.

"Your in-laws? I thought you couldn't stand them. Wasn't that why you left Hawaii?"

"I wouldn't say I couldn't stand them, exactly. They helped me a lot when I needed it and I'll always be grateful for that. Let's just say I found living with them difficult. They were so possessive about my son that it seemed I had to take him away from there or lose him."

"So you want to know how to handle possessive grandparents? I don't mean to pry, but if you really want me to get helpful information for you, I'll have to understand more about your situation than this."

"I've already decided I couldn't handle them, as you put it, if I continued to live under their roof," Jeannie admitted seriously as they started down the deserted hall. "But I want to understand them. Now that Bruce and I are gone, I hope they'll come to realize they can never have my son for their own. If possible, I'd like to resume some kind of relationship with them for Bruce's sake. After all, next to me they're the only family he has."

They emerged into the heated outdoors silently while Jeannie seemed to be struggling with her own sense of privacy. She was choosing her words carefully.

"I probably should have anticipated problems," she eventually resumed quietly. "It had bothered me those few months after we were married, that we lived with his parents—bothered me because Bruce seemed to be so dependent on them."

At Karen's movement of confusion Jeannie explained, "Bruce was my husband's name. That was another mistake, naming my son a junior. Well, anyway, we knew he was due to be drafted soon so I thought once he got settled in the army and we had a place of our own it would work out."

"But he was sent to Vietnam instead?"

"No, he was killed in an accident while he was still in basic training in the States." Her voice was curiously flat. "His parents tell everyone Bruce was a war hero, but he never saw war. Actually he was driving too fast and turned an army truck over on himself. It was senseless and preventable."

"The Vietnam thing fouled up everyone's thinking," Karen said cautiously.

"I know that, and I'm trying to understand their need, in their grief, to make his death seem worthwhile."

"You were saying you should have anticipated problems?"

"Right. I always sensed they were obsessively fond of their son. But fairly soon after he was killed they inherited a small cottage in Hawaii and insisted I move there with them. By then I knew I was pregnant and would need some help. I'd never worked; I had no home, no family to go to. So I disregarded my instincts and went along. And I'll admit it, I had visions of getting my own apartment after the baby was born, of working part-time in glorious Hawaii and playing with my little child among the palm trees and rolling surf." She frowned at her own naive dreams. "That's probably why I married so young in the first place, to have a home of my own. I'd lived with a distant cousin's large family several years after my parents died and I couldn't wait to be in a place of my own. But it didn't work out in my marriage or in Honolulu. I didn't realize I was so ill-equipped to earn my own living there."

"Didn't your husband leave any insurance?"

"Very little. I used some of it to attend nursing school. But I felt I should hold on to most of it for health emergencies and for Bruce's college. Still do, for that matter, though I've had occasion to fall back on it a time or two already. Anyway, in reality the Rasmussens took over my new baby while I worked at a full-time minimum-wage job and also went to nursing school."

"Couldn't they have helped you financially for a few years?"

"Perhaps. But they didn't. They only had Dad Rasmussen's pension as far as I know, no cash inheritance along with the house in Hawaii."

"But still, many families seem to work out temporary child care by grandparents pretty successfully,'' Karen pressed.

"I kept thinking it would get better when they got over their grief. But if anything, it got worse. It was only gradually that I realized how completely they were taking over my son. I made every effort to have some free hours to be with Bruce. But they would object when I played with him, interfere when I corrected him; they even began keeping him up while I was at work so he would be sleeping when I got home. I found myself relegated to visitor status."

"Is that when you left?"

"No, I couldn't afford to. Hawaii is, as you know, an extremely expensive place to live and I was basically stranded there. But once I got my R.N. I took an evening shift so I could be with Bruce in the daytime. I learned to get by with very little sleep. And I learned to be obnoxious about insisting on my rights as his mother. That was hardest. Family scenes are just not natural to me."

"I can see why you're looking for books. Your in-laws do sound peculiar."

"Things got worse the last few years. There was a terrible time when a lonely man next door mistook my friendliness and made a pest of himself. It's rather hard to get rid of a neighbor. And all the time this was going on, the Rasmussens were righteously indignant that I had attracted a man's interest."

"Why should they feel that way? Your husband had been dead for years!"

"That was my thought too. In fact I had become concerned that Bruce was never around young men, the sort of father figures he could look up to, you know. So eventually I began dating some of the friends I had made at work. They were nice men, people who seemed to enjoy taking Bruce places with us. But my in-laws threw some terrible scenes every time I went out."

"That's unbelievable!"

Jeannie shrugged her shoulders sadly. "I made matters worse then by a stupid mistake. One night I guess I was feeling more alone than usual and I stayed out all night with a man. I didn't love him, but I thought I knew him well enough. Actually I did know him well enough, he was a good friend. I knew immediately that a continuing affair wasn't right for me, but I let it drag on several times before breaking it off. Then he was confused and hurt. I came to dread hearing the telephone. He'd call and plead with me, and my in-laws would be hanging over my shoulder berating me for my indecent behavior. That's when I knew I had to get out. I'll probably make other mistakes like that in my life, but I've got to be free to sort them out myself."

Jeannie paused by her car and glanced back at the University Research Center. Her look was almost adoring. "You know, this job was a godsend. I had just decided to use all my savings to supplement the rent on an apartment in Honolulu when I got this job offer—they added a transportation and resettling allowance, and once school starts the hours will be shorter than what I've had in the past and at a higher salary. It was like—like 'somebody up there likes me,' if you know what I mean."

"I'm surprised the Rasmussens didn't try to stop you from leaving."

"Oh, they did. Things got pretty messy and I had to invest a bit in legal fees before finally getting on the plane with Bruce. When I first got here, I thought I would never have anything to do with them again. But once I'd been safely on my own for a while I could see things more dispassionately. I'm writing to them regularly now and I hope I can find a way to mend the fences so Bruce can see them again sometime. After all, they are his grandparents. And besides, if I understand them better, maybe I can avoid some of their mistakes. I'm raising an only child myself and I don't want to mess him up the way they did their son."

"I don't think you have any need to fear that," Karen reassured her.

"Bruce is one of the nicest kids I've been around. You're doing something right. I wish I could advise you on the in-laws, but they're really out of my expertise. I will talk with my colleagues, however, and see if we can come up with some similar case histories for you to read."

"Thanks, I'd appreciate it. No rush, though. I have a feeling understanding can take a long time."

"Forgiveness too," Karen observed perceptively.

BY THE TIME Jeannie finally pulled up outside her home, however, all thoughts of researching her family problems were temporarily set aside. Her primary concern at that point was to get Bruce to help her carry the numerous packages upstairs to air-conditioned comfort. Next year, she vowed, she was going to splurge and air-condition the Ford, if the temperamental old thing didn't present some major repair bills in the meantime.

She·had just started in with a precariously balanced armload of parcels when a woman she had never seen before came striding purposefully from their building— a rather attractive tall woman with reddish-brown hair and a pleasant face. As the woman bent over a lopsided pile of cartons and crates at the curb, a lovely red-haired girl, graceful as a swan, came running out of the building to help. Not wanting to be in the way of their tasks, Jeannie carried her own load toward the breeze-way.

But when she heard Bruce come tumbling down the stairs, she called out in relief, "Oh, good, son! You're just who I need. Help me carry these—"

"Can't it wait, Mom?" he yelled back. "Right now we've got an assembly line going. They bring 'em in from the sidewalk and we tote 'em up the stairs. We're almost as quick as the movers were, getting in the furniture."

She did not make sense of his garbled excuse until she rounded the corner and saw Greg Raymond standing at the top of the stairs, looking, from her angle, like a young red-haired giant. And at that moment she realized whom the graceful girl had reminded her of, knew who the red-haired woman must be. A warm rush of happiness left her smiling foolishly as Greg said amiably, "Hi, Mrs. Rasmussen. We're moving in today. Dad brought some stuff in his car."

"So I see," she laughed, crazily pleased like a kid herself.

Soon they were all standing awkwardly in the stifling breezeway, the three women and the two boys laughingly interrupting each other with introductions, until Jeannie suggested they all finish their unloading, then get together again in her apartment for a cool drink.

"Something cold would taste wonderful," the woman who had introduced herself as Lucille Raymond agreed. "We probably won't have any cool food or drink in our place for a while. Somehow the refrigerator got put in with the other furniture Paul stored at the warehouse, and they've all gone back over there to locate it."

It was not much later that Lucille Raymond was ensconced on Jeannie's couch with her feet propped up and a glass of iced tea in her hands. She was approvingly surveying the living room.

"Your apartment is so pleasant, I must say it gives me real hope," she said. "Frankly, when I first saw this place Paul rented, I had my doubts anything homey could be done with it."

"Mine was just like yours originally," Jeannie admitted. "When I showed Mr. Raymond through last week I warned him that the decorator must have preferred 'early institution.'"

"I'm going to cover the walls and ceiling of my room

with musical scores," Becky announced. "I didn't think I'd ever have enough collected, but since my room is so small I'm sure it will work."

"I thought all teen-agers hung up pictures of rock stars."

"Not Rebecca, of course," Lucille commented. "She's a serious artist. Ballet, you know."

Jeannie didn't know, but she took no offense, having already noticed that Lucille spoke in this vague manner all the time.

"Are you thinking of a dancing career?" she asked Becky politely, just making conversation.

"I'm not sure yet, but Dad wants me to be a dancer. I did win a place as one of the soloists with the Saint Louis Civic Ballet this season."

"You really *are* good, then."

"I'm just a minor soloist," she corrected modestly. "They import their principal soloists from New York. But it will be good experience."

"And maybe it will help you and your father settle once and for all just how serious this ballet career really is," Lucille inserted blandly.

Hoping to avoid becoming involved in what sounded like a sore subject within the family, Jeannie walked over to where the boys were sprawled on the rug examining Bruce's collection of hot-rod magazines.

"Your family may want to take a swim later," she diplomatically changed the subject. "The complex has a pool, and it will be open all weekend."

Her suggestion brought all the Raymonds to their feet, and they were gathered at the living room window, trying to follow Jeannie's directions to the swimming pool, when they heard men's voices coming from the stairwell.

"Oh, dear! That must be the refrigerator," Lucille exclaimed, horrified. "I should have known Paul would get them back here before I've even made a path to get through." The harassed woman rushed across the hall barely ahead of the movers struggling up the stairs.

"I'm staying out of the way," Becky laughed. "When Lucille starts getting efficient, Dad doesn't need any extra help."

Just then Paul Raymond's dark head appeared above the banister. "Hi, punkin." His eyes warmed momentarily as he saw his daughter with Jeannie. "Meeting the neighbors?"

"Sponging off the neighbors already, Dad," Becky grinned, holding up her empty lemonade glass.

"Looks as if there are two spongers," he observed to Jeannie, noticing Greg sprawled on the floor beyond them.

"Not at all. Your children are—"

"Ah, sir." The movers coughed discreetly. The refrigerator was out of its packing box, ready to be rolled into the apartment, but even though Lucille was still fluttering distractedly around inside, several piles of books and boxes barred the way.

"I think I'm needed," Paul Raymond apologized. "Greg and Becky, come on along. Mrs. Rasmussen probably is going out soon." He looked at Jeannie questioningly.

"They're not in the way. Bruce and I don't leave until eight."

"Ah, a civilized hour." He grinned.

She looked back at him in puzzlement a moment before remembering that when last they met she had made some caustic comments about her six-thirty date with Bill Hannah.

"That's right. A civilized hour this evening," she mumbled self-consciously, wondering what it was about this family that seemed to loosen her tongue.

She was to wonder the same thing again after she stopped by the Raymonds' apartment on her way out that evening. She had sent Bruce on down to the car while she dropped off six-packs of Coke and beer for the new neighbors. It seemed a suitable gesture now that Paul Raymond's wife was here too.

When Paul answered her ring, he politely swung the door wide open, inviting her in.

"No, thanks," she explained. "We're on our way out. Is Mrs. Raymond busy?"

"Oh, hello, dear." Lucille came out of the kitchen, wiping her hands on a dish towel. "The children have gone to the pool. As you can see, I haven't been much help getting everyone's things put away. Can you find a place to sit?"

"We're on our way out," she explained again, shyly holding up the six-packs. "I thought, since your refrigerator hadn't cooled down yet..."

"What a thoughtful idea!" Lucille immediately passed the drinks on to Paul to put away, smiling at her in her vaguely motherly way. Jeannie was struck with how instinctively she liked the woman, which was odd, because Jeannie was not by nature gregarious.

"I can't tell you how glad I am that you and your husband have moved in, Mrs. Raymond," she said impulsively. "It will be so nice to have a woman my own age to talk to. Most of the couples here are newlyweds."

"Well, my dear, I'm not—" Her protest was cut short when Paul Raymond laid a hand companionably on her shoulder. With them standing together like that, it was at once obvious to Jeannie that Lucille was several years older than her husband. But his look was affectionate as he interrupted her.

"You two are close enough in age for there to be no difference, Lucille." Then, turning to Jeannie, he added, "It's your fault we're here, Mrs. Rasmussen. You're a good apartment salesman."

"I hope I didn't talk you into anything your wife doesn't like." She looked anxiously at Lucille. "Bruce wanted teen-agers next door, but I was so afraid—"

Lucille was looking wordlessly at Paul, and he absentmindedly patted her shoulder as he cautioned Jeannie, "Becky and Greg are far from perfect."

"Oh, it isn't *your* kids I was worried about. This salesman who visits our office frequently was looking for an apartment like yours—" She stopped short, appalled that she had started to gossip.

"Does he have an obnoxious family?" Lucille asked, wide-eyed.

"I doubt it; I haven't met the children." Jeannie was horrified again at her loose tongue. This business of feeling so at ease with people, you could freely state your opinions had its limits. "I shouldn't have even said anything. It's just that—" Her face was red.

The couple continued to look at her expectantly and she realized with regret that she had to finish with some sort of explanation for what she had foolishly started.

"Well, he's divorced, and he has just talked his ex-wife into letting him have custody of their three children, so he needs a bigger apartment. But I've seen situations like that get out of hand. Hungry kids, dirty laundry, me conveniently next door...." It sounded awful, put that way, and she was ashamed of herself.

"That sounds selfish of me," she rushed on. "He's really quite a nice man. But he is anxious to find a new wife and I suppose if he'd taken the apartment I would have been wary—probably would have been creeping in at all sorts of strange hours just to avoid him."

Self-consciously she tried to smile, to pass the stupid conversation off as inconsequential.

Paul Raymond was absentmindedly kneading Lucille's shoulder so much by then that she pulled slightly away as if he were hurting her. But she smiled gently at Jeannie as she assured her, "Yes, I can see it is better never to get involved in the first place than to have to work your way out of something unpleasant. Now you don't have to worry about creeping in secretly, do you?"

"It would have been impossible anyway. Bruce usually trips up the stairs with thundering noise." Although relieved that they seemed to understand her dilemma, she determined to be more discreet in the future.

THERE WAS an eerie silence in the Raymond apartment after she left. Paul had walked over to a window to watch Jeannie and Bruce drive away in their old Ford, but he still stood there long after they were out of sight.

"Well, my dear brother," Lucille said calmly, "how and when are you going to break the news to her? I assumed your gouging thumb in my shoulder meant I wasn't supposed to explain that I'm only here a week helping you move in."

"You assumed right," he snapped uncompromisingly, not even looking at her. She shrugged and went back to the kitchen, where she was washing glasses; but she did not give up the subject.

"To bring up an unpleasant point again," she continued almost conversationally, "she's going to be more embarrassed the longer she treats you like a married man. I could figure a casual way to let her know tomorrow."

"No!" he exploded.

She was startled by the violence of his objection. Then suddenly comprehension dawned on her face. Unbelieving, she walked slowly into the living room to study him carefully as he continued to shift boxes around, refusing to acknowledge her presence.

She was right. Good Lord!

"Well, well!" she marveled softly. "After all these years...did you get hit by lightning in just one meeting?"

He did look at her then, exasperated, intending to deny her statement. But seeing her face, he frowned. "Dammit, Lucille, you always were clairvoyant where

I'm concerned. You make me feel like a green kid brother again."

She was shaking her head in wonderment.

"By lightning in one meeting?" she repeated.

He was silent a long time, preoccupied, troubled. "You're really going to keep at this, aren't you, like a dog worrying a bone?"

She nodded unrepentantly.

"It was more like getting a kick in the guts," he finally acknowledged grudgingly, giving up his show of moving boxes from spot to spot. He walked back over to the window and stared out dispiritedly.

"She was supposed to show me this apartment—I rang her bell, expecting an old widow lady, according to the note the landlady left me. Jeannie didn't come for a long time, and I was hot and tired and ready to give it up when she finally yelled something from inside and threw open the door. Oh, hell! I sound like a fool."

"So you rented this horrible apartment," she deduced. "I'm surprised the kids haven't complained. It was enough of a wrench for them to leave Arizona so you could open the alternative-energy laboratories here. But to leave your spacious house for this!"

"They probably would have complained if they had seen the luxury condominium I had already subleased for us."

"What?"

"Afraid so." He shrugged sheepishly. "Three big bedrooms, family room with fireplace; the building has an indoor pool. I was looking at this place for my assistant."

"Paul, I can't believe all this!"

"As it is, I guess the kids consider this place a logical stopgap. They know the architect has completed the house drawings and that it should be completed by spring."

"But this place is so small—"

"We'll make out. We've completed construction of

the warehouse at the lab site, so I had room in it to store the extra furniture."

"What happened to the condominium you sub-leased?"

Paul couldn't quite look her in the eyes. "Well, actually, I thought it might be nicer for my assistant than this place. His wife is young and they have two babies. I mean, after all, I was committed to paying that much rent anyway, until the owner gets back."

"So you let him have it at what this place is costing you," Lucille deduced. "And with your honest face he probably doesn't suspect who his landlord is."

She began to giggle helplessly and fumbled around to clear off the couch. "I've got to sit down. This is incredible, so unlike you." She tried to control herself, laughter spilling out anyway. "Well, *not* unlike you. But usually your dramatic decisions are related to business." She shook her head in amazement. "Love at first sight, after all these years!"

"Now don't make more of this than there is, Lucille," he cautioned harshly. "I'm not going to do anything rash."

"Not do anything rash?" she hooted, waving her hand at the confusion in the crowded room.

"I mean like getting married immediately. I learned my lesson on three-week courtships eighteen years ago with LuAnne." Pain crossed his face.

"But you were working it out, Paul," she reminded him, suddenly matching his seriousness.

"Yes, those last months of her life," he admitted sadly. "But then we both knew she was dying of cancer."

He walked aimlessly around the little room.

"I had to give this a chance, Lucille," he groaned, turning to her. "It's stupid, I know—at my age, and on one brief meeting. But I had to! However, as I told you, I'm not rushing into marriage. I have an eight-month lease here, which should give us time—"

"I don't think you could rush that woman into marriage anyway," Lucille interrupted flatly. "Anyone can tell she is reserved by nature, and from that conversation we forced out of her just now, I would guess she is not anxious to get involved with a man."

"I know that," he insisted in exasperation. "I sensed that when I first met her. She tried so damned hard to be formal, and it was obvious how proud she was to be independent. I just didn't realize it was quite as bad as this."

Lucille shook her head again. It was becoming a habit, with all these goings-on. She had a silly smile on her face too as she disappeared back into the kitchen.

"Lucille?"

Her look was benevolent as she stuck her head around the corner.

"Look, my dear Phi Beta Kappa sister, would you please just continue to act as delightfully vague as you always do and avoid commenting on my single status for a few more days? Give us all a little time to get acquainted normally without her throwing up a polite barrier."

"What about the kids?"

"I think they're the logical ones to let her know. When they realize that she thinks you're my wife, they'll straighten things out in a natural way. And by then Jeannie will have forgotten this evening's conversation."

"If it comes up directly, I'm not going to lie," she said doubtfully. "I may be vague, but I'm certainly not distracted enough to forget whom I'm married to. I refuse to act that senseless."

"I'm not asking you to."

His look was so anxious that she reluctantly nodded her agreement. Her grin was affectionate as she reassured him, "I'll do my best to avoid the issue. I still can't believe it, though. After all these years of you ignoring all the women who have been chasing you. Incredible! Wait till I tell your brother. I'm glad you took this rinky-dink apartment after all!"

"You have a nauseating sense of humor."

Chapter Four

At first Jeannie did not notice the car pull up alongside the curb in the No Parking Zone ahead of her. Instead she was grimly preoccupied with the little stream of sweat that was accumulating in a pool along the band of her bra. The early evening temperature was still not cool enough to be comfortable walking, at least not with a full bag of groceries, and Jeannie was regretting her decision to get some exercise...and even more, her impulsive purchase of the watermelon.

The mile walk to the store had been all right, but the worst of the return trip was the four-block hill still ahead of her. All she could think of was how good a cold shower was going to feel.

The man in the parked car almost had to shout her down to attract her attention.

"Do you need a ride?"

It took a few seconds to identify Paul Raymond hanging out of the passenger side of his Mercedes. His silvery opaque sunglasses masked his eyes and she was wary, until she saw the familiar highlights of gray in his coal-black hair.

"Mr. Raymond! I didn't recognize you," she apologized formally as she went toward his car. Her shoulder muscles felt as if they were going to fall apart and she could barely lift the heavy bag enough to rest it against the rear fender. Still, she did not answer his question.

Tempted as she was to hop right in and ride comfortably home, Jeannie hesitated to accept the favor. Past experiences had told her that favors usually brought complications and obligations she didn't always want.

"I'm headed home from work; you wouldn't be taking me out of my way," he said gently, as if reading her thoughts.

"Actually I was torn between wanting the exercise and not wanting to carry this bag," she lied, embarrassed that her reactions were so transparent.

"Then perhaps your bag needs the ride home."

"Now that's an offer I can't turn down," she gave in gratefully. "In Hawaii I could walk to the hospital, but since I've been driving to work here, I've gotten out of shape. Carrying these groceries has almost done me in!"

He came around the car to help her, and when he took the bag, his face registered shock. "What do you have in this thing?"

"A watermelon and a gallon of milk, among other things," she admitted ruefully. "I should have resisted the melon."

"Or used a back pack," he agreed as he carefully put the groceries on the floor behind the passenger seat. "No wonder you looked as if you were going to tumble down any minute. That's what made me notice you in the first place."

"Was I that bad?" Once she was relieved of her burden she was able to laugh. "I was lazy over Labor Day weekend, and I sat at my desk almost all of today. So I thought it would feel good to walk to the store. I hadn't counted on getting carried away in my shopping."

"Are you certain you don't want to ride the rest of the way? That hill up to the apartment buildings is pretty steep."

"I'll enjoy the climb if I don't have to carry anything." She almost believed it herself.

He closed the car door and leaned casually against it, apparently in no hurry to leave. "I know what you mean about inactivity," he mused slowly. "Over the years my work seems to require more and more time at a desk. It gets to you."

"But you jog regularly, don't you?" she asked. "I noticed you out a couple of mornings over the holiday." A fleeting image of the natural and controlled way he had been moving up the hill flashed across her memory. She recalled her surprise at his agility, having thought that with his muscular build he would be the stolid weightlifter-type. Instead he had looked like an Olympic runner who was aging gracefully.

"Jogging about three times a week is just enough to keep me feeling functional," he explained. "But I'm surprised you saw me. I usually run at sunrise."

"I've always been an early riser. In a way it's a plague because I need a nap by early afternoon."

"Which you probably never have time to take."

"Usually I put my head down on my desk during afternoon coffee break. That fifteen-minute doze does wonders." She was going to enlarge on medical advantages of short naps, then stopped herself, thinking she shouldn't hold him up any longer.

"Well, thank you for the ride—for my bag's ride, I mean."

"Your bag can ride with me anytime." He still did not move to leave. He was looking past her to where the sky was just beginning to change colors. "It's finally cooling down a little," he observed idly. "I may change shoes when I get home and stretch my legs a minute myself. Do you mind me joining you for part of the return trip?"

"As long as you don't jog!"

"You sound like Lucille."

"I don't blame her for not running with you. Even from my kitchen window I could tell you'd be a hard man to keep up with."

"If I join you this evening, I promise a nice, slow walking pace up the hill," he laughed.

"I've heard that before from you natural athletes," she responded skeptically. "Bill Hannah took Bruce and me on a so-called walk Saturday and almost rushed us to death. Bruce didn't tell me his coach is a long-distance runner."

"Bill Hannah is the man Bruce tried to fix you up with?" His eyes crinkled in amusement.

She was surprised he had remembered that from the day they had met.

"I guess it *was* funny, but I didn't think so at the time," she admitted. "For years I've been so busy with work and raising Bruce that I haven't dated. Apparently my son decided I should."

"Is he trying to pick out a new father?" She thought his tone was antagonistic but his composed face convinced her she had been mistaken.

"It wouldn't do him much good if he were," she eventually said slowly. "Marriage is not on my agenda. That's why I get along fine with his coach friend. Bill likes his single life."

With that Paul Raymond moved lazily from his perch against the car, apparently bored with the conversation.

"I guess I'll get your groceries on home," he said as he opened the driver's side. "I'll probably catch up with you close to the apartments."

"Maybe your wife would join us if she knows we're just walking...or the children?"

He seemed about to explain something, then apparently changed his mind. "I'll ask everyone, but I doubt that Lucille will want to come. Tennis is her addiction."

"I wish I'd known she's that good. We've set up a game for tomorrow evening."

"Now you're forewarned." His eyes warmed briefly. "If she talks you into betting, insist on odds. I always do!"

After he drove off, Jeannie felt strangely lonely. But consoling herself that she would probably have company soon, she resumed her walking. Before long she found that just being rid of her burden had greatly refreshed her. She quickly reached a natural pace, her arms swinging relaxed and easy, her body movements all in harmony. The motion felt good. Her earlier discomfort was soon forgotten, and she began to observe the developing loveliness of the evening. Gold streaks were now splitting the blue-white sky at the top of the hill. Jeannie's steps slowed and she became absorbed with the changing appearance of the clouds as their wispy shapes formed and reformed with orange-yellow linings.

I'd like to be a photographer right now, she mused, stopping completely to watch in wonder the living horizon. *Or better yet an artist who could mix colors and catch just one moment.* It occurred to her that an artist would almost have to take a photograph first to keep the scene in mind, so fast did it change. She wondered if this meant there was wind beyond the horizon, even though not a breath of air stirred at ground level. Almost while she watched, the sky began to assume a general red hue, indicative, she had read somewhere, of dust in the atmosphere. Perhaps the color and activity were nature's forecast of an approaching change in the weather.

This ought to be a regular part of the Center's therapy, she decided. *Required: A walk at sunset at least once a week. Will combine study of meteorology, art, and philosophy, with physical fitness and—*

"You haven't made much progress. Maybe I should have insisted on driving you home."

The quiet voice was startling. She couldn't believe that Paul Raymond was approaching her and she was barely halfway up the hill.

"You ran!" she accused.

"I didn't either," he retorted almost teasingly. "You've been dawdling." She looked at her watch in automatic self-defense.

"I've been watching the sunset," she grudgingly admitted when she realized how much time had passed. "I hope our children have noticed it."

"I doubt that they have. The last time I looked they were all out back playing catch." He matched his steps to her shorter stride. "I asked if anyone wanted to join us and got a lot of blank looks."

Jeannie laughed aloud. "Bruce would never trade a chance to play ball with friends for a walk with his mother! It's a shame they're not seeing this beautiful sunset though."

"Lucille's watching it from our living room. But you know kids. They aren't as aware of the need for regeneration as we adults are."

"I was just thinking about the healing powers of nature too! A walk outdoors on pretty evenings would be so good for the children I treat."

"You're involved in treatment then, not just basic research?" He took her elbow long enough to guide her around a hole in the sidewalk.

"Oh, yes. Many of our children have symptoms that doctors have been treating empirically for years with some success. We'll continue the better programs, but we're trying to understand the cause of the symptoms. We'll be taking extensive family histories and running batteries of physical tests, as well as charting dietary and personal habits. And we'll be feeding this information into computers for comparison with findings in other centers throughout the country. We're anxious to develop better treatments for dyslexia and hyperactivity."

"Dyslexia, is that the eye thing of seeing backward?"

"That's one way of describing it. But the visual shuffling is not always consistent. We really don't understand it; there may be several diseases or disabilities causing related symptoms." She stopped suddenly, ashamed that she had been talking so long about her own interests. "You said you've been at a desk too much lately," she reminded him. "I wondered if you'd been transferred here."

"No, I'm starting my own business. I hope to market products for alternative power, alternative to electricity and petroleum products, that is." With that terse reply he seemed to lapse into deep mental concentration—so much so that Jeannie walked quietly beside him, unwilling to break the silence, even though she was interested in hearing more about his work. His answer had been enlightening in one sense, though. Struggling to get a business established explained why a man who had apparently lived rather well in the past would now be pinching pennies in a tiny apartment. She admired his determination and the cooperation of his family.

When they eventually reached the grounds of the apartment complex, he broke the silence himself.

"How far is your office from here?" His personal question, coming after such lengthy preoccupation, took her by surprise.

"About five miles east."

"And you haven't had any more flats?"

"No, I had that tire repaired and put in the trunk as a spare."

He seemed relieved. "I thought the rest of your tires looked in good shape. Do you drive on the highway?"

"Yes, I get on it just past where you picked me up this evening. The office is only a few minutes from here." She glanced at him curiously, wondering why he seemed so interested in her car.

"Did you think my old Ford looked on its last legs?" she asked lightly. "The mechanic where I bought it assured me it has another three years—maybe!"

He shook his head, not totally amused by her frank response.

"I put your groceries just inside the front door. Bruce said it was unlocked so I figured you wouldn't mind."

Mentally shifting gears to his new train of thought, Jeannie was nonetheless appalled at her son's laziness.

"You mean he let you carry our groceries up yourself? I'm so sorry!"

"It was no problem."

"I'm really sorry about our imposition," she insisted, "And you probably haven't even eaten yet. Look, would your family like to have some watermelon with us later? As you noticed, there's lots of it!"

He appeared uneasy at her determination to even up their favors.

"Thanks, but we can't tonight...ah, we have other plans. I think I'll take one more turn around." He seemed uncharacteristically nervous and couldn't get away fast enough.

Puzzled at his sudden change of behavior, she climbed the breezeway stairs alone. The friendly encounter with Paul Raymond had ended so strangely that she wondered if she had said something offensive, or if he was just a moody man.

Somehow the question troubled her.

A WEEK later Jeannie still had not discovered the truth about the Raymonds.

As Paul drove home from seeing Lucille off on the plane, that realization bothered him a little. He'd had a perfect opportunity to tell her as he was loading Lucille's suitcase into his car. Jeannie was just leaving on a date with that coach fellow, and he could tell by her greeting that she thought it was he going on a trip, not Lucille. He should have casually remarked, "No, I'm just seeing my sister off. Lucille's got to get back to her husband."

But he hadn't. It had been so pleasant getting acquainted informally all week, seeing her son cavorting with his kids after school, hearing about her conversations with Lucille. She even had no barriers up with him. They usually met on their way to work in the morning—

they actually left about the same time through no machinations on his part. Lucille warned him he was making a mistake in letting the misunderstanding continue this long. But he didn't want this natural friendliness to end yet.

Every casual contact with Jeannie had only increased his fascination with her personality, with her looks. True, she was not a beauty in the accepted sense of the word; fashionable clothes would never sit quite right on her short, curvaceous frame. But his interest in her was becoming a hurtful ache.

Seeing her leave with that coach Bruce talked about had grabbed at his insides like a wrenching cramp. Even Lucille had noticed his jealous anguish. How sophomoric!

One thing about it, he thought bitterly: He would feel better if he saw her with several men instead of just one. Damn that jock! If he got a commitment from her before she could learn to trust Paul —

The honking of a horn brought his attention back to the traffic, and he cursed himself for his carelessness, but before long his mind was wandering again.

He wondered if he was wrong to approach his relationship with Jeannie so slowly. But she seemed to be at a stage in her life when she should not be rushed. He didn't want that for himself, as a matter of fact. He had married LuAnne after only three weeks of mad courtship, and what a disaster their marriage had turned out to be! He doubted he could survive a second love relationship like *that*.

Perhaps if he and LuAnne had not married so quickly, or if they had recognized the strains in their relationship before they decided to have Becky, they might have realized that LuAnne was *born* to be a dancer, that her talent was so superb she could never be happy without a major soloist's career. Then maybe they would have started differently and could have worked it out. But they had thought she would be satisfied as a wife and mother, still having short dancing roles with ballet companies in the cities where Paul was currently working. They had thought Paul would not resent cutting back on the high-paying traveling assignment as an engineer troubleshooter, thought it would not matter if he delayed his own timetable for accumulating the money and experience necessary to start a research business of his own.

It hurt Paul to admit he had regretted having to change his career, yet in fairness to himself he knew he could have accepted that choice had LuAnne been happy. But before long it had become clear that local dance companies, no matter how long Paul arranged to be in one major city, did not offer the challenges LuAnne's talent needed. He eventually took a routine job in New York City so she could dance with the best. But their lives became a miserable mess. Their new baby daughter was left in the care of a bored housekeeper. He vegetated in a stultifying job and saw the possibilities of creating his own firm fade farther from reality as urban living expenses ate up not only his salary but his savings as well. And worst of all, LuAnne came home late every evening, unhappy and exhausted from trying to make up for the two years of disciplined training she had missed since their marriage.

It had been no one's fault. Blame, if it could be placed at all, might be attributed to their superb talents — both were one of a kind in their fields. They had not even indulged in arguments as time went by; instead their loving relationship had slowly atrophied.

Occasionally their original love had surfaced — unfortunately, for it was in one of those rare, unplanned moments that Greg had been conceived. LuAnne had never considered abortion, thank God. But having to give up her dancing once again, even temporarily, had been the final straw. Her depression was everything one might expect from an artistic temperament, and this time even the prospect of having another healthy baby to love had not cheered her up. Paul suspected it was only his suggestion that after the birth she leave the children with him and pursue her career unencumbered that had maintained her sanity. Even then, they had not considered divorce.

It was just days after Greg's birth that doctors discovered the fast spreading malignancy. And that had changed everything. LuAnne had accepted the hopeless diagnosis with relief, as if she knew she had no chance of happiness in the future anyway. She did not want to give up her family, but she could not live without her dancing either, and the two appeared incompatible.

They had salvaged all the love they could out of those final four months she survived. And he hoped LuAnne had not given up her young life with too many regrets. He suffered her loss deeply. But he also suffered scars from their tragic marriage—scars almost as destructive as LuAnne's own illness.

He had never imagined he would want to marry again, even for companionship. He was a man who attracted women easily, and he never lacked for opportunities to ease his loneliness. And he had settled for that. Until Jeannie.

Somehow Paul managed to make it home from the airport without an accident. Later, in thinking that distracted drive over, he marveled at his luck.

Chapter Five

Jeannie had not believed Bill Hannah's claim that there was an area within easy driving of St. Louis where a person could walk nine miles and not see a sign of civilization. She had expected to find such isolation only in the desert states. But within minutes of entering the woodland preserve at the Shut-Ins Park she realized that this area of Missouri would surpass even Bill's glowing description.

If you come up with more outings like this one, I may want you to become a regular part of my weekend routine, she silently addressed Bill's back as she followed him up the narrow trail along which they had traveled for more than an hour. They had been together four weekends in a row, doing the usual tourist things in the city, but this was her favorite outing of them all.

Eager to show her the view from the lookout, Bill was setting a brisk pace along the rough trail. Although it was a little early for the trees to reach the vibrant autumn colors for which the Ozarks were noted, some leaves had begun to drop, and their crisp crunching underfoot was the only sound breaking the isolated quiet. But even as they pushed on, Jeannie inhaled impressions like life-giving air. She thrived on the brown-green contrasts in the dense undergrowth, the sudden splashes of colorful wild flowers splurging in their last blooming of the season, the hulk of the occasional massive evergreen towering above the deciduous trees that formed most of the dense patterns of sunlight and shadow. And there were impressions of scent, especially in the musky odors of the moist hollows.

When they reached the summit, she rushed to a large limestone ledge from which she could look her fill. It was fossiliferous rock, she discovered later, but at first she had no eyes for the tiny creatures under her feet, wondrous creatures deposited by an ancient sea millions of years ago on this spot that was now the top of an Ozark mountain. Instead her gaze was drawn hundreds of feet down to the powerful stream below. A creek, Bill had the audacity to call it; but how could such an insignificant word as *creek* describe the strength that had cut this magnificent gorge?

"Oh, Bill, it's beautiful," she gasped unoriginally as she dropped her backpack and sank gratefully onto the sun-warmed surface. The panorama boggled her mind.

For hundreds of years the little stream, filled with its load of spring floods and summer rains from so many hillsides beyond, had found its way to a giant vertical fault line in the uplifted limestone deposits. Time and the geologic process had done the rest; slowly the inexorable flow had cut away the stone, leaving a yawning gorge filled with natural glories. Some areas that contained more hard chert than others had withstood the grinding of the water and formed miniature chimneys, lovely in their grotesqueness. Other softer areas had buckled unprotestingly before the powerful flow, wearing down so quickly that as the relentless stream cut ever lower into the earth, great patches of pulverized rock were left behind to provide footing for stunted trees and scrub brushes randomly seeded by later winds.

"I take it you approve?" Bill dropped down beside her, resting an arm casually on her shoulders. She leaned against him gratefully, words still beyond her.

They stayed an hour or so, eating the picnic lunch she had packed, taking a few photographs, trying to identify the fossils she belatedly discovered in the limestone ledge, and periodically forgetting all diversions to stare long moments at the gorgeous panorama. But eventually they had to repack their lightweight gear and begin the return hike.

They were more than halfway down when Bill called a halt at a mossy clearing just off the trail.

"I kinda rushed us to this point because it's a good junction of several types of trails." Bill was somewhat apologetic as he handed her the canteen of water. "I thought you could pick what kind of scenery you want, and the rest of the way down I can give you a slow exploring tour."

"I'm ready for that!" Jeannie admitted as she drank deeply of the water. "What choices do I have?"

"With my great expertise," he said in what Jeannie had come to teasingly call his hearty coaching voice, "I can guide you through a tree-identification route, a wild-flower trail, the murky creek route...."

She spread her jacket out and lay back on the ground, grinning at his nonsense. "You make the murky creek route sound forbidding, but I'd like to take Bruce back a few small rocks for his collection. Would a creek bed be good for that?"

"It would be okay, but there's a bluff close to the car that would be better. It's fossiliferous limestone with a dike of granite. Why don't we just take my favorite short woodland trail back, then collect Bruce's rocks near the car?"

Jeannie agreed, thinking it was rather touching how much thoughtfulness Bill showed toward Bruce—toward most kids for that matter. What a shame that his brief college marriage had not worked out. Motherlike, she thought every adult should have a child to cherish.

Still, she was relieved that Bruce had turned down Bill's invitation and chosen to spend the day at Six Flags with Dick's nephews instead. It had been a difficult hike, even though the weather had cooled down

considerably, and he would have been weary and restless by now. Contentedly she relaxed against the mossy
coolness, eventually closing her eyes and just listening
to the sounds around her.

She knew when Bill moved over beside her.

"Have you ever just listened to the woods?" she
asked dreamily, her eyes still closed. "The wind is
barely moving those top branches, but it makes the
laziest whispering sound. Almost lulls you to sleep."

"I can think of better things to do," he said softly,
and she opened her eyes to find his face lowering close
to her own. He hesitated, giving her a chance to stop
him, and it flashed through her mind that he was really
a kind man. Overwhelmed with her own joy in the day
and feeling this strange quiet oneness with nature, she
smiled encouragingly.

It had been a long time since she had even kissed a
man, not since the ill-fated affair in Hawaii. Responsibilities and family worries had superseded that kind of
longing, and she was frozen inside, desperately needing
a kind man to help her open up the doors of her life.
Jeannie received Bill's approaching lips hopefully.

His mouth sought hers immediately, with no brush-
ing preliminaries. She felt a vague disappointment that
things were going so fast, even though he was touching
her gently, without passion yet. The kiss was not unpleasant, and she tried to make herself respond, seeking some sensitivity within her own being.

At first Bill had balanced awkwardly over her, but
gradually he lowered himself full length on top of her.
She wished it weren't so, but instead of feeling increased
pleasure as he deepened the kiss, she became preoccupied with an awareness of the pebbles and sticks protrud-
ing against her back, of the moistness of his mouth as it
pressed light caressess all over her face. She was relieved
when the approach of another hiking party startled him
into rolling off her. He ran his hand distractedly through
his hair as he tried to regain his composure.

"Wow, woman! Don't do that to me again unless you want us to make public spectacles of ourselves." He sighed softly, his usual chatty manner sounding strange in that passionate voice.

It troubled her to think about the incident as they drove home. She wished she had felt some excitement in his embrace, but she hadn't, and it was a foregone conclusion that she had encouraged him to expect more from her in the future.

Bruce wasn't due home until the amusement park closed at ten o'clock, but when Bill asked her to stop by his apartment for a drink, she turned him down. He took her refusal in apparent good spirits.

"Well, you can't blame a red-blooded American boy for trying," he joked as he parked in her apartment lot.

"Just as long as the red-blooded et cetera takes no for an answer." She couldn't keep the underlying seriousness out of her reply.

"Forever?" His voice was unexpectedly intense.

"Bill, please don't rush me."

"Rush you?" He was almost incredulous. "I've been trying to get to know you for nearly three months! We've both been married, Jeannie; we respect each other. Why two lonely adults can't—"

"Please drop it, Bill," she interrupted pleadingly. "I've enjoyed our day and I don't want it ruined." That sounded petulant even to her own ears, especially in the light of her earlier encouragement.

"I'm sorry if I misled you this afternoon," she apologized hesitantly, wishing she could manage to keep this man as her friend. But he wanted more than friendship from her and everything was happening too quickly. She remained close by his side, but the silence between them was not a companionable one.

"So here we are," she finally whispered inanely.

"More pertinently, where are we?" Bill asked.

"Is friendship for a while longer one of the choices?"

"Sounds boring." He looked at her ruefully, clasping

her outstretched fingers. Jeannie's responding look was troubled, but when he suddenly flashed her a huge, toothily wolfish smile, she burst into surprised laughter.

"Oh, Bill, you're good for me!" she said delightedly, feeling absurdly affectionate toward him at that silly moment. "I've let myself get into a terrible rut of widowhood, and I'm finding it a very awkward rut to break out of." On impulse she leaned forward and kissed his cheek.

"Gosh, for me? More, more!" he joked as he pulled her loosely into his arms. But when Jeannie did not follow up her initiative he rested his forehead against her hair and said quietly, "All right. We'll just give it time and play it by ear. Friends it is. For now."

"You must be mistaken. She can't be dead!" Jeannie had turned as white-faced as her son. "We just saw Mrs. Raymond in excellent health when she left for the airport two weeks ago."

"I didn't hear Greg wrong," Bruce denied. "When we were coming in just now I remembered you told me to invite him to go with us to the Arch this weekend, and his mother too, if she was back from her trip. And he said, 'She's dead.' Just like that, only kinda angry. 'She's dead.'"

Jeannie still could not believe it. She had crossed paths with Paul Raymond on her way to work most mornings, except when he took Becky for early dance practice, and he had never acted as if anything were wrong.

Decisively she freshened up her appearance and hurried to the Raymonds' apartment. Not wanting to upset Becky, who answered the door, Jeannie inquired for her father.

"He's gone to the store. He'll probably be home in another hour," Becky told her cheerfully, grief obviously being the last thing on her mind.

"Bruce just told me about your mother," Jeannie ventured awkwardly. "I'm terribly sorry. If there's anything Bruce and I can do to help you..."

Becky was staring at her so blankly that Jeannie faltered, wondering if she was bungling the whole thing. "I didn't get a chance to know Lucille well, but I liked her so much," she explained inadequately.

"Aunt Lucille said she would probably come see us this spring; Uncle Ben too, if he can get away." Becky's statement was carefully polite despite her puzzled expression.

"Aunt Lucille?" Jeannie wondered what the girl was rambling about.

"Isn't that the Lucille you were just talking about? You remember, you met her that first week we were getting settled—she's tall, with reddish-brown hair. She looks a little like Greg and me, which is funny because we're really not related, even though she's sort of a double aunt."

"A double aunt?" Jeannie repeated in a weak voice.

"You see, when Dad was about thirteen," Becky explained with a patient smile, as if she had made this little speech many times before, "his father married Aunt Lucille's mother, so she became his stepsister. She's four years older, but they got to be really close friends. Anyway, Dad's own brother is twelve years older and he was in South America on a job for five years. But when Ben came back and met Lucille, he married her, so then she was also Dad's sister-in-law."

"But I thought she was your mother!" Jeannie was stunned. "You mean she's...all right?" Her tremendous relief was apparent in her face.

Suddenly understanding the confusion, Becky burst out laughing. Greg, who had wandered in to hear the conversation, grinned at Jeannie.

"She's back in Tucson with Uncle Ben. I wondered why Bruce was making such a big deal about our mother. I mean, she died of cancer when I was a baby.

People say we both look like her, but we don't even remember her."

"We had been looking forward to your mother—your Aunt Lucille—coming back from her trip so she could go with us." Jeannie shook her head foolishly.

"There's no Mrs. Raymond for Dad," Becky smilingly explained.

Somehow Jeannie managed to mumble garbled goodbyes before fleeing back to her own apartment, where she leaned against the door in mortification.

Righteous indignation was gradually taking the place of the joy she had felt on learning Lucille was not dead after all.

Surely Paul Raymond knew she thought he was married. Did he think she was always that friendly with men she had just met?

"What did you find out, Mom?" Bruce had moved quietly to her side, his eyes enormous with a child's fear of death.

"That there never was a Mrs. Raymond!" she exploded. "And you are not to go over there anymore."

Later she had the good sense to apologize to the crushed Bruce and to explain the situation in a fair manner. But she remained adamant in her instructions that he must limit his visits with the Raymond children to hours when he would not be in the family's way. In other words, when Paul was not at home.

In fact, however, Paul Raymond was not home as much as he was at work the weeks after Lucille left. He was having his own problems.

"Ben, I've tried all in-state sources with no luck." His voice was impatient as he talked on the phone to his brother. "We must have electrical conduits shipped in here this week or we can't get the foundation poured—these concrete men have been waiting three weeks for our shipment, and they have a building commitment after next week. I can't even get another foundation contractor; the competent ones are all booked.''

''I can't stop the truckers' strike,'' Ben muttered, sharing his brother's frustration that although Missouri was not affected by the current stalled teamster negotiations, every state surrounding it was, choking off all shipments. ''Could you proceed without them at this point? Maybe change the foundation design? Just block in holes so that later—''

''I thought about it, but it's too makeshift for the amount of wire we want to run into this building. Remember, we're not only supplying our computers and measuring instruments, but planning on an increase of electrical consumption in the future.''

Paul spoke quietly, his shoulders hunched with tiredness. He and some staff members had worked brutal hours for two weeks to gather a local stockpile of necessary building supplies, but they had been unable to find conduits. And without them the whole building schedule was dangerously delayed. Much longer, and the labs could not be built before winter set in. The company stood to lose a whole year's data, already accumulating in makeshift trailers throughout the site.

Both brothers pondered the problem silently, unconcerned that the phone bills between St. Louis and Tucson had mounted steadily in recent days.

''Are you still good friends with George Bakewell?'' Paul suddenly asked, an idea forming in his mind.

''Sure, play golf with him every weekend. But all his conduits are manufactured in Tucson and there's no way he can get around his teamster contract, even to help me. With this strike we can't even get anything hauled across the street!''

''But doesn't he still have that strange little factory in southern Missouri, the one that makes left-handed fishing reels or something?''

''He does, and if I remember rightly, he had a railroad siding into both his plants.'' As usual it hadn't taken long for Ben's reasoning to mesh with his brother's. If Ben's friend were willing, he could load the conduits at his Tucson factory and ship them by rail directly to the Missouri factory. His Tucson union members would not object to an in-house rail shipment. Then nonstriking truckers in Missouri could haul them from the fishing reel factory to Paul.

"I may not be able to get the sizes on this specifications list." Ben could be heard shuffling papers in the background.

"We can't go down in size; just remember that, Ben. But I have a surplus of fittings, so I can adapt anything larger you get in increments of a half inch to as much as two inches."

"Stay by the phone" was Ben's characteristically curt response.

After Paul had hung up, Terry Drake, his assistant manager, unhinged his lanky frame from his own cramped desk nearby. "Sounds like we have our first hope of the season." His grinned tiredly. "Want some coffee?"

Not even waiting for a reply, Terry disappeared into the tiny kitchen at the end of the trailer that was currently serving as their office. Paul stared at the empty doorway absently, grateful that Terry had been willing to work overtime the past two weeks. He rarely asked it of him, but this had become one of those emergencies. At least Terry had a comfortable home to return to, he thought as he stood up and stretched. Terry was nicely settled in Paul's condominium.

I'll be so damned glad when we can move into the office, he thought as he walked slowly over to the trailer window. In the pastureland stretching ahead of his view was an attractive two-story office building that would be ready for his forty-plus employees within a couple of weeks. And not a moment too soon, Paul thought as he glanced around the incredibly crowded trailer. He could stand the makeshift arrangement either at work or at home. But the confusion existing at both places was about to get him down.

His tension was made worse by the huge gaping hole lying beyond the warehouse at the end of the newly asphalted parking lot: the site for the stalled solar-energy labs. Piles of displaced earth, myriad assorted large construction equipment, and numerous rented temporary buildings and trailers scarred the pastoral landscape around it. Great umbilical cords of electrical wiring connected the temporary structures with numerous experimental stations throughout the thousand-acre site.

It's going to look fine again someday, Paul thought, remembering how beautiful the wooded farmland had appeared when they had first purchased it. They had worked hard to preserve that beauty: The buildings were well designed to fit into the environment; every existing open space had been utilized so that they had had to clear only an additional fifty acres of trees beyond the two-hundred-and-fifty-acre pastureland for their buildings and experiments; and once the laboratory was completed, the wiring would all be enclosed in underground cables.

Jeannie would love the site, he thought nostalgically as he remembered the pleasure he had seen in her face when she had shown him the tiny woods behind their apartment building. How he would love to show her his own hundred wooded acres overlooking the site, and the beginning construction for his house. From its hillside location she would be able to see the whole valley, yet the family room and both bedroom wings would curl back between trees and against the hillside to provide a private tryst with nature. He thought she would agree that the architect had done a spectacular job of adapting to the site, even when confronted with the last-minute addition of a private master bedroom suite, after Paul met Jeannie.

Stupidity! What utter nonsense even to be indulging

in such daydreams, he thought angrily. The way things were going, he would probably never even show her his work, much less the house. She was so damned independent that his affluence would scare her off—if she ever started speaking to him again. It had been a couple of weeks now of this frosty avoid-him-whenever-you-can treatment. Ever since she had found out that Lucille—

"You don't use cream, do you?" Terry interrupted his rambling worries.

Paul shook his head, gratefully reaching for the steaming cup. He needed a diversion.

"Trailer offices are a great help during a building period." Terry grinned as he came around Paul's desk to join him at the window. "But every time I walk up and down that creaky hall I think I'm going through the floor. I'll be glad to get into the building."

"You're not alone," Paul agreed with the younger man. They both stood restlessly at the window, sipping their coffee, trying not to listen too hard for the phone.

The waiting was intolerable.

"We're lucky we don't have more elms on the property," Paul resolutely broke the silence. "I don't think a single tree in the country is going to survive the Dutch elm disease. We had to take three big ones down near the old farmhouse we're remodeling for eating facilities. We can't have some high wind blowing dead elm onto our lunch tables."

"What are most of the trees in the woods, oaks?"

"Right—several varieties of scrub oak, plus some dogwood and hickory." Paul grinned. "This whole farm was apparently once native Missouri woods. The groundsman says every time he starts to mow the pasture there's a rash of new little trees coming up."

"The landscape and climate are certainly different from those of Arizona. I've never quite understood why Tucson wouldn't have been ideal for solar-energy testing," Terry mused honestly.

"It *is* ideal for basic new solar research," Paul agreed. "That's why Ben is keeping his new laboratories there. And of course our production facilities are still there. But my goal is to see if our newly developed products will work under less-than-ideal conditions, and if not, what adaptations will be needed before we can market them nationwide. The Saint Louis climate is perfect for that range of testing, it has great temperature extremes. Here we can also test problems with overcast skies, humidity, precipitation, wind—all factors we can't duplicate in Arizona."

"So this complex will have no new basic reasearch?"

"Not in solar energy. But we hope as time goes on to do small-scale basic experiments with the natural resources here on the site. There are great possibilities in using wood and undergrowth as a source of mulch fuel. That stream below us is fast-flowing enough to give us good data on water-movement energy potentials, and we could replant that cornfield and experiment with gasohol production. There are any number of naturally occurring sources here, as you can see. And that's the name of the energy game in the future—we've got to find sources that can renew themselves proportionately to the energy they produce."

He had about exhausted his supply of casual chatter. It was not his nature to talk much, nor was it Terry's. But again the silence grew worrisome as the phone remained silent.

"Say, Paul, I haven't wanted to bother you with this before—" Terry restlessly walked over to his desk and picked up a large envelope, as if any action was preferable to the waiting—"but we've had a second letter from the federal government wanting us to bid on that contract for designing a sawdust-fueled generator. I thought you'd turned them down again, but—"

"You're right; we're sticking with our policy of avoiding government contracts. Tell my secretary to write a firm letter of refusal again." Seven years earlier, when the firm was just getting started, Paul had stood alone against all their advisers who wanted to seek a government contract to tide them over their financial growing pains. In the end Ben had backed him, and the decision had gone well for the company. Free to concentrate on their own projects, they had come up with a solar-energy system for West Coast vacation homes that soon became a big money-maker. Since then the Raymond firm had developed three additional specialized alternative-power sources for small users and had secured patents on several other processes. All were paying good profits.

Watching Paul fiddle with papers at his desk, Terry wondered how he always seemed to remain so outwardly calm when under pressure. In this respect Paul and his brother were alike. But in other ways.... Terry had worked with them both since the inception, but his personal loyalty wavered toward the younger brother. While it was Ben's brilliant mind that had perfected the theories making new methods of energy utilization possible, it was Paul's practical mind that could convert those esoteric theories into usable products, Paul's hard judgments that kept the business on sound financial footing.

Few other people in the firm knew that it was Paul who had provided the venture's financial base. In his young years he had taken the most difficult, highest-paying engineering jobs he could find—his mind soaked up the experience while he lived a hermitlike existence, banking part of his earnings and investing all the rest in coal and oil leases throughout the Midwest. Everyone had thought he was crazy, and there had been a period, when he was married, in which he had diverted his energies. But eventually his sacrifices had paid off. The Illinois and Kentucky investments had begun producing coal mines and oil wells. Paul's lease income from that had provided the firm's big start and still helped build up a slush fund for future expansion financing.

Terry was just speculating what he himself might have done with his earnings if his investments had succeeded when the phone shrilly broke the silence. The grin on Paul's face as he listened to his brother's terse message told the story.

"They'll be here on Tuesday!" Paul motioned Terry to get on the extension. "Help me take down these size changes he substituted."

It took only a few moments for them to get the necessary data. When they finished, Paul and Terry took one look at each other, then unashamedly began laughing aloud. The relief was incredible!

When they could finally control their nervous exuberance, Paul told Terry to clear out for home. "You can't do anything about lining up the new-sized fittings we'll need until you see my drawings anyway. I'll work on the conduit size changes this weekend and get a copy of my new drawings to you Monday."

"I'll be glad to stick around here the rest of the day and help with those drawings," Terry offered, concerned about how fatigued Paul looked.

"I appreciate the offer, but I think I'm going to have to fiddle with this myself. In fact I'll probably go on along home soon, since I've had to leave the kids alone so much recently. I can finish up after they've gone to bed."

Paul meant what he said about wanting to be with his children. But as he was driving home he couldn't help dreading the immediate confusion that would confront him when he walked in the door. How nice it would be to go to Jeannie's apartment, he thought, and to find her alone. He would like, for just a little while, to put his feet up on her couch and his head in her lap. And talk.

He urgently wanted to talk. Elation like this should be shared.

A year's work for the company had been near disaster.

And then this simple act of locating a shipment of electrical conduits—salvation! How satisfying it would be to have someone you loved understand what joy it was to have this terrible worry off your mind. But he could not talk to the kids. It wasn't the same, somehow.

His wistful thoughts about her seemed so much nonsense, though, when he got to the apartment. Jeannie was just turning up the stairs, and she gave him only the frostiest of greetings. His answering smile was more poignant than he knew.

The minute Paul walked into his living room he knew that the children were not home. The place was beautifully silent.

Looking in their usual spot, he found Becky's note explaining that she and Greg had gone to the movies with a friend. They had left him a ham sandwich in the refrigerator, and they were planning to pick up pizza on the way home so he would not have to cook. Greg had scrawled a postscript:

No more of your pickled herring and grapefruit salad. Tonight I am going to slice tomatoes.

Paul grinned at that. That herring salad last week had not been one of his better ideas.

For a while after he had eaten he just sat at the table staring at the empty plate. With the pressure suddenly off, the exhaustion had hit him. It was a terrible temptation to go to bed—he had slept only four hours a night for the past several nights. But on the other hand, if he napped now, he would have to stay up late tonight to get finished.

With resolution then, he heaved out of his chair and went to his small bedroom to get the card table from its storage spot behind the double bed. *Some desk*, he thought ruefully as he set it up in the living room. But once started, Paul worked quickly and well. When he began concentrating on his work the tiredness seemed to shift into a holding pattern—he had always had the ability to postpone collapse one more day.

It was late that same afternoon when Jeannie stood hesitantly in front of Paul's door, looking prim and scrubbed in her nurse's uniform. Only her agitated hands betrayed her indecision. Paul had looked so tired earlier—like a little boy who should be cuddled into your lap and comforted—it was criminal to add to his burden. But instinctively she knew that he would help her, despite how coldly she had been treating him lately. Decisively she pressed the doorbell.

He was obviously surprised to see her.

"I'm sorry to bother you," she stammered. "I just didn't know what else to do. I've tried everyone else in the building and no one is home right now."

He sensed immediately that she was in trouble. For one thing, he knew she had never worn a nurse's uniform to work. He pushed the door wide for her to enter, but she shook her head.

"I've been called in for an emergency drill. You see, I had registered at Saint Joseph's Hospital because I had been a critical-care nurse in Hawaii, and it's professional protocol to be available for disasters in your community," she began the lengthy explanation breathlessly, "and they've called this surprise training drill. It's unheard of to do it on Saturdays, but. . . . Anyway, Bruce is out with friends and I'm afraid he'll come home without a key and—"

"We'll have him with us till you get back," Paul said quickly. "And you can leave an extra key here if you think he'll need anything before you get home. In fact, he can bunk on our couch if you run late, so don't worry. Did you leave him a note?"

"No, I wanted to ask you first." She was a little taken aback at his instant handling of her problem.

"I'll tell him to come over here," he said, picking up

a pad off the littered table. "I can stick it on your door in case I don't hear him coming up the stairs."

"A note on the door! I should have thought of that," Jeannie exclaimed distractedly. "I have a date with Bill Hannah tonight and I haven't been able to reach him, either. I probably won't have a chance to call later. Could I borrow—"

Wordlessly Paul handed her the pad. He would take the greatest of pleasure in posting *that* note. That ought to slow the jock down a little.

Jeannie did not notice the malicious grin on his face as she passed him back the pad, but she did see the pile of work stacked on the table behind him.

"Oh, you're busy working," she gasped, feeling guilty at adding Bruce to his burdens.

"It will work out fine, Jeannie." He automatically called her by her first name as he exasperatedly turned her toward the stairs. "I'll post your notes. Get on to your work."

She cast him one last worried look before running down the stairs.

It was almost ten o'clock when Jeannie got off duty. The first few hours had been hectic enough—she had been the sole nurse in a cavernous meeting room to which eager, boisterous students who were simulating minor injuries were funneled. A few of the young people had been instructed to simulate increasingly dangerous symptoms and it was Jeannie's duty to locate these problems and make decisions on treatment. The whole situation had become horrifyingly real, however, when one of the adult sponsors accompanying the students had collapsed with a real heart attack. The students had not called attention to him at first because they thought he was teasing them. By the time Jeannie had noticed their jovial remarks and rushed across the huge room to him, his heart had stopped.

She had started C.P.R. immediately and ordered two

students to rush to the emergency room for help. Probably not more than a few minutes had passed before the complete E.R. staff had reached her with all their lifesaving equipment, but it had seemed hours. Jeannie had not had occasion to use C.P.R. for a year, and she only hoped her old skill had not failed her. She was certain she had reached the man before the critical four minutes after heart stoppage had elapsed; if her C.P.R. had been good enough he had a reasonable chance of survival without brain damage. The E.R. crew had successfully revived him within minutes and hastened him on to intensive care. Then Jeannie had shakily resumed her work with the greatly subdued students.

Trudging up the stairs that night, she felt as exhausted as Paul Raymond had looked when she had seen him earlier that day. After the episode that afternoon she was ultrasensitive about overworked men who did not take care of themselves. Nurselike, she wondered if Paul had gotten any rest before Bruce had been added to their household. But her habitual reserve did not let this concern show when he answered her light tap at the door.

"All done?" he asked calmly, insisting that she come inside.

She stepped gingerly into the tiny room, which seemed to be overflowing with people. Bruce and the two Raymond children were huddled around the card table, studying what looked like house blueprints. All signs of Paul's earlier work were gone.

"Hey, Mom, you should see these plans of the house they're going to build!" Bruce exclaimed enthusiastically. "Boy, it's going to be neat!"

"I'll teach you to read these plumbing sketches later," Paul suggested before Jeannie could respond. "Your mom's probably ready to sit down right now. How did the emergency drill go?" He did not look at her until he had casually tossed the blueprints on the top of the couch.

"Yeah, Mom, what happened?" Bruce asked eagerly.

"They simulated a tornado," she explained reticently, not wanting to talk about the teacher—not until she had learned if he would survive without brain damage. "I guess such storms are fairly common occurrences in this area in the spring and fall."

"How did the drill work?" Becky asked. "We saw something on the TV news about it just now, and it showed ambulances bringing in all these cute guys with ketchup on their faces."

"Cute guys!" Greg objected. "Those were victims, stupid!"

"Why don't you sit down and have a drink with us? Then you can tell us more about it," Paul invited casually, at the same time quelling his son's teasing with a stern look. Becky promptly disappeared into the kitchen.

It was then that Jeannie noticed Paul's bare feet, his loosened shirt collar, and the open can of beer on the table near the couch. She stood there awkwardly, wanting to share some aspects of her recent experience with them but hesitant to further prolong Paul's day. Her lips were just forming a polite refusal when Becky came out of the kitchen, carrying a full tray.

"I was just bringing in snacks and Cokes for us when you came. I opened you a beer; I hope that's okay."

So the decision was taken out of her hands. She accepted the cool, frosty can and sank gratefully onto the couch. Paul returned to his place at the other end, grinning at how quickly the boys had folded away the card table and sprawled out on the floor in front of the food tray.

"I hope you're not hungry," he commented softly, subtly drawing her attention to how quickly the boys were devouring Becky's food.

She sank her head back and let the cool beer flow down her throat. It tasted wonderfully refreshing.

"Not really," she finally answered.

"So tell me about these cute guys," Becky directed, munching a chip she had rescued from Greg's overloaded hands. "Were they high school or college students?"

It was a lazy conversation. There were some funny incidents she *could* tell, and the children seemed especially interested in the mechanics of how such a drill was set up. This one had been unusually long. Jeannie had learned that a few years previously a violent tornado had hit the county on a weekend, catching some hospitals unprepared. So this area-wide practice had been thorough.

The boys asked the most questions, pausing periodically to argue good-naturedly with Becky over who was hogging the most food. Paul sat wordlessly through most of the conversation, listening to it all as if he were enjoying himself. Jeannie did not stay long, but oddly it felt a rather comfortable and right way to end her confused day.

"Don't forget you owe me nine thousand two hundred dollars," Becky called out mischievously to Bruce as they started home. "You'd better practice up on your twenty-one."

"I'll get you the next time!" Bruce rejoined happily as he ran ahead with the keys, proud to be the one to unlock the door.

Since Greg and Becky were already beginning to pick up the mess from the snacks, Jeannie was relatively alone with Paul at his open door.

"I really appreciate your caring for Bruce..." she stammered, feeling suddenly self-conscious.

"He's a good boy," Paul brushed off her thanks. She looked at him anxiously, wondering if he was angry with her, but saw nothing of that in his face. She couldn't help noticing, even in the dim light of the breezeway, that his coloring was almost gray with fatigue.

"Look, it's none of my business," she ventured, the incident from the afternoon still haunting her, "but anyone in health care could take one look at you and see you're not getting enough rest." He seemed surprised at her concern. But she was undaunted by his reaction, feeling that, since he was obviously dead on his feet, someone should try to talk sense to him. "For your children's sake you really should take better care of yourself."

It shocked her when, instead of being angry at her interference, he smiled warmly; a vulnerable expression passed briefly in his eyes before he controlled it.

"I'll be letting up," he assured her quietly. "We've just settled the problem at work that has created all the overtime—today! Things will be better for me from now on."

"That's good, I'm glad." She sighed. She was finding it very wearing, this being her neighbor's keeper. "Well, get some rest now." Her hand fluttered briefly, as if she couldn't decide whether to point an admonishing finger at him, shake hands, or give him a comforting pat on his shoulder. Oddly, she saw nothing incongruous in her present concern compared with her usual aloof treatment of Paul.

Closing the door behind her, Paul felt suddenly relaxed—rested, almost. He grinned wryly. Indeed, he had not been able to put his head in her lap, or his feet on her couch. And they had had an audience of three young faces. But she was speaking to him again. So what if she *had* been more bossy than loving? It was a start. . . .

Chapter Six

A house of their own!

While Bruce pondered her suggestion, Jeannie allowed the precious dream to tumble around in her own mind, a kaleidoscope of shapes emerging, each poignantly appealing in its own way: the little ranch-style bungalow with an apple tree in the backyard; the tiny split-level contemporary with its attached carport; the ancient brick row house, stately in its onetime ethnic neighborhood. They were all realistic dreams, she reassured herself practically. She wasn't hoping for a mansion.

"You mean, if you took this extra job, we might buy our own house?" Bruce asked, a little awed by this idea.

"Not immediately," she explained, "but not so long from now, either. We didn't have to use up all my savings in this move, and I've been adding a little more each month. If we're careful, we could put the whole paycheck from this hospital job in the account. Within a year or so we should have enough saved for a down payment."

"But I thought you said you were glad you weren't in the hospital emergency room anymore, that you were too old for such hard work?" Bruce looked worried.

"This job at Saint Joseph's Hospital is only two short evenings a month," she pointed out, regretting that she had been open with her son in the past. "I can take the pressure again for that little bit of time."

He still looked perplexed as he tried to sort out the possibilities in his own mind. The job idea came as no more of a surprise to him than it had to Jeannie herself. When she had called the hospital that morning to check on the condition of the heart-attack patient, the hospital administrator had asked to speak to her. After the usual polite comments about Jeannie's fine handling of the emergency, the man had shocked her by offering her this work. It was a perfect moonlighting job, if you could discount the wear and tear on your nerves. The shift was designed to augment the hospital's emergency-room staff during peak hours, and secondarily, it allowed former E.R. nurses to keep their skills updated.

"And you're asking if I can get along by myself on Thursday nights?" Bruce had returned to her original question.

"Just the first and third Thursdays. I'd have to go to the hospital straight from work. Of course you'd be at Scouts several hours during the evening anyway; I can still handle my car-pool for that by driving the Thursdays I'm off. And I'd be home by eleven. Or if you'd feel better having Mrs. Westerdale from downstairs come—"

"I don't need a baby-sitter!" he objected irately. "I can get along fine if you're sure you won't be too tired. It would be nice to have a house!"

"It's settled, then," she said decisively, trying not to show her own misgivings about how she would hold up with the extra job. But for a house? Of course it was worth it.

"So, with that decision made, it's time to get to work here." She glanced at the groceries still on the table and the can of gasoline in the middle of the floor where she had set it as she came in. "I was so excited I just had to talk it over with you right away. But we'd better rush now if we want to have our stuff ready for Greg and Becky's barbecue."

"Is this gas for them?"

"No, that's for Doctor Matthews's power mower. She needs it tomorrow and I was stopping at the service station anyway. So remind me to give it to her when she comes by—she's dropping off some work for me. I think what I need you to do now is bring in the other sack of groceries from the car."

"Couldn't she stay for our barbecue? Greg and Becky won't mind. Their dad won't be here 'cause he's working late."

"I don't think so, son. She's behind on some of her cases this week. And besides, since this is the Raymond kids' first time to try cooking out, we'd better not add any extra mouths for them to feed."

"It's going to be a good dinner," he said confidently as he ambled out. *It can't be too bad, since I seem to be assigned most of the side dishes.* Jeannie thought humorously as she carried the gasoline out to the breezeway storage room for safekeeping. Somehow when the Raymond children had decided yesterday to have this cookout, Bruce had volunteered her services for the salad, cake, snacks, and baked beans.

But she didn't really mind. It would be a way for her to let Paul Raymond know she was available to help his family in emergencies, just as he had helped her Saturday. She had left on time for work this morning, thinking she would see him and could thank him, but somehow she had missed him.

The cookout with his children would probably be fun. And besides, it was good to have something to keep her mind off this extra job and the possibility of owning a house. It was probably just coincidence, but ever since Bruce had stayed with the Raymonds he had been babbling about blueprints. His talk had filled her with the most restless resurgence of the old dreams for her own home. And then this job offer....

She made Bruce help fix some of the food. It was her belief that in this day and age a man needed to know how to cook as much as a woman did. But she was questioning her wisdom in putting her good intentions to practice that particular evening by the time Bruce had excitedly talked nonstop about house plans through cutting up celery, washing lettuce, and stirring up a cake mix.

"Bruce, I think you have oral diarrhea," she said in exasperation when she thought she would scream if he said one more word.

"But it's just so neat, us going to have a house! You know what I'd really like to do? Help build it. It was really something seeing those blueprints of Mr. Raymond's. He said he'd teach me how to tell which lines and marks are for electricity, which are for plumbing—"

"That cake is mixed enough. Grease your pan."

Obligingly Bruce plopped a spoon of grease in the loaf pan and flattened it with the whole of his hand. Jeannie groaned disgustedly.

"Mr. Raymond said if you know how to read blueprints"—Bruce had barely paused in his talking long enough to draw a deep breath—"you can build a man's house just right even if you have never talked to him about what he wants or seen any pictures of what the place is supposed to look like. But that's what blueprints are, you know, sort of pictures in a way."

She experimented with shutting his voice out of her hearing. It was hard to do. She couldn't believe how obsessed he was with blueprints since his visit next door. She understood that it had been Greg who had got the house plans out in the first place; Paul had said he was not ready to show them around yet, but had relented when he realized how disappointed Bruce was. She could understand Paul's reluctance—if, as Bruce reported, he was having troubles in starting up his own business, the likelihood of his building his dream house was probably even farther in the future than her own house dream.

"You know, you can send off in magazines for house blueprints," Bruce continued enthusiastically, her efforts to shut him out failing completely. "I've seen ads in *Popular Mechanics.* Maybe I could get some, and we could plan to build our own. . . ."

Dutifully Jeannie absorbed five full minutes of explanations on air-conditioning systems and support beams, interrupting only when necessary to rescue the food from her bumbling cook. But finally she'd had her fill of being the understanding mother who always shows an interest in her child's thoughts. In desperation she began assigning Bruce other tasks to get ready for the barbecue, most of them unnecessary and far away from her ears.

Unfortunately, the extra work had not worn him out at all by the time the Raymond children emerged from their own apartment with fixings for the fire. His excitement seemed contagious, and Jeannie was so concerned about the three kids' hyperactive behavior that she insisted on coming with them while they started the fire. She wasn't about to have any accidents; she had treated too many burned children in her life.

They got the charcoal going, but just barely.

"I think we didn't have quite enough charcoal lighter left," Greg said regretfully. "We did everything just like Dad showed us last time, but this stuff isn't catching as fast as it did then."

"Maybe we should add some paper to it?" Becky offered the suggestion.

They began discussing what to do next, and Jeannie left them at it, thinking that if they didn't come up with a solution by the time she brought the food down later she would intervene with her own suggestions. But in the meantime she would let them try to work it out for themselves.

She was just heading back into the breezeway when Karen arrived.

"Smells like you're cooking out tonight," Karen greeted her.

"Bruce is helping the kids next door," Jeannie explained, taking the briefcase of files Karen had brought her. "They decided to try barbecuing hamburgers, since their father won't be home until late."

"So those are the neighbors you said Bruce liked so much." Karen walked across the open breezeway to look at Bruce and his friends. "Nice-looking kids. Say! I've seen that girl before!"

"Really? I'm surprised. I thought you serviced only elementary schools in our district."

"I do. Now, let me see, where was it? There's something about the way she moves. Look at that! She literally glides when she walks, and holds her head almost like a swan....That's it! I remember now; she was the soloist with some ballet group that gave a show at one of the grade schools where I was testing. She did *Swan Lake*, if you can imagine—you know, the solo for the dying swan. She's really excellent. Have you seen her dance?"

"No. I know she's considering it for a profession."

"I wouldn't wonder. She put the other kids in the chorus to shame. I mean, they looked like regular klutzes next to her."

"Do you have time to come out and meet them?"

"Not this evening. I still have to get Dick fed and off to the airport. I hate these hurried business trips. Tell Bruce hello for me."

She had dashed off with a hasty apology for being late with the files, and Jeannie was back in her own apartment before she realized that Karen had not taken her can of gasoline. She glanced out the window to see if she could catch her, but Karen's car was already gone.

It was some time later when Jeannie came out again, carefully carrying a tray of stuffed celery. The celery was sliding all over the plate and she was walking gingerly, wondering if she should go back and cover it with plastic wrap, when she almost knocked someone down.

"Careful!" Paul Raymond's exclamation shocked her.

"You're not supposed to be home!" she exclaimed, hastily rescuing her slipping celery. Her involuntary response sounded deliberately rude.

Anger dominated Paul's weary expression, but his voice came out icily controlled. "Frankly, I was so relieved to finish early I forgot about the kids' barbecue. Isn't it enough for *you* to avoid *me*? Do I have to stay out of your way too?''

"I haven't been avoiding you!" Jeannie protested. "At least not today. I came out on time and you weren't there." Her aggrieved voice made it sound all his fault.

"Why the he— Why did you ever feel it necessary to do otherwise?"

"You let me believe that you were married!" she blurted defensively without thinking.

"Good Lord! Most women complain because men let them think they *aren't* married."

"That's not the point," she objected childishly, not liking to be in the wrong. "You knew how I felt." The justification sounded weak even to her own ears.

He had started toward his own apartment, but at that statement he whirled back, furious. His anger was overwhelming in its intensity. She faded away from him, uneasy at what she had unleashed and wondering how she had gotten herself into the argument when she really felt nothing but gratitude toward Paul Raymond now. But her second thoughts were too late.

"Sure, I knew how you felt," Paul bit out, advancing menacingly toward her. "You made that clear the day I moved in. You didn't want to live next to a single father who would push his kids, his sex needs, and his dirty laundry off on you. So what was I supposed to do?" His face was close to hers by then, his eyes piercing in their fury. "If you had known I'm single, my children wouldn't have had a prayer of a chance of making friends with Bruce quickly."

Jeannie flushed as she realized how accurate he was. She raised one hand protestingly, but he seized it in a harsh grip, shaking it as he went on emphatically, "And whether you needed friends or not, Bruce and my kids did!" Then he tossed her hand aside as if it offended him.

"Just don't tell anyone I came home," he muttered, going back toward his door. "I'll slip out for supper and come in later. You can still have your party in peace."

He seemed to be glancing wistfully over the railing toward the scene at the fire braziers when suddenly he froze.

"No!" he yelled wildly. "Stop!"

White-faced, he threw aside his things as he ran to the railing.

"Don't move that can! Stay right there!" He seemed to be willing obedience as he shouted the commands in an unyielding voice.

Momentarily Jeannie was shocked motionless as he brushed past her, but she recovered her senses and rushed downstairs after him. What she saw as she burst out of the breezeway halted her in horror.

Bruce stood directly over the charcoal brazier. An open gasoline can, moisture clinging to its tilted lip, was suspended in his hands. A rolled-up newspaper was blazing on top of the stubborn charcoal, waiting for him to complete his toss of the volatile liquid.

The whole scene froze in Jeannie's mind: Paul slightly in front of her, Greg standing at the trash barrel several feet away, Becky bending over the gaily colored picnic cloth that was just fluttering down on the table. Her throat constricted into agonized immobility.

"Very carefully back away from the fire, son. Don't let any gas drip." Paul spoke quietly, all the while walking steadily toward Bruce. "That's right. Carefully."

His sigh of relief was audible as his hand closed around Bruce's arm, moving him even farther from the flaming paper. No one said anything as he took the can of gasoline Jeannie had bought for Dick Matthews.

Paul was obviously trying to calm himself as he haltingly explained. "If you had tossed gasoline on that open flame, chances are it would have flashed back and exploded the whole can." His hands were shaking as he recapped the container.

"I—I didn't know," Bruce stammered, his eyes saucers of fear. "I'm sorry." He was almost frightened speechless.

Some of the whiteness had left Paul's face.

"Charcoal lighter doesn't flash as quickly as gas," he relentlessly continued the gentle explanation. "But it still isn't a good idea to throw any flammable liquid onto something you've already lighted."

He looked sternly at his son and daughter then. "You two *do* know better."

"I'm sorry. I wasn't watching," Becky said.

"I didn't think, Dad," Greg apologized lamely.

"Next time *think*!" he shouted.

Tears began to trickle down his son's contrite face.

Jeannie made a constricted noise in her throat, but she had this strange inability to move. And the ground seemed to be undulating up and down. Involuntarily her fingers unclenched and the plate of celery tumbled unheeded to her feet.

Perceiving her difficulty, Paul walked reassuringly toward her as he calmly asked Bruce, "Where did you get this gasoline?"

Hurry, Jeannie thought, panic-stricken. *I don't want to frighten the children more by fainting in front of them, but . . . help!*

"In the storage closet upstairs," Bruce squeaked brokenly, not sensing his mother's distress.

"I'll put it away for you." Paul had an arm around Jeannie's waist now. Automatically her feet began to move in step with his.

"You kids had better do your best on those hamburgers, because Mrs. Rasmussen is starving." Paul was able to toss the inanity out lightly even as his arm tightened its support on the wobbly Jeannie. "We're going to have a drink upstairs while you get the food cooked."

"But, Dad, the fire?" Greg brushed at his wet face.

"Make a bonfire of sticks and dry leaves on top of the charcoal and keep it going for a while. Gradually transfer pieces of charcoal on top with the tongs. It will take a while, but it will work fine.''

"Are you going to eat with us, Dad?" Greg's voice sounded strangely wistful.

Paul hesitated only briefly before answering, "Sorry, son, I have to go back out."

They had made it to the breezeway and out of sight by then, and he drew Jeannie completely to his side as he literally dragged her up the stairs with him, kicked aside his briefcase, and cursed violently while fumbling for his keys. Nausea and blackness wanted to overtake her, but he virtually threw her onto his couch and thrust her head between her knees. She could feel the roughness of his callused hands through the soft hair at her neck as the dizziness came and went. Vaguely she was aware of his voice mumbling, "He's all right, Jeannie, he's all right."

At last she felt better, no longer restive against the restraining hand. Her vision focused on Paul's shoes, then on her own hands clutching her knees. As he gradually allowed her to raise her head the nausea and dizziness receded, but her pupils were dilated with shock.

"Are you going to make it?" he asked as he watched the color returning to her face. She nodded mutely, automatically, wishing she could understand his expression.

Then a voice not at all like her own grated out from her inner soul. "We had burn patients at the children's ward in Honolulu. Terrible pain! So hard to survive...." Was that her own voice, she wondered, her own voice beginning to sob? "Gasoline explosions are almost hopeless to—" Yes, of course it was she. Sobbing, covering her eyes, finally being given blessed relief in crying.

Helplessly he watched her. Then, blowing tension out of himself, Paul stepped to the open doorway. He could see the children down below at their work, much subdued. Muttering an oath, he flung his briefcase inside and locked the door behind him.

She wasn't aware of when he took her in his arms. She knew only that she had been racked with this terrible anguish, suffering alone as always, then suddenly she wasn't alone anymore. *He* was there, prying her hands away from her face, encouraging her to accept his strength as if she were a hurt child. She was too spent to care that she was clinging to him, almost lying across his lap.

He patted her back, he stroked her soft curls, he rocked her awkwardly as if she were a baby. She couldn't get enough of the comforting until she had buried her face in his neck; when she reached that warmth, she was finally eased. The crying eventually subsided into dry, aching gulps, Jeannie then lay quietly against him, thinking she might never move again.

The sun was going down. She could tell by the changing play of the light patterns in the room as her surroundings gradually began to take on day-to-day shape again. How unbelievable that life could go so suddenly from the mundane scope of dream houses and colored tablecloths to disaster. Instant desolation. She felt an urgent need to talk. To listen. To be comforted.

"Parents are damn vulnerable." It was Paul who finally broke the silence.

She understood his feeling of impotence. She had never felt her own helplessness with greater clarity.

"We were talking today about buying a house," she mused weakly. "We were so excited. And then...it's too real! I almost lost twelve years' total investment of my life. My son! All my love and dreams."

She couldn't go on. That he understood what was unsaid was evident when he tightened his arms, not letting her move away from him. She acquiesced immediately, so greatly did she need his strength. If only someone had the power to promise her that her son would always be safe. Dejectedly she remained huddled against Paul, both of them knowing that parents were never given such assurances.

"When Becky was about seven," he said pensively, his chest moving slightly against her cheek as he spoke, "she wanted to clean the car. I remember that it was a warm Sunday afternoon. I had just opened a beer, Greg was taking a nap, and I was very close to falling asleep myself. But I got out the tank vacuum and hooked it up for her outside. I guess I eventually dozed. I heard her turn on the vacuum, and then I heard her using the water. But it never dawned on me that she wouldn't know not to use electricity around water."

Jeannie lifted her head slightly to look up at him. His jaw, covered with blue-black stubble, jutted out above her. She couldn't see his expression, but she knew it must be tense because his hands were tightening hurtfully on her shoulders as he remembered.

"I started to lie down on the couch, but for some reason I decided to go check on her first." His voice was grim. "She was rooted in a pool of water with the electric cord trailing alongside her to the house. The metal vacuum rod in her hands was banging up and down with the current. She was trying to scream, and she was trying to let go, but she couldn't do a damn thing."

Jeannie shuddered against his harsh hold and he loosened his grip, absentmindedly stroking the areas he had bruised as his voice went on.

"I got the thing unplugged and carried her inside. Becky was shaken up, but didn't even have a burn on her hands. Nothing. And she started talking a mile a minute. Why did her hands feel tingly? she wanted to know. Did she look funny when I came out? Her tongue wouldn't work at first. Daddy had sure looked funny!

"I couldn't believe her chatter. I made her lie down on the couch, and then I went to the bathroom and was sick." He laughed ruefully. "I've never been so sick in my life. If my toes had been loose, I'd have lost them. When I was finally able to stumble back into the living room, I found her talking on the telephone—she couldn't wait to tell her best friend about the experience."

He threw his head wearily back against the couch, a smile softening his expression. The gray in his dark hair seemed doubly intense at that moment.

Jeannie straightened beside him and tried to smooth down the unruly whitened sideburns. It was a silly gesture related to her futile wish that she could remove the strain of responsibility from his face.

And then his head was resting weakly against hers, and somehow she was rubbing her lips against his rough beard, almost taking pleasure in the hurt it caused her as she tried to return the comfort he had given her.

It was an odd moment of true giving, of two-way extended understanding in which one doesn't see, doesn't think. But everything was there, the involvement of all the senses, and yet no awareness of any one of them. Both Jeannie and Paul experienced only the sensation of helping, of being no longer alone, of... rightness.

They didn't realize that their hands were gently soothing and touching, their lips planting soft reassurances, unmindful of where they landed; didn't realize that her tears were blending with the sweat on his face. There was no reality except this urge to ease the other's burden.

They must have been kissing. His breath was within her when the contentment of her bruised mouth was interrupted. She moaned in mindless protest as she felt herself being lifted away from him. She clung to him desperately, anguished that someone wanted to take away her comfort.

Finally his whispers broke into her consciousness.

"Jeannie, we have to help the children."

Only then was she aware of the knocking at his door, of Becky's anxious voice.

She jerked her head back and focused on him; he was crouching above her, loosening her hands from his arms, obviously as shaken as she. Embarrassed, she slumped back in mute contrition as he gently pressed her hands together in her lap.

"Gratitude makes us damn vulnerable too," he sighed, gazing at her with no censure in his eyes. "Do you want to fix up a little bit?"

Conscious then of how disheveled she would appear to the children, she moved toward his bathroom.

"We're pulling ourselves together, Becky," she heard him explaining to his daughter as Jeannie closed the bathroom door behind her.

In the living room Becky had paused undecidedly in the doorway, the empty celery plate in her hand.

"I threw away the stuff Mrs. Rasmussen dropped, Dad," she said hesitantly, her face worried. "Bruce said there was stuff left in the kitchen, that we could make more. I could...I mean, if you'd stay with us now?"

"No, I have to go back to the labs, but I won't be very late."

At her look of disappointment he patted her shoulder awkwardly. "This is the last time, I should be able to have normal hours from now on, that's a promise."

He glanced back toward the bathroom.

"See what you can do to help Mrs. Rasmussen when she comes out, Becky. That was a pretty close call out there."

"I know, Dad. We all feel terrible about it."

"Just so you've learned from it. I'll check on the boys before I leave. Oh, and Becky?"

"Yes?"

"Tell...Mrs. Rasmussen I'm taking this gasoline with me and I'll dispose of it."

"All right, Dad. Dad?"

He turned back inquiringly.

"I love you."

He smiled at her. "I love you too, punkin."

Chapter Seven

By early November Jeannie's life had settled into a routine. She left for work about 7:00 A.M. and was home shortly after 4:00 P.M. Two Thursday evenings a month she worked in the hospital emergency room. Except for an occasional date with Bill or an evening with the Matthewses, she spent her free time at home.

By and large she was satisfied with what Bill dubbed her sterile routine. Certainly Bruce was happy; he was well settled in school and he loved having the Raymond children for friends right in his own neighborhood. Jeannie teasingly argued with Bill that he wasn't really opposed to routine—he was just annoyed because she wouldn't plan to go out with him every Saturday and Sunday, no matter what.

Actually she saw nothing sterile about her life; certainly it was glorious compared with what it had been in Hawaii.

If occasionally a strange restlessness engulfed her, if she felt a vague sense of emptiness, she shoved it to the back of her mind. Jeannie had already discovered that, fond of Bill as she had become, accepting his affectionate caresses had not filled the void—it had only necessitated more zipping and buttoning to correct her appearance after their dates. That was one of the reasons she did not see him more frequently. She was still refusing final fulfillment, and she knew his patience was not unlimited.

Sometimes she wondered if there was something wrong with her, if her emotions had atrophied even before her husband went off to the army. Some people seemed to meet all of life with ecstatic passion; it was only recently she had been able to meet it with subtle joy.

There had been years when she rarely laughed, but now, even in her little routine, she was beginning to discover so many simple pleasures, so many causes for laughter. Foremost, there was the enjoyment of her son. Since the ill-fated barbecue she was doubly aware of how fragile life was, and she cherished Bruce all the more. There was the satisfaction of maintaining her own apartment, the small successes in her job at the research center, the rich friendship with Karen and Dick. She even appreciated the challenge of the new hospital job.

Jeannie could not honestly say it was good to get back into emergency-room duty—her earlier conclusion that the job was for young people with no other major responsibilities still held true. But she liked the feeling of competence she gained with each night's work. And if some Friday mornings she felt a little tired, she justified the strain as she proudly watched her savings grow, realizing that her dream house was coming closer to reality.

But her friends seemed to worry about her. Karen and Dick in particular thought she was working too hard, that she didn't have enough fun.

"But I'm really not the fun type," Jeannie objected one crisp November morning when Karen expressed concern at how tired Jeannie had looked the previous weekend. "Certainly, sometimes I *am* tired. Like last Thursday, in addition to the usual routine stuff, emergency had a fatal heart attack, two big car wrecks and a drowning. And I saw you two the next night—no wonder Dick thought I looked exhausted! But it's not always like that."

"But it is always steady work, isn't it?" Karen asked. "I'll bet you never have time to get acquainted with any of your colleagues there, not when you rush in just ahead of the clock and have to hurry home to Bruce the minute you're off."

"Well, no, but—"

"You see what I mean? You don't get to visit with people enough. Not here at work, either. You need to be seeing people socially where everyone has time to...just talk!"

"Karen, you're not going to start this fixing-Jeannie-up-with-eligible-men routine again, are you?"

"No. I figure between Bill Hannah and Pete Randing you have all you can handle. But seriously, you'd enjoy being with other couples and families socially. You and Bill ought to help me with this community-center project I've been telling you about. I know of a fun job you both would like and—"

"I thought you said I was working too hard!" Jeannie couldn't help laughing at Karen's inconsistency.

"But this wouldn't be work, it would be play! And you would meet so many nice people of all ages."

"I'll bet your friends all regret the day you became a YMCA director," Jeannie said suspiciously. "How many of them have you already drafted to work on remodeling that old schoolhouse?"

"Well, a few...a few," Karen admitted. "But truly, they're all loving it. They bring their kids and grandpas and old-maid aunts along and—"

"I can see I'm going to get a hard sell," Jeannie groaned. "Why don't you just get on with the nitty-gritty? What is *this* friend who's working too hard supposed to do that's so much fun?"

Even after Jeannie had heard Karen out, she wasn't convinced that she would feel comfortable mingling with all the families Karen so enthusiastically described—Jeannie always felt a little odd at family gatherings. But in the end she agreed to join the group of professionals Karen had drafted to select exercise facilities that the center would make or purchase. It didn't sound as if the assignment would take much time, and Jeannie suspected Karen was right: Probably she did need to meet more people socially.

That same evening after supper, armed with a list of classes the center was considering offering, Jeannie dutifully settled down to study the equipment brochures. She had pictures and catalogs spread all over the kitchen table when Becky Raymond dropped by looking for Greg.

"Have you taken up ballet?" Becky asked, forgetting about her brother when she saw some shots of dancers among the things Jeannie was studying.

"Not I. These are for a project of Dr. Matthews's. The YMCA board of which she's a member is considering offering ballet classes in their new community center. I'm supposed to be helping them decide on exercise equipment of all kinds."

"A real ballet studio could be expensive," Becky said thoughtfully, toying with the photograph. "How serious are the students?"

"That's hard to say. This area of the county where Dr. Matthews lives was farmland five years ago, but now houses are mushrooming by the hundreds. The Y is remodeling an old school to provide recreational facilities until the public services catch up. I suspect that the center would be used primarily as a social and recreational outlet for families."

Becky hesitated momentarily, then blurted, "I wouldn't recommend ballet for people who are just seeking good exercise and an emotional outlet." A slow flush crept up her neck.

Not wanting the girl to think that her suggestions were unappreciated, Jeannie looked at her questioningly.

"Why not?" she asked.

"This probably sounds conceited"—Becky's face became even redder—"but it takes too long with ballet to become good enough to express yourself, especially if you don't start until you're an adult. Modern dance would be a better course to offer."

"Modern dance?"

"They teach it in most colleges now. It takes a long time to be really good, but reasonably athletic people can learn the basic moves quickly; they can *feel* expressive as they dance, so it's a good emotional outlet along with providing exercise."

"And you think it's a good way for adults to keep fit?" Jeannie was fascinated with the girl's interest.

"As good as any amateur dancing. But if you want to give joints and muscles a good workout without injury, I think karate would be better."

"Becky, you move so gracefully, I can't imagine you ever taking karate!"

"Dad used to teach classes, but he wouldn't take me as a student at first," Becky admitted. "But often when I would be stiff after dance practice I'd try some of the martial-arts exercises I'd seen him do when he would work out. It helped limber me up so much that I finally convinced him to let me in his class."

"Was he afraid you'd be hurt?"

"No, he thought karate might interfere with the artistry of the dance."

"And it didn't?"

Becky shrugged nonchalantly. "I'm still practicing karate, and I'm still getting soloist roles."

"It sounds as if you're an all-round athlete, not just a dancer," Jeannie commented.

"I'm really interested in the effect of exercise on the human body," Becky admitted seriously. "Sometimes I wonder if I might like to be a physical therapist."

"I'll be working with one on this committee. If you like, you can come along to our meeting tomorrow and meet her. Dr. Matthews said family and friends are welcome. But I warn you, she's likely to hand you a hammer and paintbrush!''

Jeannie had not really expected Becky to go to the meeting. But the girl did. Her interest in exercise appeared to be genuine, and she readily agreed to Karen's suggestion that she help out on the project too.

And there goes my so-called sterile routine, Jeannie thought after the meeting. The group was frantically trying to finish the center by Thanksgiving, which gave them only about three more weeks. Becky enthusiastically offered the services of her brother. *And that means Bruce will want to go, too*, Jeannie figured, foreseeing herself spending many evenings chauffeuring the kids out to the center, even if she didn't do any work herself. Somehow she couldn't imagine Paul Raymond having the time to drive his kids out there on a regular basis.

Oh, well, she thought philosophically, *Bruce will love a chance to hammer and paint and tote. And Karen was right. These people are nice. At this rate I may as well ask Bill if he wants to help out too.*

PAUL didn't really have the time.

When Becky originally suggested that he join the work on the center, he had mumbled a noncommittal answer and appeared busy with some other problem at the moment. But as he gradually became aware of how much time Bill Hannah was spending on the project with Jeannie, he quickly gave in.

As Paul saw it, Hannah was poaching on *his* territory; it was just that Jeannie didn't realize she was his territory...yet. She was still treating him like a kindly stranger and calling him Mr. Raymond to his face, for God's sake! He was determined to put a stop to that, even if it did mean adding hours of manual labor to his heavy day.

Unfortunately, for Paul it didn't take long at the

center for his great mechanical skills to become known. The short job list to which he had agreed grew. When he wasn't helping Jeannie's group set up the excercise equipment, he was being called upon constantly for various mechanical emergencies throughout the building. It was almost too much, the demands coming on top of doing problem solving all day at work. But he was determined to outlast Bill Hannah.

By the Saturday before Thanksgiving it was apparent, that everyone's efforts were paying off—the center would be ready for opening right after the holiday. Karen ordered an impromptu spread of hot coffee and snacks as a sort of come-and-go celebration for her friends who were at the building, finishing up last-minute tasks.

Jeannie had dropped Bruce off early in the morning, and when she came back late in the afternoon to pick him up, she found that the crowd around the party table had dwindled down to Bruce, the Matthewses, and the Raymond children.

"Do you know what I think I'd like to be?" Becky was asking as Jeannie joined the group. "I'd like to be a doctor specializing in muscular problems."

"I thought you were interested in physical therapy. You've just added five more years to your education!" Jeannie teased as she found a seat at the table.

"What about dancing?" Karen asked as she watched the boys wander off to find some friends. "I've never seen anyone better at it than you."

"Dad is interested in my being a dancer," Becky admitted, "but lately I've begun to think it isn't right for me."

"Where is your dad, by the way?" Karen broke in with a self-conscious laugh. "They're having trouble with a couple of those windows they rehung, and I thought...."

"That poor man is going to regret the day Becky got interested in this project," Dick warned. "You've made him the unofficial maintenance man."

"Do I hear a vaguely familiar description?" Paul seemed to come from nowhere as he settled down beside Jeannie.

"You'd better leave." She looked warningly at him. "Karen has found one last little job for you."

"I thought that the unstable balance beam was the last job," Paul commented, unconcerned that his broad shoulders were crunching Jeannie into the corner. She eased sideways against him for a little more comfort.

"By now you know Karen better than that—" Her teasing stopped in midsentence. "Good heavens!" she gasped involuntarily.

They turned to look in the direction she was staring, but all they could see was an innocuous-looking tall man standing hesitantly in the doorway with a huge box in his arms.

"Oh, it's Pete with those paper products I ordered." Karen waved her arms and he smilingly strode over to join them.

"Pete Randing's a salesman for a paper-packaging company," Karen explained, "and he was able to get what we needed at a good discount."

"Karen, you should have warned me," Jeannie whispered miserably, trying to crunch down out of sight behind Paul's body. He looked at her questioningly.

"An unwelcome admirer." Karen couldn't resist whispering in Paul's ear. "He has three kids, and his eye is on Jeannie as their future mother."

"Aha! Do I recognize that description?" Paul's face was perilously close to Jeannie's, a malicious grin on his face. "Does he chase you around his new apartment?"

"He hasn't found one yet," Jeannie snapped at him belligerently.

Dick watched the by-play in confusion. He had never heard of Pete Randing, and he could not comprehend what Karen and Paul were saying.

"Hey! What a surprise to see you here, Jeannie," Pete exclaimed jovially as he set the box on the floor. "I thought you had work to do at home today."

"I finished earlier than I expected to," she responded quickly, her face red. "I'm here to pick Bruce up. Do you know Dick? And…"

By the time they got through all the introductions and glad-to-meet-yous, Paul had somehow thrown his arm around the back of Jeannie's chair, practically engulfing her. When she moved protestingly against him, he said innocently, "Just thought I'd make room for Hannah. He's on his way over to join us."

Bill obviously did not like the cozy picture he saw, judging from his grim face as he started to sit down. His face hardened even more as he heard Pete say, "That's great you're finished early, Jeannie. Now you can go out with me to dinner after all, can't you?"

"But I have Bruce with me," she stammered uncomfortably.

"Go ahead and keep your date, Jeannie," Dick blustered affably, not noticing his wife's frantic gestures behind Pete's back. "You work too much anyway. We could take Bruce home with us, and you two can pick him up after you have dinner."

Noticing the jealous look on Bill Hannah's face, Paul studied Pete Randing. He looked the prototype of a competent salesman—friendly, good-natured. Probably harmless enough for a short evening.

"Sure, Jeannie, keep your date," Paul emphasized heartily, giving her a brotherly thump on the shoulders, reveling in the distressed look on Bill's face. "I tell you what: I'll just take Bruce on along home with us. Then Pete won't have to make a trip to pick him up."

"That's great! Just great." Pete reached across the table to shake Paul's hand. "I've got this new apartment I want Jeannie to see. But we won't run very late; it's not far from your area." He seemed utterly oblivious to the undercurrents around him.

Honestly! Pete is just like a big dumb puppy dog, Jeannie thought angrily, resenting how they both had been maneuvered. Paul ignored the malevolent look she shot him. Wordlessly she tried to convey her apologies to Bill, but he was staring stonily ahead and wouldn't look her way.

BY THE TIME Pete brought Jeannie home a few hours later, she didn't think of him as a big dumb puppy dog.

Dinner hadn't been so bad—they'd been in a public place. But when they'd got to the vacant apartment Pete had just rented, the puppy dog had become an amorous octopus that chased her not only around the new apartment but across the balcony as well.

With the firm insistence that her neighbor was a busy man and she could not possibly leave Bruce with him late, Jeannie had been able to get headed home at a decent hour with her honor reasonably intact. She had used some feeble excuse to forestall Pete from walking all the way to her door with her because she was determined to get Paul Raymond alone and give him a piece of her mind.

"You really are too much!" she stormed at Paul in the breezeway after she had sent Bruce in to their own apartment. "You know you forced me into that date!"

"How could you have said such terrible things about that man?" Paul responded unsympathetically. "He looked good-natured and harmless enough to me."

"He's about as harmless as a six-handed snake-oil salesman!"

"Well, at least he has marriage on his mind," Paul said mildly, reassured from her appearance that while the struggle might have been hectic, it had not been too serious.

"I don't have marriage on *my* mind. I have murder on my mind—yours!"

She had started to flounce away when she realized that Paul was having trouble restraining his laughter.

Disbelieving, Jeannie turned back to stare at him open mouthed. He was brimming with self-satisfaction.

"You rat!" she finally wailed. "What a terrible way to get even...." But then she began to chuckle helplessly herself.

"What are you doing Thanksgiving?" Paul asked abruptly, his tone casual.

She looked at him suspiciously, not trusting the mischief in his eyes.

"I don't have marriage on *my* mind, either," he reassured her. "Nor murder, for that matter. I have not having to cook our own turkey on my mind."

"You're perfectly capable of cooking a turkey," she said ungenerously.

"It was raw last year." His mouth screwed up with distaste.

It had taken a great deal of effort for him to get the invitation out in such a light vein. Paul hoped she could not see how anxiously he was waiting for her answer.

Jeannie hesitated briefly before sighing unenthusiastically.

"Oh, all right. I suppose you want dressing and all the rest too."

"Of course." His quiet answer did not revel his rising excitement.

"It figures," she snapped, closing her door without looking behind her.

Paul's slow grin burst into a huge smile as he stepped back inside his own place.

Chapter Eight

After the Thanksgiving Dinner in Paul's apartment the two families naturally drifted into spending more time together. On the next Saturday the first snow of the season fell and at Becky's suggestion they went to the zoo to watch the polar bears. On other evenings the children would occasionally decide to watch television or to eat together.

But the more Jeannie saw of the Raymonds the more she told herself that Paul was a solitary man by nature who only came to their impromptu gatherings for the sake of his children. So she was always correctly polite around him and made certain he was never maneuvered into being alone with her. She didn't want him to be uncomfortable about her living next door—she had been through that problem herself and wouldn't wish it on others.

It was disturbing to her, therefore, that her formality seemed to irritate, rather than please him.

The matter came to a head on a mid-December morning when he discovered her standing forlornly in their frozen parking lot, watching a tow truck haul her car away.

"It looks as if you've lost your transportation," he observed sympathetically, tossing his briefcase into the Mercedes before reaching into the back for an ice scraper. "It will take me a few minutes to get this stuff off the windshield, then I'll be glad to run you by your office."

"Thanks, but that won't be necesary, Mr. Raymond," she refused quickly.

"For God's sake, Jeannie," he exploded. "Are you ever going to quit calling me Mr. Raymond? I keep feeling I should hand you a steno pad and start dictating. My name is Paul."

"I think it's disrespectful for Bruce to—"

"Bruce can call me Mr. Raymond. I'd appreciate you calling me Paul." His words were little short of a command.

She stared at him rebelliously but he turned away. "What's wrong with your car?" he asked abruptly as he sent chips of ice flying with his angry motions.

"They think it's the starter switch. I have a new battery but they couldn't even jump it."

"Will it be ready after work?"

"No, I plan to walk over to their shop tomorrow. It's not far."

"Go on in and get your things. You don't even have a coat on. I can drop you off now and swing back by your office whenever you're ready to come home."

"You don't have to do that...Paul. I've already planned to call a cab."

"Jeannie, your pride is nothing short of foolish sometimes." He seemed to have reached the end of his patience. "You are not taking advantage of me by accepting a ride. What's twenty minutes out of my day? Now give me one reason you should deprive Bruce of a new shirt, which is about what a cab will cost you, just for the sake of your own pride?"

She bit her lip childishly, beginning to shiver in the cold. Finally she flounced back to her apartment, unable to fight his logic.

It was an uncomfortable trip. Not physically, for Paul drove expertly and his car held the road like a whispering dream. But the tense silence was terrible. He asked about the decorated cake she was balancing awkwardly on her lap, but her snapped explanation of bringing it for coffee break was so harsh that he didn't venture any more conversation except to seek directions.

Paul had agreed to pick her up at the center's front entrance at five o'clock. Therefore Jeannie was astounded when at four o'clock he walked into her office, carrying two bottles of wine.

"They're Californian Sauvignon Blanc," he said without preamble. "Since it is BYOB I thought this would go well with Dick's fondue."

"How did you find out about the office party?" She couldn't hide her dismay.

He almost looked proud of himself, fleetingly. "You acted so guilty trying to hide that fancy cake I couldn't resist checking it out with Karen Matthews. Why couldn't you just tell me you needed to stay?"

"I don't need to. Besides, this thing will probably run late. There's a band and entertainment—"

"But you had planned to attend before you had car trouble. Karen said you already had a sitter. She claims if we don't stay, Dick won't know anyone here."

"You're not planning—"

"My ego loves your enthusiasm. If I embarrass you, you don't have to sit with me. I do very well at parties by myself."

Her eyes moved from his firmly molded features to his striped shirt, open casually at the throat and showing the strong lines of his neck and the dark hair covering his chest. Ashamed of him? The man was insane.

"You know it's not that. I just don't want you to go to any trouble," she explained belligerently.

"Jeannie, why is it so difficult for you to be around me without our children?" He leaned toward her seriously. "Have I made some off-color remark and offended you?"

"Of course not! It's just that I'm your neighbor."

"That's a problem?"

"Stop being so obtuse. I don't want you to feel... chased."

He laughed sarcastically. "I assure you, you *never* give me that feeling. Quite the opposite."

"Now you're saying I've been rude."

"What would you call it? I haven't had a break from work in weeks. The only social talk I've heard is from teen-agers. Yet the moment I take off early for a party and look forward to adult conversation, you tell me to go the hell back home."

"Damn you!"

Carefully he set the bottles of wine on her desk, his face impassive. "No matter. I'll pick you up at the entrance at nine o'clock. Karen said that's how long the party is to last."

He was almost at the door before she called him back.

THERE WAS a period when Jeannie lost sight of Paul completely. At first she had tried to stay by him and make introductions, but as the party became confusing and she was meeting new people herself, she gave up. Besides he seemed quite comfortable introducing himself if the need arose, and he exhibited no apparent need to cling to her side. He was deep in conversation with a pathologist when she left him to meet the husband of one of her colleagues.

Since the festivities had been set up in the series of lounges spread across the third floor, it was easy to get separated. When Jeannie eventually rediscovered Paul, he was standing at a window talking to the center's administrator while chivalrously serving wine to two women with them.

"I didn't realize you'd be such a dangerous man to bring to a party." She joined him once he was alone again. "I've already had three women bribe me to introduce you."

"Liar." He smiled, selecting two clean glasses from a nearby table before reaching behind a curtain at the window to retrieve an unopened bottle of his wine.

"Your colleagues finished off the other bottle, but I've been keeping this cold for you."

"Mmmm," she murmured approvingly after she took a sip from the brimming glass.

"How is it?"

"Mellow and dry. You mean you haven't had a chance to drink any yourself? You were serious when you said you wanted some adult conversation!"

"You work with nice people. I just got an idea for a new product while talking to your boss."

"You mean the administrator? What product?"

"Energy supplements for computers. He's having too much trouble losing data during fluctuations in electric current. We need to develop some kind of continuously recharging battery that's in partial service at all times, and not dependent upon utility power."

Jeannie stared at him in delight. The man had actually been enjoying himself.

"You devil." Her face broke into a smile. "You didn't come here to converse, you came here to connive!"

"A man has to keep his hand in." He grinned back at her, tucking the bottle under his arm as he held his glass in one hand and took her elbow with the other. "I saw Dick Matthews a minute ago. He said Karen was dragging him off to his one duty dance. I think he wants company."

"I'm sure of it." She let him guide her close to his side as they forced their way through the crowds. "Dick's as bad a dancer as I am and Karen loves to dance. That's their one mismatch. I suspect he hopes you'll dance with her and let him sit with me."

"We can probably arrange a little of that."

"You surprised me about the computers," she returned to his earlier remark when they had to wait for a group of people to pass.

"Hmmm?"

"I thought your new business was a store to sell other people's products."

"I'm an engineer; I help with development of new ideas too," he answered vaguely, his eyes scanning the people seated around the dance floor. "There they are, over to the left."

Jeannie had been right about Dick's motives. They had barely gotten seated at his table and dipped some bread in the cheese fondue he was hoarding for them before he suggested that Paul might like to dance with Karen.

It was all Jeannie could do to avoid laughing out loud.

"You have no shame at all," Karen reprimanded him hotly. "You can surely stand to dance twice with me."

"He can monopolize you later, Karen." Paul's face revealed none of his earlier conversation with Jeannie as he gallantly drew Karen to her feet. "Do an old man a favor and dance with me."

They were a well-matched couple. Karen was almost as tall as Paul and fit nicely against him as he led her expertly to the intricate Latin step. They looked just as good when the band switched into light rock.

"He doesn't dance like an old man," Dick grumbled.

"You can't have it both ways, Dick," Jeannie laughed as she forked another piece of bread. "You can either dance with Karen or take a chance on someone else. Oooh, your fondue is good. I'm glad you didn't put it on the potluck table, you hog!"

A number of people wandered by to visit, while Paul and Karen remained away for several numbers. But Dick's conversation seemed distracted because he was constantly looking around the dance floor, trying to locate his wife. Jeannie was amused at the feeling of relief evident on his face when he finally saw Paul leading Karen back toward them.

It was while Jeannie had her guard down waiting for their return that the stranger asked her to dance. She tried to explain she was waiting for her friend, but the man cheerfully dragged her along with him, unmindful of her protests.

In the movies a heroine's steps always matched the hero's, Jeannie thought dispiritedly as she stiffly struggled to match her feet to her partner's movements. But she just couldn't get the feel of him and she bumped his toes frequently. Amazingly he was so flushed and contented with whatever he had been drinking that he seemed unaware of her mistakes. He held her closely and seemed to be having a wonderful time.

She was painfully embarrassed, knowing that Paul could see her appalling awkwardness.

"I said I couldn't dance, but he wouldn't believe me," she mumbled when her jovial partner finally returned her to her seat.

Paul's eyes were narrowed harshly as he watched the man weave back into the crowd.

"He was too far gone to lead correctly."

"That's chivalrous of you," Jeannie appreciated his remark. "But I assure you I'm that bad with everyone. Dick and I make a good match."

"Dick's not a bad dancer." Karen had overheard their conversation and was looking pointedly at her husband. "He's just lazy."

"That does it, I can't let that pass," Dick objected, firmly grabbing Karen's wrist. "I'll show you who's lazy."

"I'll bet he dances half the evening now." Jeannie smiled at Paul. "Did you plan it, dancing so long with Karen? Your expertise out there made him jealous."

Paul laughed aloud. "It's been years since I've made anyone jealous. I'm complimented."

"You are good, though. We couldn't help but notice."

"I learned in self-defense," he explained lightly. "My wife was a professional dancer. Becky tries to keep me updated but I draw the line at acid rock. That's her current craze."

At his questioning look she let him refill her glass.

"You're a light drinker," he observed as he served himself from the bottle, which was still more than half full. "Remind me to take you to a party again. What is this event about, by the way? One couple we passed wished us Merry Christmas but someone else congratulated Karen on her un-graduation."

"I haven't the foggiest what we're celebrating!" The noise level was increasing so much that Jeannie had to lean close to Paul to be heard. "It started out as a Christmas party, but our one atheist suggested we salute the Great Pumpkin instead, and Alice Quan suggested observing early Chinese New Year. Then my boss said it was his son's birthday, and the party exploded from there."

"That explains the eclectic decorations." Paul looked curiously around the room. "Dragons, Santa Claus, Snoopy, a canoe...a canoe?" His laughing question hung unanswered as he slid closer to her to make room for two couples who were drawing up chairs. The band was taking a break and almost immediately more than a dozen noisy couples were crowded around their small table for six.

"The only trouble with dances," Paul said into Jeannie's ear as he laid his arm loosely along the back of her chair, "is that even though the music stops, people still think they have to shout."

She nodded her head but didn't even bother to answer, knowing that they would both be hoarse if they tried to converse under those circumstances. It was not unpleasant, though, leaning back in the circle of his arm and sipping her wine in the relative quiet of their own making. There was so much to watch.

It didn't occur to her that he might be bored until the music resumed and the table cleared out once again.

"If you want to dance with someone, I certainly don't mind."

"I do at that!" He curved his arm about her waist and took her hand.

"No! I didn't mean me," she protested sincerely, trying to pull back.

"You know I can't dance. I'm too rusty. I'm no match for you, I really don't—"

She was saved from further protests when the lights suddenly dimmed, announcing the entertainment. People were scrambling to their chairs as a slow, tension-building roll began on the drums. Paul still had his arm around her as they sat back down and watched the spotlight circle the smoke-filled room.

There was a strange hush when the drum roll finally reached fever pitch, then suddenly broke off. The spotlight shifted to multicolors as it settled on a statuesque woman posed ethereally upon the stage.

"A belly dancer!" a voice close to them enthused.

The woman was beautiful—tall and voluptuous in her harem pants, scanty bra, and fragile gauzy veils. Her hands were frozen aloft in the classic pose of the exotic dancer, her chin tilted in queenly disdain. She had everyone's rapt attention when she finally broke her pose, her sequined navel glittering as she slowly began her graceful undulations. The only sound in the room was the faint metallic tinkling of her finger cymbals.

The band began to pick up her rhythm, gradually adding the exotically disharmonic music as she bent her body backward, the veils falling away briefly to show her costume. A murmur seemed to spread over the group, then die as she snapped suddenly erect and resumed the classic, strangely beautiful arm movements.

Jeannie was enthralled with the sensuous beauty of the dance.

Even as the woman stretched her toes delicately and

stepped down to move among the crowd, her demeanor maintained a subtle blend of eroticism and purity. Rather than attracting admiration only to herself, the dancer seemed to be a catalyst to the passions laying dormant among the couples watching her. One could sense the emotions building as she swayed, her bowed head letting her shining brown hair fall in a mysterious cloak about her. She would remain only a short time in one place, not letting the tension build beyond a certain peak before, with a disdainful wave of her veil, she had drifted away. The whole audience seemed to sense in her dance a pattern of growing intensity and seeking.

Jeannie was crushed so close to Paul at their crowded table that she could feel his every movement against her own body, so she was aware when he drew some paper from his pocket, folded it, and placed it on the table beside his lighter and cigarettes. She did not have time to wonder about his action, though, for the spotlight just then caught them in its outermost edge. Paul fell perfectly still, almost as if waiting. The moment the light teased across his shining black hair the dancer's eyes seemed to brighten with noticeable fire. The audience noticed her change in demeanor. She clattered her finger cymbals, signaling the musicians into an even more erotic refrain as she honed directly to Paul and Jeannie.

His muttered "Damn, I knew it" was so out of character that she looked at him to see what was wrong. But his impassive face convinced her she had not heard him correctly. His blue-black beard was evident even in the muted colors of the dancer's light, intensifying the stern masculinity of his face. Paul's lips curled knowingly before he looked the woman in the eye, then turned slightly away. Deliberately he raised his arm intimately around Jeannie's shoulders, his hand moving to play inside the soft collar of her V-necked dress.

Surprised by his public fondling, Jeannie at first started to draw away. Then instinctively she realized,

He's doing this for a reason... all for the dance. She remained motionless as she felt his hand caress sensuously across her neck. The dancer's eyes flashed and she arched her body invitingly, as if teasing Paul's attention back to herself. A murmur of reaction swept across the room as people became aware of the erotic game. Almost feeling vibes pass from Paul's warm body to her own, Jeannie was totally engulfed as a necessary participant in his mysterious ability to aid the dancer in her performance.

"But what do they want me to do?" she wondered momentarily. The dancer was circling her hips before Paul slowly, temptingly, throwing out a mock challenge—his choice between herself and his own woman. The audience loved it.

I should act confident, yet try to compete.

Once again Paul was pointedly ignoring the dancer. He had lowered his head to place a cigarette in his mouth with one hand, his other still playing across Jeannie's neck and shoulders.

In what she hoped was just the right combination of encouragement and confidence, Jeannie daringly elevated her body, as if inviting his hand to move lower. Immediately Paul flipped open his lighter, setting a brief glow on both their faces before hiding them in a curl of smoke. Only after taking a slow, full draw on his cigarette did he raise his head, as if announcing to the dancer that she might momentarily have his attention.

The woman pulsated before them, sliding her veils gracefully across herself, then letting them glide slowly down, urging the eyes to follow the curvaceous line of her body from the creamy fullness of her breasts to her low-slung, bejeweled hip belt. Paul drew another long drag off his cigarette, and Jeannie temptingly moistened her lips with her tongue just as he let the smoke form a cocoon around them. Their actions seemed to incite the dancer, who flicked her veils wildly. The erotic game was drawing all viewers into its spell. Jeannie could feel the woman's grinding undulations echoing within herself as Paul's hand slid just inside her sweater and spread fully across her collarbone, his thumb settling in the hollow of her throat. His touch seemed to dominate her.

Changing the mood yet again, the dancer twirled completely around twice, her arms gloriously graceful in their odd movements as she expertly let her veil glide like a thin white cloud between them. She turned Paul's face toward herself, but he drew back at the last moment, allowing her to tease her garment off his face in the slightest promise of a kiss.

Then the woman's movements became frenzied, her mood picked up and repeated by the musicians. A thousand colors sparkled off the jeweled beads lining her hips. The swirling of her gauzy harem pants emphasized the beauty of her long legs. Just as it seemed her audience could stand no more tension, the dancer broke her rhythm completely. She paused motionless before Paul, a warm, curvaceous statue, so close she could almost fit against his knee. Instantaneously Jeannie froze the scene in her mind—the gauzy fabric, the shape of the creamy ankle contrasting Paul's dark socks and black shoe.

It was her move.

Instinctively she slid her free hand caressingly down his arm, from his elbow to the powerful wrist, then cautiously over his fingers. He turned his hand to capture hers, letting his elbow slide below her breast as he drew her closer to him. It was a slight gesture, but effective. The audience murmured in anticipation as the dancer initiated the slow, flowing movements of her belly, turning gradually in a circle so that everyone could enjoy her pulsating beauty. The room was unearthly still when she finally faced Paul again. Her head fell back suddenly, her breasts lifted high as she let her hair drag the floor behind her just before she flipped forward so that her gorgeous hair formed a momentary curtain around Paul's face. Immediately she stepped back, posed vibrantly erect before them with aloof question.

His only movement was to tilt his head slightly in a noble sign of approval. Then in a gesture so natural it was as if he had arranged the whole performance for his own benefit, he tucked a folded ten-dollar bill within the edge of the dancer's gauzy bra. Immediately she kicked her leg high above her in a magnificent movement, then in a flutter of veils ran out among the crowd again.

The applause was spontaneous.

The remainder of the dance was almost anticlimactic to Jeannie, although obviously not to others. The dancer moved around the room, pausing only briefly in her routine if a man held up a folded bill he wanted to tuck into her garments. Her gestures were still lovely but the wonder and tension had relaxed into enjoyable play involving all couples.

"None of the men can tuck money as disdainfully as you," Jeannie whispered to Paul, who was still crushed close to her. He raised an eyebrow as if daring her to try teasing him anymore.

"I've had some practice," he admitted wryly. "Belly dancers have honed in on me before. Thanks for your cooperation, by the way!" His appreciation pleased her.

It was not until the woman returned toward the stage in an obvious finale that the eroticism of the opening music began again. It started in the band with a softening and slowing, then was repeated as a second colored spotlight roved the audience before catching Paul's black head, highlighting his features as the dancer honed toward him. Her costume was now filled with money, yet her face had the same fiery aloofness that she had maintained throughout. Her final challenge was brief and beautiful. She swayed a few moments before throwing her veils around both Paul and Jeannie, drawing their heads together in a sensuous gesture of blessing before slowly trailing the fabric off their shoulders. Then she ran gracefully to the stage, her colored veils blowing behind her, paused, fell into a deep bow, and disappeared.

The applause thundered on for minutes.

But true to her aloof image, the dancer did not return.

Eventually the band shifted back into dance music and the houselights were raised slightly, encouraging people to return to their partying.

And it was then the comments exploded all around them. Instantaneously, loudly, and in mass confusion.

"Jeannie, you'd better watch that man!" "Hey, Paul, did that dancer know...?" "How'd you get that money out so...?"

The reaction was volleying around them in such a mood-shattering shambles that Jeannie willingly allowed Paul to lift her to her feet. She scarcely heard his laughing rejoinders to the group as he led her away and she was in the middle of the crowded dance floor before she realized his intentions.

"I can't dance with you," she gasped in terror, trying to tug away. But he ignored her protests, drawing her so close against him that her body had to move involuntarily in harmony with his.

"It's so crowded out here all we can do is stand and hold on to each other anyway," he reassured her quietly, his lips close to her ear. "I could do without all those questions for a few moments, couldn't you?"

She realized he was right about the dancing; it was not possible to move—she could only embrace him. Nodding her head in agreement, she let her hand settle against his neck, grateful that he didn't want to talk either. Although she had known all along that the exotic dance was just a game, she was gripped in a resulting vulnerable mood that was made even more euphoric by the warmth of Paul's unavoidable closeness and the mellowness of the wine she had consumed. It felt soothing just to sway with him, his cheek against her hair, as the band played one, then another haunting melody.

"Are you going to sleep?" His gentle question was almost caressing. "Belly dancers are supposed to stimulate you." His hand moved idly up her back, encouraging her to relax even more, and she knew there was no criticism in his words.

"You don't seem all that frantically active yourself." She let him tuck her head against his shoulder. "You were magnificent, you know. You'd make a wonderful Arab sheikh."

"I try to please." She could feel his smile against her hair as his arm completely enfolded her and she let her own arms slip under his shoulders.

"If you were my husband, I would have been jealous."

"No, you wouldn't. I'd never give you any cause for jealousy." His mouth felt like a light kiss against the nape of her neck. But she couldn't be certain. She stirred slightly in his embrace. As if sensing her sudden wariness, he loosened his hold and guided her into a pocket of space suddenly opened to the side of them.

"I've enjoyed this break with your friends," he said gruffly. "I don't make myself get away from work often enough."

It was such a casual remark that it put her rising doubts at rest. She leaned back slightly. "I guess I'm glad you made me come too," she admitted. She started to say more, but the light mood was shattered quickly and effectively. They had worked their way toward the cooler area at the edge of the dance floor and a large group of partygoers nearby had recognized them. They were immediately surrounded, as everyone loudly congratulated them on stealing the show. There were numerous teasing remarks before one doctor grabbed Jeannie's hand and insisted that he and Paul exchange partners for the next dance.

Jeannie had become separated from Paul in the crush and she looked about, panic-stricken. "We really have to leave now. Paul said that—" She was trying to prevent being swung out on the dance floor and was almost shaking in fright when she felt Paul's arm around her, heard his voice making cheerful explanations as he led her away.

"Do you really want to go home now?" he asked her quietly once they were free of their admirers.

She nodded dumbly. She was overcome with such frightened shyness that she hardly knew how Paul made their good-byes, collected their things, and got her away from the party.

"Jeannie, you need to give yourself therapy for confidence," he said calmly, his hand reassuringly at her back as they walked toward her office where they had left their coats. Their steps echoed hollowly in the empty corridors. "I take it this flap was because that man wanted to dance with you?"

Her annoyed shake of the head gave him his answer.

"You did just fine with me. That man wouldn't have eaten you alive."

"You and I didn't dance. We just stood there and held each other. I certainly wouldn't do that with someone else," she fumed illogically. She angrily smacked her keys into her lock and didn't see his self-satisfied smile. And he didn't renew the subject as he helped her into her coat, then shrugged on his own heavy parka.

They were walking arm-in-arm along the sidewalk, braced against the bitter winds flowing across the open lawns, before he remembered the cake.

"I left your pan behind." He stopped suddenly.

"I can get it another day." Jeannie urged him forward again. Letting him draw her close, she could sense him shivering.

"Coward!" he chuckled. "Why aren't you cold? A Hawaiian should have as much trouble adjusting to this weather as an Arizonian."

She watched his breath make patterns in the icy, star-studded night. "I thought you were an Arizonite."

"No more wine for you," he groaned at her nonsense. "Why aren't you cold?"

"You forget I didn't always live in Hawaii. I'm accustomed to Kansas and Minnesota."

He bundled her inside his car and she reached across to unlock his own side for him. It felt good to remain huddled against him in the frigid interior, but once the luxurious automobile began to get warm she gradually retreated back into her own corner.

And with the return of her body heat the euphoria of the whole pleasant evening began to wear off. She watched Paul's large hands manipulate the wheel, his competence making her strangely nervous. Recollections began to worry her.

How could I have been so...friendly? She questioned her behavior. *Did I overdo at the party? Is he going to think I expect...*

Her smile gradually dimmed and her replies to Paul's casual comments were stilted at best, so her distress was painfully evident. But she could do nothing to stop her reactions. By the time they reached home, she was too upset even try. She scrambled out of the car, as spooked as a teen-ager on a first date.

"Jeannie, what am I going to do with you?" Paul's tolerant question was gentle as he grabbed her hand and prevented her from walking ahead of him.

"We've been great friends all evening. Now all at once you're obviously afraid of me. Do you think that belly dancer got me so lustful I'm going to force my way into your apartment? That's hardly logical, you know. The minute we start up those stairs I'll bet there will be three faces peering over the banister."

She felt a little foolish.

"I just thought...maybe I'd been over-friendly tonight."

"I needed friendship tonight." He let go of her hand

as his steps matched hers. "Now relax. We're just two adults who've been to a pleasant party."

She was trying to frame an apology when they reached the breezeway, but the opportunity never occurred. True to his prediction, all three children had tumbled eagerly to the top of the stairs, full of questions.

"Did you bring home any cake?"

Bruce's eager query seemed uppermost in their minds as they all crowded into Jeannie's apartment. She was so busy answering their questions that she didn't even notice Paul help Mrs. Westerdale into her coat, pay her, and see her safely downstairs. Only when the apartment was empty of visitors and Bruce was rummaging in the kitchen for a snack to make up for the missing cake, did she wonder how she could ever have thought Paul Raymond would want to kiss her good night.

Chapter Nine

It was Paul's suggestion that Jeannie and Bruce go with them to see Becky dance the annual Christmas-season performance of *The Nutcracker* with the St. Louis symphony.

After she accepted the invitation, Paul warned her not to plan to be home early, because the families of the cast were all invited to an after-performance party at the Chase Hotel.

"Wear something pretty," he advised humorously. "I think Becky plans to look quite theatrical for the occasion."

Upon hearing of the party, Jeannie almost reneged on her enthusiastic acceptance. She had objected that she and Bruce weren't family and that they could drive themselves to the performance so Paul could go on to the party. But he ignored her protests, leaving her committed to both occasions.

After a dissatisfying initial search of her meager dress-up wardrobe, Jeannie had impulsively bought a rather daring sweater dress for the occasion. But when she tried it on again the night of the performance, she decided that the plunging neckline was not suitable after all and changed to an old, long black printed skirt and demure white blouse. Then right up to the time to go she worried about whether *that* choice was acceptable.

As she flipped off the lights, leaving only the Christmas-tree colors glowing in the living room, Jeannie tried to quell her rising nervousness. She couldn't imagine why she was so restless and wondered if she was getting excited about the Christmas season in general. It was the first time in her life that she could do as she pleased on the holiday. She decided that after the party she would invite the Raymonds to spend Christmas Day with them; maybe the Raymond children would like coming to her apartment for dinner this holiday, since they had entertained on Thanksgiving.

Jeannie was pacing around the dimly lighted room, patting and repatting her hair and urging Bruce to hurry up with his tie, when Paul arrived to get them.

Later she wondered why she had been all that concerned about her appearance anyway.

When she opened the door to Paul, he was not alone—a tall gorgeous woman was fitted to his arm as if she had been there all her life. They made an elegant couple, the fashion-plate blonde and Paul, overwhelmingly virile-looking in what was obviously a tailor-made dark suit and matching overcoat. Jeannie had never perceived him in quite that way before, perhaps because she had always considered him a solitary man. The intimate glances the woman was giving him tossed that misconception right out of the window.

Her name was Carol Sasser and she was from Arizona. While Paul was making the introductions Jeannie was taking in the long scarlet tunic beneath Carol's fur cape. The garment was split to the knee, revealing shapely legs and high-heeled sandals made of the wispiest of fabrics. Jeannie hoped her own long skirt hid the low-heeled pumps she had sensibly chosen in case they had to walk in the snow.

"Is she a model?" Bruce whispered in awe to Greg.

"No, I'm a ballet teacher," Carol charmingly explained, not at all put out by overhearing his question. "I was in Saint Louis for a convention that ended yesterday, but when I called Paul and learned that Becky was performing tonight, I stayed over to see her. She is the best pupil I've ever had. Have you seen her dance?"

The question seemed to be directed at Jeannie, and

when she shook her head Carol added, "You'll love her."

"I already do," Jeannie answered belligerently. It seemed a strange answer, even to herself. But then, she was feeling strange about this whole evening. As she led the way down the breezeway stairs, hugging her serviceable cloth coat to her, she was grateful she had not worn the sweater dress after all. Her attempts at glamour would have been ridiculous beside this lovely creature.

A strange, sad feeling of disappointment was nagging her when they entered the elegant foyer of Power Hall— so much so that she hardly noticed the famous crystal chandelier glistening in their thousands of facets over the heads of the milling symphonygoers, hardly looked at the ropes of greenery and huge red bows that wound their decorative way up the three balconies. She had seen the pictures of the hall in the St. Louis papers— thousands of area residents came to see its traditional Christmas finery during the numerous holiday concerts, and she had thought she could hardly wait to see it for herself. But now that she was here, everything seemed to go flat. She wanted to get into the darkened hall and retreat into a corner.

Jeannie tried to slip into a seat beyond Greg and Bruce, but somehow the boys were too fast for her, and she found herself between Greg and Carol, caught in the aura of the woman's understated perfume and dazzling smile.

If it weren't such a genuine smile, Jeannie realized angrily, *I could hate her.*

But she couldn't drum up much comfort that way; the woman obviously sensed Jeannie's discomfort and did everything she could to put her at ease. Oddly, that didn't help Jeannie's feeling a bit.

It wasn't until the houselights dimmed, however, that Jeannie realized her anguish went far beyond concern about her own appearance. In a sudden rush of nervousness her thoughts became focused on Becky, that darling young woman she had become so fond of. The curtain was opening, the lush sounds of the orchestra were echoing the excitement created by the glittering setting on the stage, and a new emotion engulfed Jeannie: fear.

She was swamped with a realization of the enormity of Becky's undertaking. Say what Becky would in all modesty, it was obvious from the program that she was the major soloist among the local performers. And there was a full crowd in the hall, an elegantly dressed holiday crowd seeking excellence in entertainment. Jeannie looked across at Paul in panic.

But he was staring stonily ahead, his tightly compressed lips a little white. It surprised her that he was clutching the armrests of his seat as desperately as she clutched hers.

And so it was not Paul who gave her reassurance, but Carol Sasser, offering aid to both of them. Calmly Carol lifted her elegantly manicured hands and gently patted both Jeannie's and Paul's, a confident smile warming her face as in a noisy burst of gaiety the dancers filled the stage. The age-old story of the children's Christmas party and the gift of the nutcracker was on.

Waiting through the gay little dances and the familiar music was sheer anguish for Jeannie; she felt sick with the suspense, wanting only for Becky to appear and end this agony.

But from the moment Becky sailed onto the stage, Jeannie was completely lost in the beauty of the girl's performance. Her talent was so inspired, her movements so flowing, that Jeannie was absolutely shaken when the solo was over, unable even to join the thunderous applause that came spontaneously from the audience. She could not move, she could not look at Paul; she could only clutch Carol Sasser's hand.

The waiting for Becky's second solo was not as bad. And in this final act Becky seemed even better, if that were possible; she seemed to glow with a stage presence that was shared only by the professional soloists. Jeannie was able this time to join the applause with a pride of possessiveness that puzzled her. Fleetingly she sympathized with Paul's apparent determination that Becky should become a professional dancer; talent such as hers was rare indeed.

Once it was all over and they had made their way to the Chase Hotel for the party, Jeannie was a shaken bundle of nerves. And that didn't make sense. She was no longer uncomfortable with Carol Sasser; indeed she had to admit she liked her. She was not worried about Becky any longer. But as Paul tucked Jeannie's hand under one arm and Carol's under the other and they followed the triumphant Becky, who was hauling Bruce and Greg with her, Jeannie wanted to escape. They had no time to talk, no time to unwind from the tension—there had been too much laughing confusion as everyone piled into the car to drive to the hotel. Then suddenly there Jeannie was in the midst of the beautiful people of the ballet world, feeling very much out of her element. Had Carol not stayed by her side most of the evening, intervening when people insisted on talking too much ballet, Jeannie would have withered into misery. As it was, she was an automaton.

Somehow she and Carol got separated from Paul and the three children. But Jeannie was sure she did all the right things: She helped herself to the champagne and little sandwiches, she did not spill anything on the Oriental carpets, and she repeated the correct nothings to the people she met. But she wanted to go home. It seemed like an eternity before Paul finally shepherded Becky and the boys toward her.

Maybe it was the unaccustomed flush from the champagne. Or the surprising discovery of Becky's great talent. But when Jeannie saw her young neighbor again, the enormity of the whole evening absolutely closed in on her. She was horrified to find her eyes spilling tears.

"Oh, Becky," she croaked achingly, trying to explain away her crying. "It's just that I was so worried for you . . . and then so proud!"

Paul looked at her steadily over the heads of the partygoers.

"We're going home," he announced abruptly.

He dropped Carol Sasser off at her motel first. When he came out from seeing her safely inside, Jeannie could not help noticing the smudge of lipstick on his face. The children, however, were too engrossed in their conversation to notice.

Carol's motel was near Lambert Airport, and it was a long drive across county to their apartments. Jeannie kept telling herself that the lipstick smudge made no difference; it was none of her business. But it bothered her. She could think of nothing to say the whole way home.

Finally they were all walking up the stairs of the breezeway, but she had not even managed to issue the invitation she had been planning for Christmas Day. She wasn't even sure if she wanted to—now.

The children were unmindful of her preoccupied silence; their cheerful chatter went over her head until she realized Greg seemed to be asking her a question for a second time.

"Could Bruce come in for a minute?" Greg asked again. "We want to give him his Christmas present now, since we'll be leaving tomorrow to spend the holiday in Arizona."

She literally stared at him openmouthed.

"You can't go!" Bruce wailed. "I'm not picking your present up till tomorrow evening. I thought we'd be spending Christmas together just like we did Thanksgiving...."

"I can get it when we come back," Greg said cheerfully, not waiting for Jeannie's permission as he dragged Bruce into his apartment. "We'll be home right after New Year's. Wait till you see what Becky and I picked out for you!"

Blindly Jeannie moved to her own door. Of course nothing had been said about Christmas, she thought. But like Bruce, she had just assumed....Christmas seemed a time for sharing.

She was fumbling for her keys when she realized with surprise that Paul was right behind her. Belatedly remembering her manners, she turned awkwardly and began a stiffly polite little thank-you speech.

Exasperatedly Paul tore the keys from her hands. "We'll freeze out here," he swore, shoving her in ahead of him and closing the door firmly behind them.

She leaned against the wall as she looked up at him, and he moved close enough almost to pin her there.

"Look, Jeannie I just want to wish you Happy Christmas," he said gruffly. "I'm taking the kids to Tucson tomorrow to see Ben and Lucille...." His voice trailed off as he studied her sad face in the gay colors of the Christmas-tree lights. He had no words to explain that he wished he could stay, that he had not told her before because he couldn't bear the thought of leaving her. But Ben and Lucille were so alone, and they loved his children as if they were their own.

"I know it will mean a lot to Lucille to have them." Her voice had a forlorn little-girl quality as she tried not to stare at the lipstick smudge nestling too near his mouth. She was all eyes, the champagne lessening her ability to hide her disappointment.

"Look, have a nice holiday!" He tried to smile, determined to keep this good-bye casual. "Don't stand under too much mistletoe."

Her eyes moved to his mouth.

"You're the one who has to watch out for mistletoe," she said in a too sophisticated voice. "That lipstick isn't exactly your shade."

His eyes narrowed.

Dammit! He couldn't explain that it had been a good-bye kiss. A *real* good-bye kiss. What had Carol said? "I'm glad I was able to meet your Jeannie. You deserve the best, dear friend." And she had kissed him quickly—perhaps a little regretfully?

Paul's angry silence alarmed Jeannie and she would have moved away if she could have. She wished she had kept quiet about the lipstick.

"In that case," he said cryptically, eyeing her trembling mouth, "I may as well try another shade."

He had intended to keep it friendly, a cheerful mistletoe-nonsense kiss. But the instant his lips touched hers it was all there — his longing, his frustration. Both he and Jeannie caught the fire.

Their lips clung, burned, pleaded.

He slid his hands through her hair to cup her face so that he could lift her mouth more deeply into his. Instictively she opened her soul to him, not understanding what was happening, but at that moment not caring. This kiss went on and on, then started afresh even more sensuously. As his hands absorbed the pulsing in her throat, Paul could not control his desperation to feel her against him. He spread both their coats aside and eased her against his aching body, his lips never leaving hers. But her softness and warmth had barely penetrated to his body when his vulnerable senses were startled by the noise of children's laughter in the hall.

"Damn!" Paul groaned.

It was cruelty. It was a vicious joke.

He leaned away from her reluctantly. She didn't move, rather like a helpless wild-eyed little creature pulsating before him.

Momentarily they were suspended there — he looking at her yearningly, his fingertips seemingly unable to leave her body completely, pausing to rest sensitively on her breasts. She did not try to remove his hands.

"You've had too much champagne." She blinked away tears.

"So have you." He could feel the rapid rise and fall of her breathing through the fabric of her blouse.

Then abruptly the moment was over.

"Hey, Mom!" Bruce objected loudly. "You've locked me out!"

Later, alone in the kitchen, Jeannie scrubbed angrily at her mouth. She noticed that one button of her blouse had strained open, and she hastily rebuttoned it. Then decisively she went to the memo board by the telephone, scrawling a message she was unlikely to forget anyway: "Ask Bill for Xmas."

Chapter Ten

I'm going to have to work out something better for this company. God help us if Ben or I ever have an extended illness, Paul thought disgustedly as he continued his slow progress through the stack of papers on his desk. It was into the second week after New Year's, and he was still tackling work that had piled up during his Christmas holiday.

While Terry had been able to take some of the load off his shoulders, there were still many areas of expertise that required Paul's judgment; as yet he had no employee qualified to take over certain complicated financial and technical decisions.

If I could just hire one accountant who has a real grasp of engineering, and one... scientist? No, an inventor— that's what I really need. That would do me; my staff would be complete and there would not be such near disaster every time I take a few days off.

His thoughts were becoming repetitious and he leaned back to take a little break from the grind; these fourteen-hour days since he'd returned were beginning to get to him. It had been nice, the sunshine in Arizona; and the holiday hadn't been a total loss business-wise. He and Ben had gone over all the data Paul had collected thus far, and they had decided on the modifications necessary to make their newest products suitable for unstable weather conditions. Paul had already turned many of those modifications over to his engineering staff.

If only it weren't so damn cold! After basking in the sun he was having trouble adjusting again. Paul was unconsciously shivering slightly as he looked out at the snow-covered fields stretching away from the office. The sight of the other permanent buildings, all fully occupied now, gave him great satisfaction. The company could never have made it through the winter in those temporary facilities. The little trailer that had been Paul's office was now being used for some nonpriority work, and its heating system was fighting a losing battle to keep interior temperatures above 50°. This latest winter storm had been registering close to zero for five days now.

Too bad a winter tan doesn't keep you as warm as you look, he thought as he glanced down at the newly acquired brownness of his hands. Lucille always swore that if you felt perpetually chilled you were coming down with some illness. But he attributed his present problem to the change in temperature—his body still thought it was operating in desert warmth when it was actually back in Missouri during the state's worst winter in more than a century.

It was quiet working at the office on a Saturday with only Terry and a couple of other employees around the building somewhere. Usually Paul insisted that all his staff take their weekends off, but this was one time he had welcomed offers of help. They were getting a lot done with this freedom from routine office interruptions. He really should continue working until late tonight. But that thought no sooner occurred to him than he dismissed it.

He'd hardly seen the kids for ten days. Even in the confusion at home he could surely find time to get through the work that absolutely had to be finished this weekend. And if he just kept up this fourteen-hour pace for a few more days next week, he should be caught up. Then he could resume his personal life.

Resume it! You may have to start from scratch again, he thought ironically. *Jeannie probably thinks you're dead.*

Of course he had called her as soon as they returned, and she had sounded glad to hear from him. But it had been impossible to ask her out; his work was too pressing. Ruefully he thought of the days in his twenties when he had regularly spent twelve grueling hours on construction crews in blistering heat, then come home to shower and party all evening. And even in that first ecstatic year of marriage the workdays had been long—but so had the nights!

Lord, he was getting *old*, couldn't even summon enough energy after a long workday to be with the woman he loved. Well, not exactly that; it was the lack of privacy too. If only his house were completed; if he could just come home exhausted but know that later he would be alone with her in their private world. But with three wild ones always underfoot? No way! Now if he wanted to see Jeannie alone, he had to shave and shower, put on a suit, take her to a public restaurant, and hope for a chance to have a quiet conversation together.

He'd be an unrealistic fool if he resented sharing Jeannie with their children, but it was becoming urgent, this need to have her to himself occasionally. They needed to talk. He was not a poet; he had no words. But given privacy and time to piece his thoughts together, he was hoping to tell her what she meant to him, urge her to think about their future.

Next week. He determined he would get to it then.

Somewhat heartened by that decision, he turned his attention back to the papers on his desk, determined to leave the office at a decent hour.

Becky and Greg were delighted when he got home shortly after six o'clock. Not only were they glad to see their father, but his arrival meant they could escape the confines of the apartment and the boredom of each other's company.

"Hamburgers from Burger Chef, and eat them there!" Greg suggested, putting the can of deviled ham he had been examining back in the kitchen cabinet.

"Pizza from Pizza Inn, Daddy!" Becky danced around him cajolingly. "Then you can get a beer!"

"I'll tell you what," Paul said on impulse. "We'll call the Rasmussens. If they want to come along, we'll let them decide."

I should have done this last week, he thought as he eagerly dialed, *not let so much time go by before we got together. My nerves can take three children too; that's better than nothing.*

But that decision to face an outing with both families had been an intellectual exercise only. Jeannie had other plans.

He thought she sounded a little tense on the phone. Not unfriendly, because she asked about all of them and even shared a couple of funny incidents about her work before hanging up. *Like the best of old friends*, Paul thought glumly. But still, he knew he had not imagined that tenseness. He felt a vague worry as he returned to the teasing entreaties of his children.

EVEN though it had been good to hear from Paul, Jeannie replaced the phone sadly, half wishing he had not called this particular night. During that long Christmas holiday when he was in Arizona, she had missed being able to count on his presence across the hall if she needed him. It had shaken her to realize that Paul had become one of the best friends she had. Yes, *friend*, she told herself firmly. She had dismissed that romantic incident on the night of the Christmas party as champagne nostalgia. Paul needed no one, least of all her. It had been an illusion on her part to consider him a solitary man; obviously he already had Carol Sasser to provide joy in his life. But self-sufficient? Yes, she had been right about that: He was the most self-sufficient individual she knew.

And he was her good friend.

But she did not want to hear from a good friend just then, not when she was making up her mind to spend the night with Bill Hannah. Until that moment when Paul called, she had not considered what her friends might think of her behavior. And she still didn't want to think about it, didn't want to worry about whether or not Paul would think ill of her.

She and Bill had a date for dinner, and he had suggested that if the snow didn't get too bad they could drive downtown later to hear a name band that was appearing at Stouffers. What Bill did not know was that Bruce had gone for an overnight with his Scout troop.

All week long Jeannie had been reasoning that their relationship could not continue much longer in the adolescent limbo she had insisted upon thus far, so if she was ever going to get started in this thing, tonight was the time. *I'm approaching this affair like medicine I have to learn to take*, Jeannie thought bitterly. *Why, when I like Bill so much? Isn't affection enough for a start? With practice surely desire will come....*

She was mad at herself for continuing to waver back and forth at this late moment. She had already dressed in the daring sweater dress she had originally bought for the dance concert. She had spread on the makeup, squirted the perfume, and discarded the jewelry as too awkward to get off quickly. With a come-on like that, Bill's patience and control were certainly going to give out if she backed out of what she was so obviously suggesting.

She fervently wished that Paul Raymond had not called, stirring up all the old inhibitions and misgivings.

When Bill arrived, she was still wearing the dress and still wavering.

"You seem different," he said softly, obviously enjoying looking at her.

From the look on his face she realized that she had better make up her mind fast, because once she let any-

thing get started tonight it was not going to be easy to
stop. And she found she liked being able to inspire that
feeling in a man.

"I think I *am* different," she answered softly, the
decision quickly made. She picked up a light knit cape
that she thought furthered the gorgeous image she was
trying to create.

"Are you sure you'll be warm enough?" Bill asked,
lingeringly settling the lovely garment on her shoulders.

"Of course," she lied, not wanting to wear the heavy
corduroy car coat that was her only other choice. "Anyway, if your car is cold, I can always huddle against
you," she added impulsively, then immediately wondered if the words sounded as corny to him as they did
to her.

They must not have, because he tucked her especially close under his arm as they went out to his car.

For a while she enjoyed herself thoroughly, basking
in pleasure at her success as a seductress. Bill had never
been more attentive.

Luigi's restaurant was well known for its steaks and
there was a large crowd there when they arrived, despite the fact that snow was falling heavily. They were
able to get the last two stools at the intimate little bar,
so waiting for a table was fun. As is frequently the case
when strangers are thrown together in a winter storm,
all the patrons were visiting together as if they were old
friends, and it was almost a disappointment to have to
pick up their half-finished cocktails and move on to
their dining table.

They ordered Luigi's famous toasted ravioli, but
Jeannie turned down a second cocktail, determined
that any euphoria she felt on this night would come
from her new relationship, not from overindulgence in
alcohol. And for a long time she did feel quite euphoric. They were seated at one of the leather-padded,
high-walled booths that lined the room on an elevated

walkway, and the intimacy in the tiny candlelit cubicle was pleasurable. They felt no sense of hurry, and it was a long time before they progressed to their delicious steak and salad, choosing even to linger over second cups of coffee.

Suggesting that they had better look at the weather before they decided to drive downtown, Bill had just called for his check when a small combo began to set up instruments in one corner of the dining room.

"Are you having dancing?" he asked the waiter, surprised because Luigi's was not known for having entertainment.

"During January we have been," the waiter explained. "Late-dinner business always lets up because of the weather, so we've found that serving fondues and providing music helps take up the slack. Want to change your mind and stay?"

"I'm not much of a dancer, Bill."

"Neither am I. But we could do lots of listening."

At Jeannie's nod Bill handed back the check and told the waiter to bring them after-dinner drinks.

It was a nice end to their evening out. Once the clatter and confusion of clearing out the tables to create a small dance floor ended, the lights were dimmed and the trio began to play soft music. The logs in the huge fireplace fronting the room blazed cheerily, providing as romantic a setting as anyone could want on a stormy night. Bill was as self-conscious about his dancing as Jeannie, and only asked her to dance during the slow, crowded numbers. That suited her fine, and she enjoyed listening to the band with him.

It was after midnight when they left.

Bill's car was quite cold after standing idle so long in the freezing temperatures, and Jeannie, not even remembering her corny remark earlier in the evening, gratefully huddled close to Bill until the car warmed up. When she eventually started to move away, he threw an arm around her shoulders to keep her there.

Despite the storm, or perhaps because of it, the drive back was heartbreakingly beautiful. Lush music from the car stereo cast its own aura, augmenting the rainbow-colored beauty of the city lights sparkling off the falling snowflakes.

During the drive Jeannie had no doubts, no concern about where things were leading. Not until Bill finally broke the relaxing silence.

"Jeannie, I want to be with you a while longer"—his hand tightened on her shoulder—"and it's so damned adolescent and difficult to kiss you in the car. Surely your sitter could stay a bit later while we stop at my apartment for a drink?"

She was surprised at the lurch in her stomach, the tightening in her throat as she realized that the moment was here. Her voice did not seem to be working quite properly as she forced out the quiet response: "I don't have a sitter tonight. Bruce is at Boy Scout camp."

"You're kidding!" Bill exploded. "He'll freeze his b—"

She giggled nervously at that.

"That's what I thought too, but it's the truth—he's on a Scout overnight. His leaders say they have a heated winter cabin complete with electricity and beds."

"Well, I'll be damned," Bill murmured reflectively, the possibilities of the situation fully dawning on him. He said nothing else, not until he had parked outside his own apartment building. And then he merely placed his hand over hers and murmured, "I thought you might prefer my place?"

She nodded her assent, feeling strangely disembodied.

His arm slipped possessively inside her cape to draw her to him as they walked inside. Her panic heightened and she couldn't seem to make herself lean against him naturally as she wanted to.

Once inside, he flicked on a soft lamp and she

formed a quick impression of a couch, a few pictures, before he was removing her wrap and drawing her to him. Maybe if she had walked around the room a bit, settled herself, talked, worked up to it. But his urgency, controlled as it was, gave her no time to adjust, and she could barely still the panic and force herself to stand quietly in his arms as he began kissing her hair.

Sensing her reticence, he did not rush her. His mouth nuzzled her ear, explored her face, before finally coaxingly teasing her lips. She closed her eyes, reminding herself how much she liked Bill. But just as she reached up to touch him back he pulled away from her. Confused, she blinked at him, wondering miserably if she had been that inept.

But the ardor was still there in his eyes.

"Ah, Jeannie...." His face was flushed and he seemed to be struggling for words as she watched him numbly. "I mean, well, do you take the pill?" he blurted. "I'm not being very sophisticated about this after all. But if you might need...I mean, I could go out and get something—something for myself. I wasn't prepared—"

"Yes, that would be best," she mumbled, lowering her head against his chest momentarily before turning away. "If you could get something for yourself, I..." Her voice trailed away nervously.

"Right." He picked up his coat and moved quickly to the door. "Can you make yourself at home, find something to drink, whatever? I'll be back within ten minutes."

"Yes, I'll do that."

She wandered around the room restlessly, detesting herself. She had already taken precautions against pregnancy; she should have said so. But she had seen a chance for delay and grabbed it. *I've got to quit thinking so much*, she lectured herself.

In one corner of the room was a liquor cabinet. After a little rummaging she poured a small amount of wine into a glass. Her first sip of the warm liquid tasted heavy and sweet. Nothing could have made her more aware that this whole evening was not at all her usual style.

"Oh, God, I can't do it!" she sobbed, setting the glass down. "I can't go through with it."

Grabbing her purse and cape, she ran to the door. Surely she could catch a taxi at the corner. Concern that Bill might worry when he found the apartment empty prompted her to scrawl a hasty note on his desk pad:

Bill, I'm sorry. Don't come after me.

Jeannie

It was a poor apology but she had to get away.

His building was in a commercial area and she had expected to find a phone booth nearby, but she had to walk a couple of blocks in the blowing snow before she discovered an all-night launderette where she could make a call. Then she was horrified to realize that when she had changed purses she had not transferred billfolds. She had no money.

The deserted laundry made her uneasy, but she stayed there, desperately needing shelter from the cold. It had been foolish to wear the cape—just one of the many foolish things she had done that night, Jeannie thought dispiritedly. The stink of the laundry chemicals and the ugly litter left by uncaring patrons seemed a perfect setting for her purgatory. She wondered if she would be safer trying to walk the long distance home; she was a sitting duck to every passing idiot here—they only had to look in the glaringly lighted window to see an overly made-up, underdressed woman cringing alone.

Aping what she had seen countless aggressive children do, she began a systematic search of the washers, dryers, phones, and soda machines. All she needed was one quarter in a coin return. Finally she was successful.

Automatically she dialed, not even realizing whom she was calling until Paul Raymond answered.

"Paul?" she said weakly.

"Jeannie, where are you?"

"At a launderette on the corner of Gravois and Elm in Fenton." Her voice broke slightly.

"Shall I come for you?"

"Please. Oh, please do!"

Paul almost didn't recognize Jeannie when she ran out of the launderette. Her open cape was totally inadequate for the weather, her dress was obviously not her usual taste, and she had been a little heavy-handed with her makeup and perfume.

But as she slid into the seat beside him he noticed that her appearance was not rumpled, so apparently she had not suffered any mishandling. Questions were on the tip of his tongue, but he left them unasked as he headed in the direction of their apartments. They had driven several blocks before she finally broke the silence.

"I owe you an explanation." The words seemed to come grudgingly.

He waited patiently while she blew out several shuddering breaths.

"I decided I was going to become a sophisticated woman at last and—and have an affair."

His hands clenched white on the wheel. Her voice was extremely weak, but he was sure he had not heard wrong. Was it that damn jock? he wondered helplessly. Had he hurt her?

"I blew it. Before we . . . he went out for . . . well, anyway, I left while he was away."

"He's going to be one hell of a shocked man when he gets back." The relieved response was involuntary.

"I know. I'm not very proud of how I handled it all," she responded sadly. "Everything was my fault."

He drove on unthinkingly, hurting inside himself, not knowing what to say.

"It was just when Becky—"

"Becky!" he interrupted in amazement.

"Oh, not her directly. But a few days ago she made a remark about my husband. She saw a picture of him in Bruce's room and called him a 'hunk.'"

Her lips curved sadly as she saw Paul flinch.

"That was her exact word: 'hunk.'"

"I've heard her use it before," he admitted gruffly.

"But don't you see, it was so right! That picture was taken a few months before he died and for the first time I saw my husband for what he was—a cute teenager. And certainly no more that that!"

Paul shifted restlessly, trying to make sense out of her explanation since it seemed so important to her. She seemed aware of his puzzlement, because she lowered her face tiredly in her hands.

"I suppose it's hard to understand," she sighed, anxious for him to comprehend her troubled thoughts. "But, you see, I'd reached a point where I really hated my husband's memory. It was a terrible feeling, all bottled up guiltily inside me. It was because I wanted to give Bruce an image of his father that he could be proud of. But as the years went by I couldn't remember any strengths to build that image on. My husband had never had a job or even been trained for one; he was drafted right out of high school. He didn't even have any special interests except driving cars as fast as possible."

"Few nineteen-year-olds do have much ambition," Paul commented quietly.

"That's what I suddenly realized, when Becky felt so badly about her comment and apologized, saying she just had always thought fathers were men. I realized that hard as I tried, I could not make my husband grow up. Time was my enemy, not him.

"That night I really wallowed in nostalgia. I got out my high-school yearbook and looked up all our pictures; I couldn't believe what adolescents we both were. Sure, we got married and legalized our necking, spent the government paychecks, and played house like grown-ups until he was killed. But we were still babies!

"And all at once I felt free! It was as if all the enforced loyalty and guilt were gone because I could forgive my husband for not becoming a man. It was such a release for me...."

"So it released you right into an affair," he commented gruffly, deeply hurt that she did not see him as her man. "I can't say I follow your reasoning."

He regretted the words as soon as he'd said them, even before she cringed in shame.

They had just pulled up into their lot, and she frantically jerked the door open. But he scrambled out too, catching her before she could dash around the car. At his touch her face whitened.

"Jeannie, I'm sorry, that was just jealousy lashing out," he groaned, trying to enclose her in his arms, but she backed away from him as if he were disgusting. Angrily he slammed a hand on each side of her, pinning her between himself and his snow-covered car.

"I'm not letting you go in without listening to me," he insisted harshly.

She raised her head defiantly.

"I tried it once before in Hawaii," she jerked out, trying to shock him. "An affair."

He was deadly still.

"I followed through with it too. And I knew immediately, that night, it was a ghastly mistake. I tried to break it off politely, but he pestered me for months. All because of those few times...." She was forcing it all out, determined to make her shamed self-condemnation complete. "So you see, you're right," she sobbed. "You're damned right! Adult romance is not for me—I don't have what it takes. I was foolish to try it."

"You're not foolish," he attempted to soothe her. "But, Jeannie, most adults don't just make love to order. You should wait until you want one person so badly that—''

''Then that will be never!'' she almost shouted. ''And quit giving me your fatherly lecture! I *know* there must be something wrong with me....''

Something wrong with her? This time he grabbed her roughly, thoroughly exasperated, certain that she was hysterical, absolutely beyond making sense. The only thing wrong with her, he thought desperately, was her inability to recognize the passion smoldering in her body. He began to drag her up the sidewalk.

''We're going to get you inside quietly and you're going to pull yourself together.''

The snow-clogged night was oddly hushed. There was no light visible from his apartment, and all remained still as they passed his door. The children were undoubtedly asleep. He wondered if Mrs. Westerdale was taking care of Bruce as usual. She would probably be dozing on the couch by now.

''I'll see your sitter home,'' he whispered when he led Jeannie quietly inside her darkened living room.

''Bruce is at overnight Scout camp.'' She was almost listless now; she looked exhausted, incapable of making any further decisions for herself. With a concerned grunt he found a light, locked her door, and pushed her toward the bedrooms.

''I want you to get out of that dress and scrub off that warpaint. Before I go home I'll make you some coffee to warm you up.'' Obediently she moved down the hallway as the phone rang, and rang again—then a third time, with Jeannie remaining frozen where she stood.

''Shall I answer it?'' Paul asked.

''No!''

''He's probably worried sick about you.'' Jealously Paul wondered who the man was.

Only when the phone quit ringing did she move on toward her room.

''You owe him peace of mind, Jeannie,'' Paul reprimanded her. "If I were he, the next thing I'd do would be to start looking for you, all night if necessary. You obviously didn't wear enough warm clothing; it's freezing. It was late and you were alone—"

"All right, all right!" she almost shrieked, pushing past him to the kitchen.

As she shuffled through her phone listings he considered acting as if he were busy making the coffee. But that would be a ridiculous gesture; there was no way he could not be listening, for the phone was right there. He wondered if he should just go home right then; to hell with the damned coffee. Undecided, he shuffled aimlessly down the little hallway, loath to leave her while she was in this distraught state.

The first room he glanced into was obviously Bruce's. With a shameless curiosity he moved on to the second. It was dark, but enough light reflected off the snow through the window for him to make out the shape of a bed and a table nearby. He walked over to it and switched on the lamp. It was a neat and pleasant little haven— proof of Jeannie's occupancy lay around: a soft seagreen robe over the back of a chair, gorgeous color; her jewelry on the dressing table; a book on the bedside table. He looked around a brief moment before lowering the shades and turning back the covers for her.

When he returned to the kitchen, she had already made her call.

"I told Bill I'm home safely," she announced flatly.

"Good," he responded noncommittally. So it had been that jock. At least she had had the good sense to choose someone who genuinely cared about her. He hoped she had also told Bill she wanted his forgiveness. Paul felt sympathy for what the poor fellow had suffered at her hands.

He began opening doors, looking for a pan to use for the instant coffee.

"I'm not drunk, Paul." She sounded almost belligerent as she started toward her bedroom.

"I didn't say you were. Do you want to get something warm in you or not?"

"Oh, I guess so." Her tone sounded disinterested.

She was still splashing noisily in the bathroom when he finished making the coffee, so he carried the steaming mug to her bedside table. Noticing that her dress and slip had replaced the robe on the chair, he decided it was time he left; he had invaded her world enough for one night.

"I've left your coffee by your bed, Jeannie," he called softly as he passed the bathroom. She did not answer, but he hadn't really expected a chipper goodbye under the circumstances.

Chapter Eleven

It had never been his intention to return to her room.
But immediately after he had darkened the front of the
apartment she turned off her bedside lamp. It wasn't
sensible, he thought, her fumbling with that steaming
cup in the pitch dark. Concerned that she was not yet
stable enough to be alone, he walked slowly back to her
door, trying to adjust his eyes to the blackness.

"Are you going to be all right, Jeannie?" Stupid
question. The silence was unsettling.

Unable to stop himself, he walked toward where he
thought the lamp was. Finally gaining some vision from
the moon glow slipping under the shade, he could
make out her form on the edge of the bed. She was
huddled dejectedly, her robe draped loosely around
her, trying to muffle the sound of her crying.

"God damn!" he swore impotently, furious with her
even as he yanked her up into his arms. He was almost
shaking her, trying to stop the anguished sobbing.
"What the hell do you have to cry about?" he muttered.
"Your... *honor* is intact. Everything is going to be fine."
But she wouldn't stop sobbing. She couldn't stop.

Helplessly he sat down on the bed and folded her to
him, resigned to letting her wail her soul out. But in his
compassion he still tried to reach her reasoning, to stop
her, soothing her in the only way he instinctively
sensed might work. His hands found their way inside
her robe, providing the comfort of flesh against flesh.

Eventually she grew quieter, the sobs slowing to awkward hiccups, but she stayed huddled against his now soaking shirtfront. She seemed to want his comfort still, or perhaps to give back reassurance of her own. Her lips moved restlessly around the opened collar of his shirt, but when her mouth brushed his throat, the essence of their mutual comforting changed. There was that gradual encroachment of the...magic?

In a moment of clear sanity he *knew* he should go home. Right then. And he stiffened. But before he could set her aside, her hands had slipped under his shirt cuffs, searing the coarse hair on his forearms. And he was lost. It was as it had been that other time in his own apartment—a moment of magic.

The sweet smell of her filled his nostrils. Seeing better now, he could discern the patterns of moonlight on her creamy skin. He pushed her robe away because it had become absolutely essential for his fingers to trace those light-on-flesh patterns, so hauntingly lovely were they. Her lacy bra offended him; clumsily he removed it, desperate to discover the softness it so ruthlessly kept from him. His eyes caressed the beauty before him, beauty he waited so long to see. Almost worshipfully his hands shaped her breasts until his wanting grew hurtfully urgent.

In a tangle of her discarded robe he was stretching down beside her, pressing her full against him, kicking off his shoes. As he gloried in their closeness another fleeting thought of pregnancy came and went. He wanted her, everything about her: their babies, their love, everything. They belonged to each other, and he would never let her go.

At first he didn't seek her mouth. There was so much about her his eager lips needed to discover...the shape of her shoulders, the hollows of her smooth arms, the sensitivity of her fingertips. His hands joined the joy of this exploration, and before long she was writhing against him, not seeming to know how to please but eager to obey his directions. Finally he found her mouth but couldn't get his fill. Nor could she. Frantically they were kissing and touching, and he was struggling out of his clothes.

Nothing else mattered to him except her soft gasps of astonished pleasure and his own intense, ever increasing desire.

Jeannie was even more helpless than he in her unexpected need for him and him alone. Willingly she let him remove her last garment. She pressed grateful kisses on his face, at the same time instinctively stretching herself as long as possible, feeling a demand all the way to her toes to give him free access to her body.

She wanted to be pleasing to him.

Without shame she encouraged him to touch her wherever he wished, her tortured soul demanding his caresses. Her sobs of anguish had transformed to breathless moans of delight such as had never emitted from her throat before.

"God! I knew you'd be this lovely," Paul breathed hoarsely as he leaned back to look at her, obviously pleased with the throbbing willingness he had reduced her to. Even in the darkness his eyes seemed to be deep pools of raw hunger that visually devoured her.

Jeannie had never felt more beautiful.

Her skin seemed a new part of her, suddenly created lush and sensitive, solely to respond to Paul Raymond's kisses, only Paul's. She said his name aloud in wonderment. As if sensing her awareness, his mouth brushed between her breasts and settled in her navel, shaping her soft belly with light kissess.

If he doesn't take my breasts soon, I'll die, she thought wildly, the agonizing fullness of longing becoming so unbearable she began to writhe again, frantically wondering what to do to tempt him. Her hands fluttered, shyly hesitant to force his head against her, but...

"Please, Paul," she pleaded involuntarily in a voice unlike her own. Her fingertips in his hair followed his

movement as, of his own volition, he lowered his head.
Slowly his tongue encircled one swollen nipple, then
the other. Her sigh of pleasure seemed to excite him
and his tongue rasped over her nipples again and again.

"That's not enough," she groaned mindlessly, obviously frustrated.

Glorying in her need of him, Paul slid his hands beneath her hips and pressed her moistness against his
intruding thigh as he paused above her, teasing her for
long moments before finally suckling at her breast.

The beautiful relief, more intense because it was
postponed so long, racked her whole body.

She felt helpless in wave after wave of loving response, her hands caressing his strong back and arms as
she tried to absorb the tempting masculinity of him in
every pore of her body. Her need of him almost frightened her, for she had never trusted so much of her soul
to any man. But the fear fled as quickly as it came, so
lost was she in the magic of belonging to Paul Raymond.

His mouth finally abandoned her sated breasts, leaving them tingling with sensitivity as he lay heavily
against her and pressed light kisses over her face. She
kissed him back, thinking it was not possible to feel
more wonderful than this. But suddenly, ecstatically, it
was as if the love beauty was just beginning again when
he lowered himself into her and reached to guide her
own hands. Engulfed in the intense heat of his thrusting body, she grasped his muscular hips and lifted herself against him, wanting to learn how to satisfy him.

All rational thoughts vanished as she was transformed to another world...a world where nothing existed but heated spheres of love radiating over and over
again from deep within her. The extent of her commitment to this man was overwhelming. Paul kissed her so
deeply as they clung together that she felt at one with
him along the entire length of her body. The sensation
was humbling, fulfilling, enlarging. She couldn't ab-

sorb the meaning of it. She only knew she wanted him to be as intoxicated with her as she was with him.

When he shuddered against her and moaned her name, she knew he was out of control and it made her proud. But not yet satisfied, for unbelievably their erotic intensity immediately built even higher. So high, that she too lost control and her voice melded with his in cries of mindless, wordless love.

The silence followed.

And the trembling and awe, natural aftermaths of that slow, incredibly beautiful release.

But even then their fulfillment was not over. For a long time they lay quietly together, the vibrancy of their lovemaking gradually easing as they lazily caressed one another protectively.

Warmth! What a delicious thing it was. Soft, mellow warmth of their own creation, slowly enveloping them as the pulsating of their final ardor eventually subsided and they drifted into dreamless sleep.

THERE was frost on the inside of the kitchen window, attesting to the subzero temperatures of the night before. Jeannie had got as far as rinsing off her face and pulling on jeans and a warm sweater. She was vaguely aware that it was midmorning, but she couldn't pull her thoughts together beyond that. Her hair was still rumpled, her face flushed with the lethargic beauty that is the natural aftermath of lovemaking.

It felt so good to stand near the stove as the coffee water boiled, her shaken body absorbing the heat. And shaken she was. Never in her imaginings had she thought lovemaking could be like that—natural, affectionate, and then suddenly beyond reasoning, unbelievably timeless. She quaked at the memories of Paul's work-roughened hands stroking her as if he couldn't get enough of the feel of her; memories of her own incredible response to the smell, the warmth, the texture of him. It must have been the once-in-a-lifetime experi-

ence poets wrote about. She felt humbly grateful that it
had happened to her.

Her fingers curled around the freshly filled coffee
cup as she walked over to the icy window. They were
well into winter. The squirrels and birds tenaciously remaining in her little woods would have trouble finding
food; Bruce should put out a feeder. She sipped idly at
the hot liquid, feeling her body come further down to
earth with each swallow. She wondered who claimed
coffee did not have a sobering effect.

Sprawled in a chair at the table, not really wanting to
bother with anything to eat, she began thinking again.
She wished she could stop it, could just be grateful for
life's little pleasures, with no regrets.

But the thoughts were persistent. She was torn between delight at her initiation into fullest womanhood
and chagrin at her own shameless role in making it happen. She wondered about what Paul must think of her,
wondered why she had clung to him when it still would
have been possible for him to go home as he had intended to do.

In embarrassment she tried to recall her unguarded
conversation with him the night before. Hadn't she
talked about her loveless decision to have an affair?
Would he think that since she had failed with Bill, she
had decided he would do as well? Horrible thought. He
was the father of her son's best friends, and she had
never looked on him in that way; the idea seemed almost incestuous.

Restlessly she went over to the cabinet. Maybe she
would have some cereal after all. When she reached
up to the high shelf, her sweater stretched hurtfully
across her breasts. Astonished, she ran her hands self-
consciously over herself, shamed to discover that her
nipples were achingly hard. Lord! Even the memory of
the man was arousing her. She clutched at her stomach,
trying to deny the hot, moist waves of need beginning
to vibrate from within her.

This disquiet was worse than it had been last night

when they had lain sleepily together so long in the curious afterglow, enjoying their naked closeness; satisfied, yet unable to stop the awareness or the occasional soft caresses and featherlight kisses they needed to let themselves down from that incredible high. She scarcely remembered when they had both drifted to sleep. When she had awakened, the only evidences of his presence were her swollen lips and the fact that her robe was neatly folded on the chair. His place beside her had not even been warm.

She was still stuggling to gain her composure when the doorbell rang. *It could be Bill*, she thought frantically. *And he will know. One look at me and he will know. . . . Or worse yet, it might be Paul.* She couldn't handle facing him yet.

The ringing continued relentlessly. Determined not to answer, she remained in the kitchen, but the ringing went on and on. Then he was pounding.

She didn't even bother with caution then. Angrily she swung open the door.

"Go away!" she snapped defensively before even identifying the victim of her anger.

Paul leaned against the doorjamb, his overcoat collar turned high against the gusting winds.

"When does Bruce get home?" he asked softly, ignoring her furious greeting.

"Oh, no!" she cried in agony, backing away from him. He *couldn't* think so poorly of her that he was coming back for a quick—Her hand flew to her mouth.

"Now, Jeannie, always thinking the worst of everyone," he reprimanded her, not moving from his place except to shove his foot slightly into the opening. She stared at his shoe pointedly.

"I'm not going to let you slam the door in my face," he said firmly.

"What do you want?" she asked ungraciously, trying to hide her alarm that her love-awakened body was throbbing longingly at the very sight of him.

"Not what you apparently think," he objected, "although the idea does have its appeal." His face was curiously softened, nostalgically relaxed, almost.

She snorted inelegantly.

But his face had sobered, the fun and games obviously over. "We've had an equipment breakdown at my labs," he said briskly. "I'm on my way to get the kids from church and then I'll have to go in. Usually I wouldn't mind leaving them alone, but I've had to work every night since we got back...."

His own glow of satisfied love could no longer hide the weariness in his face. She responded instantly to that fatigue.

"You've been working too hard again," she accused, feeling exhilarated to be on the attack. "Even if you do have your own business you should have someone you could turn over—"

"I don't have time to argue about it," he stopped her cruel pleasure curtly, glancing at his watch. "The children will be waiting. I'd appreciate it very much if you would just look in on them sometime this afternoon, help break up their day alone."

"What time is it?" she asked suddenly, her eyes open wide. He had said his children were already at church.

"Eleven-fifteen."

"Oh, no! I was supposed to get Bruce at eleven!" She began looking around frantically. "Where did I put my boots?"

"Where is he?"

"They were going to drop him off at the high school. He must be standing outside in this freezing—"

"It's only twenty minutes from here; I'll get him. My kids will be waiting inside. A few more minutes won't hurt." He was already on his way to the stairs.

She padded out into the breezeway in her scanty clothing and bare feet, her gratitude overwhelming.

"Paul, just drop them off here. They can stay with me. I'll give them lunch. And supper. And if there's

any laundry or housework you need done, we can—''
She knew she was rambling, but she wanted him to
know how much his help meant to her.

"Now get this straight!" He lunged back up the
stairs, shoving her ahead of him all the way to her
apartment. He slammed the door shut, closing out the
cold and the curiosity of neighbors.

"Now get this straight," he reiterated, his anger still
smoldering. "I'm not asking you to baby-sit or do my
laundry. Not until we're married. I just want—''

"Married!" she objected stormily. "Then *that* will be
never—''

His face went white. "And why do you say that?"
His voice was deadly still, too still, a warning that she
had better watch her words carefully. She drew a calm-
ing breath.

"That's obvious." She was reasoning clearly now.
"Because you don't need a wife."

"Who says I don't?"

"Paul, you don't need anybody."

"Is that so?"

She stared at him, perplexed, until angry comprehension flooded her.

"Well, if you're worried about my being pregnant,
forget it. I am a nurse, you know." She gulped, tears
pricking at the backs of her eyelids. "I'm sure the precautions I took for one man work just as well for
another."

He shook her then. "You stop that! I won't have you
cheapen what happened between us, especially not in
your own mind."

"That's very chivalrous of you," she said bitterly,
stiffening in his grasp to prevent her head from flop-
ping back and forth. He let her go.

"We'll talk about this again," he said, pressed for
time.

"There's nothing to talk about."

"The hell there isn't!"

Chapter Twelve

"Greg! Turn that radio down!" Paul abandoned his search through the papers littering the card table, wondering how he had ever thought he could get the specification sheets finished at home. With the distractions of Greg's radio and Becky's endless banging around in the bathroom, he was misplacing more work than he was completing.

"Becky, finish up in there—it's bedtime! And, Greg, this is the last time I'm telling you about that radio—" A fit of coughing cut short his intended diatribe.

"Gosh, Dad, I always have it this loud." Greg stuck his head out of his room, unaccustomed to such complaints from his father. Becky also came scurrying out, with cream on her face and her hair in huge rollers under an outlandish yellow plastic bonnet.

"I haven't dried my hair yet, Dad," she pleaded.

"You've been in there long enough to dry it three times!"

She glanced wonderingly at her brother, but Greg quickly ducked back in his room to mute the disco music, abandoning her to their father's unexpected anger.

"It took me longer to do the mud pack than the directions said, Dad, and then—"

"Mud pack?"

"It's good for my complexion, helps prevent wrinkles." She was edging nervously to her room, the electric base of her hair dryer balanced precariously on a stack of cosmetic boxes and fashion magazines she had used in her glamour routine.

Paul's mouth was open in amazement. He was ready to storm at her again, but she looked so vulnerable, his baby—so close to being a woman—that he caught himself.

"Dry your hair," he mumbled, looking back down at his papers to hide his affection. As she hurried into her room, however, he reasserted his authority momentarily to add, "And make it snappy!"

"I will, Dad," Becky promised, the rest of her words lost in the roar of the appliance.

I shouldn't have bothered to complain about the radio, Paul reflected ruefully. *I can't hear a damn thing anyway.*

The realization filled him with a strange restlessness and he glanced at his watch. Five to eleven. Jeannie should be returning from the hospital about now, but with all the noise he wouldn't be able to hear her come in, couldn't reassure himself she was home safely, as he had got in the habit of doing the nights she worked. He had little confidence in her old clunker of a car even since she'd had it fixed.

Her safety seemed especially urgent to him now that—

Saturday night had *not* been a mistake, he reflected angrily. What did *she* know about it? All her pseudosophisticated babble about how she had been ripe for anybody, so their night together didn't really mean a thing. If she had been ripe for *anybody* she would have fallen into Bill Hannah's arms earlier in the evening. What kind of husband had she had that she was so unknowledgeable about her own response?

Damn, they were only kids. Why think the thing to pieces? he reminded himself.

If only he could get this work off his back so he could take the time to force her to talk reason. You could not seriously discuss marriage on the telephone, especially if the proposed bride-to-be kept hanging up. And phone calls were all he had been able to manage.

The lab breakdown had increased his holiday backlog even further. And these particular specifications he was doing now, the modifications for a solar-energy product, had to be finished this weekend if they were to be installed in time for adequate winter testing. Otherwise the product could not be ready for marketing in the coming season. The company stood to lose thousands of dollars in potential business in the next year alone. And if someone else beat them to the patent.... He buried his head in his hands, tired to death and constantly irritated by the rasping in his throat. What a mess!

But even exhausted and preoccupied with the responsibilities of work, he ached for Jeannie—unbearably, like some fool in the daytime soaps. He resented his weakness.

Unaware even that he was dozing until sudden silence of the once droning appliance jarred his consciousness, Paul jerked erect as Becky noisily stuffed objects away in her room. He heard her flop and turn in her bed for some time before she finally settled down and called out a good-night. He guessed she probably could not get comfortable wearing those miserable curlers, though why she didn't take them out after she dried her hair was more than he could fathom. Women were confusing creatures.

"Night, Dad," Becky called again, a little-girl question mark on the end of her greeting—she had always hated to go to bed thinking he was upset with her.

"Night, Dad," Greg also called out gruffly.

Paul sighed deeply, ashamed of his earlier anger.

"Night, kids," he responded, love creeping into his hoarse voice. "And sleep tight," he impulsively added, as in the old days. Sheepishly he wondered if he was getting senile, treating those big lugs as if they were babies.

"You too, Dad." Becky sounded happier then. After some hesitation she firmly added, "You ought to get to bed too, Dad."

Paul grinned at that. She was certainly getting bossy lately, telling him he looked tired, fussing that he should see a doctor for his cough. Kids!

"Yeah, Dad. You should take some cough medicine and go to bed," Greg seconded.

"Okay, okay! Go to sleep. I'll wind up here right away."

"Night, Dad."

"Good night!"

He had restacked his papers in his briefcase for the third time before he heard Jeannie come up the stairs. Only then did he give up and head for his bedroom.

WORKING with seven children at a time in a physical therapy group was certainly possible. But as Jeannie studied the charts of the patients assigned to the Friday afternoon session she realized that the therapist was right—some transfers should be made immediately. The disabilities of these particular seven children were too diverse, and two of them needed one-on-one instruction.

Jeannie replaced the chart and watched Carrie Lynd at work. The young therapist was good, and she was doing her best to give a thorough workout to all the children. But it was an impossible task, under the circumstances.

"I've had some experience with joint functions," Jeannie walked over to where Carrie was manipulating the leg of an arthritic child. "Perhaps I can help him with the knee and hip stretches, and that would leave you free to demonstrate for the others?"

Carrie nodded in relief as she introduced Jeannie to the little boy and showed her what to do. "Mike does a good job," she said, "but it sometimes helps to have an adult push too, doesn't it, Mike?"

The child's cheerful grin in spite of the pain he must have been experiencing with the manipulation of his swollen knee tugged at Jeannie's heart. As she worked carefully with him for the remaining fifteen minutes of the session she said mental thanks for her own son's excellent health. It was a blessing she had recounted on numerous occasions during her nursing career.

Once the young patients had all gone home, she and Carrie relaxed over cups of coffee and discussed the situation. "You're right; your grouping just won't work," Jeannie agreed. "But I guess I understand how it slipped through Authorization. The two children originally added to this session will work fine. But when their mothers both insisted on switching siblings from other sessions to cut down on their driving, we got our problem. Both those siblings require individualized therapy. I'll get Scheduling to work out a different time with the mothers."

"Thanks for looking into it so quickly, Jeannie," Carrie said in obvious relief. "I really don't mind a full assignment, but I do want to do a good job."

"I'm glad you called it to my attention so soon. Otherwise I wouldn't have caught the problem until I start my routine follow-up in several weeks. But it raises a question I've been thinking about."

"Oh?"

"Our departments are all working blindly. We don't know enough about the activities and needs of other sections, so we tend to foul each other up."

"You're right about that. I was late getting some adjusted reports in last week and I threw one of the secretaries into unpaid overtime to change the monthly report she had already typed. I felt terrible about it."

"I think I'll try to set up an orientation day of some sort—get the heads of each area to give us a brief explanation and distribute printed information to help us adapt to each other's functions."

"Sounds good. I'd like to know—" Carrie cut short her comment to answer the phone.

"It's for you."

"Who would go to the trouble of tracking me down here?" Jeannie handed Carrie her cup for refill before answering the call. Her face registered shock when she recognized Paul Raymond's gruff voice, and she was grateful Carrie's errand to the coffeepot had put her out of hearing range.

"Paul, I can't talk now. I'm not even in my own—"

"If you dare hang up on me this time, I'll come to your office right away!" His immediate threat was so firm she had no doubt he meant it. "I'm perfectly willing to raise hell in public, if necessary," he continued.

"I can't talk from here," she insisted, her face flushed in guilt. Admittedly she had been rude in hanging up on Paul's calls to her home.

"I'll give you exactly five minutes to find some place where you *can* talk. If I haven't heard from you by then I'm on my way over."

"This is no place to settle personal—"

"I agree. But I've had enough of this goddamned hanging-up game. We can either involve our children by getting together. at home, or you can call me back."

"What's your number?"

Her hands were shaking as she copied it down. For a few brief moments after replacing the receiver she contemplated leaving work immediately. But the futility of that idea was so apparent that she abandoned it. Waving aside the second cup of coffee Carrie offered, she mumbled explanations as she rushed out the door.

It took her exactly four and a half minutes to get back to her own office, tell her secretary not to let her be disturbed, and dial Paul's number.

His voice sounded hoarse and tense, but his temper was in fine form.

"Jeannie, I don't want to discuss our private lives on the phone any more than you do. But running away from the issue is not good for either of us. We have to get together and talk this out."

She was horrified to feel tears in her eyes as she hugged the phone against her, aching painfully in every inch of her body at the sound of his voice.

She didn't want to feel this way about him. Wouldn't let herself.

"What do you suggest?"

"I want you to have dinner with me next Tuesday. Right now I'm so swamped at work I can't even get home to sleep much. But it will let up soon. I could drive by the Center Tuesday and we could go some place quiet where we can get this mess settled."

"There's no 'mess' to settle. You and I just—"

Her objection was cut short by his coughing.

"You probably shouldn't even be at work, much less staying out late." She attacked him hotly. "Why are you such a fool about your health? You should—"

"I just have a cold," he snarled. "Now, about Tuesday?"

"Paul, I'm not getting married again. I was lonely Saturday night and—"

"Don't give me any more garbage about it being a mistake. What we had together..."

Her flesh grew clammy cold and her guts lurched with longing as memories swept over her—memories of such pure beauty that she never wanted them touched. She wished that Paul Raymond were a stranger who would disappear forever from her life and leave her with her beautiful remembrances. She knew too much about the reality of daily human relationships to entrust the fragile beauty of that night to the test of time. And yet....

"All right, all right! I admit it was... well, no matter. We can't go on."

"I'm not suggesting an affair, dammit! Even if that were all I wanted from you, I wouldn't do that to our children. But we could have so much more, Jeannie. We'll talk about it Tuesday."

"I want it ended now. We're just friends."

"The hell we are! We haven't been 'just friends' since the day I met you, and you know it."

She was shocked into stillness. She didn't want to listen to him, couldn't believe that the attraction had been there all along, even when she thought he was married. It had to have been a temporary weakness. And there was the problem of her future, of the life she wanted to live, alone, in control of her own affairs. What about all those dreams she had struggled so hard to gain?

"Paul, I'm just beginning to get my own life in order. I'm not going to mess it up again by getting married."

"Marriage doesn't have to mean giving up control of your life." He seemed to be forcing himself to speak rationally. "If you share your life by choice, your independence is enlarged, not lost."

His reasoning confused her.

"Paul, I don't even want to think about the commitment of marriage." Her voice was weak.

"Don't think about it. Just plan to meet me Tuesday. We've got to straighten ourselves out one way or another, Jeannie. For the children's sake as well as our own. We can't go back to how it was this fall when you scuttled into hiding every time you saw me."

"Oh, leave me alone!" She was almost in tears. She couldn't understand how the man could do this to her. No one else ever made her cry. No one else made her hang up on them.

"What time shall I come for you on Tuesday?"

She hesitated momentarily, then surrendered to the inevitable. "Five o'clock," she snapped, slamming down the phone.

She immediately grabbed it back, but the connection was broken. She regretted her impulsive reaction, but she knew that Paul would be satisfied with their appointment for Tuesday and would not come by her office.

Sighing, she leaned her head back against her chair and closed her weary, tear-soaked eyes. It was hard to act sensibly when you were lonely.

There, she had admitted it. She was lonely.

But surely the emotion was temporary? She didn't need Paul Raymond in her life, not that way. And he didn't need a wife. Still, she couldn't shake off that plaguing longing for him. And she cursed Paul for causing that very human vulnerability.

Trying to force herself to think clearly, she vowed she would fight him and win. She had until Tuesday to strengthen her resolve.

Chapter Thirteen

"Mrs. Rasmussen? Oh, I'm so glad you're home."
Becky sounded relieved at finding her in. "I know
you're always busy on Saturdays and I hate to bother
you, but we've been so worried...."

Jeannie's professional sense was alerted by the concern in Becky's young voice. "What's wrong, Becky?"
she asked as she wedged the phone firmly on her
shoulder so she could cap the fingernail polish she had
been using. She had a feeling she would not be finishing that job right away.

"It's Dad. He's been coughing all day, and he
wouldn't go to bed. He just kept working on those
drawings—" Her voice broke.

Jeannie remained silent, helplessly wondering if
Becky realized how unlikely it was that *she* could do
anything about Paul's tendency to work himself into
exhaustion.

"Mrs. Rasmussen?"

"I'm here, dear."

"What shall I do?"

"What do you usually do when he's sick?"

"He's never sick." Becky sounded like a frightened
child, and Jeannie could just picture the scene: Paul
had a cold and was tired; he was probably irritable over
trying to finish his work.

"Dad's been working too hard ever since we got
back from the trip," Becky rambled distractedly. "He

said that things got so behind. And then there was the lab breakdown last Sunday. He had a firm deadline on these drawings—someone came and picked them up an hour ago—and he wouldn't go to bed until that was done."

Jeannie suddenly felt relieved.

"Then I think you should keep things quiet and comfortable for him and encourage him to stay in bed over the weekend. He'll probably feel much better with some good rest."

"Dad kept saying he'd be fine once he got to bed. But he's still coughing all the time. He finally said we could call a doctor, but Greg and I haven't been able to reach one yet."

It alarmed Jeannie that Paul had agreed the children should call a doctor. She did not imagine that Paul asked for help lightly.

"I'll drop over, Becky," she said with more calm than she was feeling. "Just to keep you company until you reach your physician."

She was fuming angrily as she walked the short distance across to the Raymond apartment. *Damn, damn, damn that foolish man,* she thought stormily. *Absurdly foolish, waiting until six o'clock on a Saturday night to get medicine, scaring his children to death. . . .*

Becky must have flown to the door.

"Oh, Mrs. Rasmussen, I'm so glad you could come!"

"He's talking out of his head some more!" Greg came running from the bedroom hall. "Becky, you had better try that doctor's exchange we saw. Oh, Mrs. Rasmussen!"

Jeannie could hear Paul's coughing from the other room. It was a dry, painful sound, and he seemed to be murmuring too. She moved past the panic-stricken children to his bedroom and was immediately shocked by what she saw.

"He must be burning with fever." Jeannie was

barely able to keep an impassive face as she placed an experienced hand first on his neck, then on his chest. He didn't even realize she was there. Jeannie needed no thermometer to know that his temperature was probably close to 104°. No wonder he was out of head! He looked dehydrated too, as if he had been quite ill for several days. She marveled at the self-discipline that had kept the man on his feet this long. He had not sounded that near exhaustion when she had talked with him on the phone yesterday. Once he had turned in his work to that messenger, his system must have collapsed completely.

"Have you given him any aspirin?" She forced her voice to sound confident.

"No, but we have some, I think." Greg was already headed for the bathroom.

"Get me three tablets and some water. Do you have a vaporizer?"

"Not here; I think it's in the warehouse. We haven't used it since we were little."

"Becky, in a minute you can go and get ours from Bruce. What doctor does your father use?"

"He never got around to having his physical here. We were trying to reach the doctor who gave Greg and me our school exams."

"An internist?"

"Yes. We didn't like him much and were going to change, but—"

Jeannie made a quick decision. "Do you mind if I call my own doctor?"

The bewildered children were willing to turn everything over to her, so with a confident manner she was far from feeling, Jeannie sent them scurrying on errands while she called her internist. She had to have him paged at the hospital and at that moment thanked the fate that had sent her to St. Joseph's for employment. Under normal circumstances red tape would not have allowed her to reach him so expeditiously.

"I would guess bronchitis or possibly pneumonia," she verified when he finally was able to answer the page. "Fever near a hundred and four. He's delirious, dehydrated. I would suspect you may want to start intravenous tomorrow if we can't get liquids down him. His color is bad; dry cough. He's already exhausted from overwork." Jeannie hurriedly ticked off symptoms, hoping the children would not return before she finished.

"I was going to give him three," she responded to the doctor's question about aspirin. "Yes, we have one," she went on with a nod to Becky, who along with Bruce had just come in with the vaporizer. "We'll start that now too."

"Do you know if your father is allergic to any antibiotics?" she asked Becky.

"I don't think so." The girl paused at the kitchen sink where she had started to fill the vaporizer. "But then, I don't remember him ever having to take any medicine."

"Uncle Ben would know," Greg contributed eagerly. "We could call him."

Promising the doctor she would call him back if the antibiotic had to be altered for allergies, Jeannie finished receiving her instructions. Then she began her cheerful professional-nurse routine of treatment.

It was not an easy facade to maintain; Paul's condition greatly concerned her. There was a near epidemic of viral and bacterial infections sweeping the county, and the doctor, tied up with some of those emergencies, probably would not be able to see Paul until late that night.

"First we're going to make your father more comfortable," Jeannie explained as she returned to the bedroom, all three children following pathetically close on her heels. She held out her hand to Greg for the aspirin, deliberately moving slowly.

"Greg, you and Bruce hold your father up while we

get this aspirin down him. It won't cure him, but it should lower his temperature so he can rest better. Becky, get a spoon just in case we need it.''

Paul was like a deadweight, too delirious to help them at all; it was impossible to get him to take the pills. Quickly Jeannie crushed the aspirin in a little water and coaxed some of the grainy liquid through his feverish lips. Instinctively grateful for the cooling moisture, he tried to swallow and she hurriedly kept trickling additional amounts into his mouth.

When he began to cough painfully they gently lowered him back to the pillows. The children looked anguished while Jeannie set up the vaporizer. She quietly explained that the cooling mist aimed right at his face would help his breathing as well as the fever. Then she covered him lightly, motioning the children out of the room.

"It's like Grand Central Station in there." She smiled gently, leading her little retinue back to the living room. "The thing he most needs now is rest and antibiotics. He probably has a bacterial infection. But even if it's viral we need the antibiotics to prevent secondary infections. The doctor has called in a prescription to the pharmacy, along with a combination decongestant that should help the coughing and make him more comfortable. And the doctor will call in when he finishes at the hospital.''

Luckily they reached Ben Raymond immediately and almost cheered when they learned Paul had no known allergies. Ben and Lucille offered to catch the next plane to St. Louis, but when Jeannie reassured them that she would stay with the children that night, they agreed to wait until the doctor had seen Paul and advised the family on what to do.

Becky and Greg were like different people once they realized they would not be facing their father's illness by themselves. Smiles wreathed their faces as they asked what they could no next.

"Bruce, you can run back to our apartment and get

my coat and purse. I'm going to Skaggs to get the anti-biotics. I should be back within twenty minutes. While I'm gone, you tote your sleeping gear over here. Oh, and bring the meat loaf and muffins I have in the oven—there's enough for all of us."

"What car are you taking to Skaggs, Mom?" Bruce asked practically.

Jeannie's mouth formed a dismayed O as she remembered that her automobile had broken down again that afternoon at the shopping center and she'd had to have it towed to a garage for repairs.

"You can take Dad's," Greg exclaimed, stepping into Paul's bedroom to get the keys to the Mercedes.

"I'm not sure I can drive it," Jeannie groaned, momentarily losing her calm. "Don't you have to shift gears?"

"Right. Dad ordered it that way special."

Jeannie looked dismayed. "I never learned to drive a standard shift."

"I'll drive," Becky said with decision, going to the closet for her coat.

"But you don't have your license yet. Maybe the pharmacy delivers."

"How long will that take?"

Jeannie hesitated. In this stormy weather, with an apparent epidemic of respiratory infections and viruses going around, she knew it might take quite some time. She could hear Paul's tortured coughing in the background. The doctor wanted the tablets started immediately and she agreed with that need.

"Let's go," she nodded to Becky. *And pray God,* she thought helplessly, *no accident!*

His breathing was a little easier, Jeannie thought as she unplugged the vaporizer. The air in the small room was close to saturation and she didn't want him wet. As she placed an anxious hand under his pajama jacket she realized that the fever was coming up again. She'd best try to get some more aspirin into him; he simply did not rest if his temperature got too high.

"How is he?" Becky came stumbling into the hall, looking about ten years old with her long red curls bouncing over the lace collar of her flannel nightgown.

"He really needs the rest." Becky stood at Paul's bedroom door, tears in her eyes as she watched her father.

"He's going to get well, Becky," Jeannie said brisky as she returned from the bathroom with the aspirin and water. "And now that the doctor has seen him we can all be assured we're doing the right thing."

"I heard the doctor say he would have to put Dad in the hospital unless you could stay, that he needed a trained nurse to watch—"

"Shh, you'll wake him up," Jeannie whispered, anxious to get the girl's mind off Paul's danger. She thought he was going to respond to the antibiotics; he was no worse, and they should know for sure by midmorning. They certainly did not need the children in a panic.

As she spooned the crushed aspirin between Paul's feverish lips she marveled at how instinctively the human body tried to help itself. Paul was beyond consciously assisting in his care, yet he automatically tried to swallow the bitter liquid, so starved for moisture was his body.

"Becky, why don't you stay here with your father a few minutes?" Jeannie moved from the small folding chair they had set up at Paul's bedside. "I'm going to crush some ice. I think we could get some moisture down him that way." She was hopeful they could avoid the necessity of an intravenous tomorrow.

Obediently Becky remained anxiously by Paul until Jeannie returned with a small bowl of crushed ice and a spoon, but when Jeannie offered to let her administer the ice, she quietly refused.

"I'm afraid I'll spill it on him or something," she confessed anxiously.

"Of course you can get a little ice into him," Jeannie said firmly, handing her the bowl. It was important that Becky regain confidence in her ability to help her father. "I'm going to pull on another sweater."

She tugged her rumpled knit shirt back down over her slacks as she quickly left the apprehensive girl. From the bathroom she could hear the clatter of the spoon against the dish, and she nodded in satisfaction. Actually, in the chill of nighttime it did feel good to pull on an added sweater. She ran a brush through her hair and splashed water on her face, then yawned and smiled wryly at her sleepy reflection in the mirror. Greg had given her his bed, since it was just across the hall from Paul's room, but Jeannie had been up more than she had been down.

Pausing at the door of Paul's bedroom, she stretched and watched Becky running the moist cold spoon across her father's dried lips. He opened them eagerly, just enough for a little of the cold chips to trickle in.

"He's taking it!" Becky whispered wonderingly, her face wreathed in smiles.

"Yes, he's taking it," Jeannie affirmed quietly. "Just give him a few chips at a time and let him rest in between."

Becky looked back at her with misty eyes. "I'm so glad you're here, Mrs. Rasmussen. What would we have done? I just wish you and Dad would—" She stopped as Jeannie made a shushing sound.

"Just keep giving him ice," Jeannie prompted, moving on into the living room because she did not want to hear what she suspected Becky, in her frightened, grateful state, might say.

There was no frost on the window. The temperature had probably stayed up in the twenties all night, Jeannie thought as she tucked Greg's exposed bare foot back in the sleeping bag and zipped the bag shut. He

moved restlessly for a few seconds but did not wake as
he adjusted to having his sprawling body confined. Quietly she zipped shut Bruce's bag too. There were drafts
on the floor and she didn't need anyone else sick for a
while. How odd, she thought, that she was feeling such
a curious sense of family well-being despite everything.

There was not very much useless puttering to be
done in the kitchen, just wiping up a few specks of ice
and putting away the hand ice crusher. Becky was trying
hard not to doze when Jeannie returned to Paul's bedside.

"I think that's enough for now," Jeannie whispered
to the girl as she repositioned the vaporizer and
plugged it in. "Let's both get some rest."

It had not been necessary to set Greg's alarm for the
next round of antibiotics. With the discipline of long
training and, she admitted it, her own real concern,
Jeannie had awakened fifteen minutes early. Pushing
off the alarm button so it would not ring and disturb
them all, she unwound herself from the blanket in
which she had wrapped herself, then threw it over her
shoulders as she went to check on the household.

The boys were sleeping soundly, looking like awkward giants enclosed in cocoons. Becky was a fairy
princess, relaxed and blessedly easy in her sleep with
her tousled hair making a red spiderweb across the pillow.

Paul, however, was moaning restlessly, his parched
lips rubbing together anxiously. Wrapping her makeshift cape more securely around her, Jeannie padded to
the kitchen to crush some more ice. Two more doses of
the antibiotics, she thought, and there should begin to
be some real improvement. There *had* to be some improvement, she insisted to herself, bitter that there was
nothing more she could do except wait it out and try to
make him easier.

It was difficult getting Paul to take the medicine
without help from the boys. He seemed such a big man

when she tried to lift him herself. Just as she thought she was going to have to wake Greg to help her, however, Paul opened his eyes and, in a moment of lucidity, focused on her face.

"Paul, open your mouth," Jeannie ordered him quietly, forcing her arm behind his back and easing him against her. He leaned on her shoulder, trying to help her raise his own weight. With one hand she slipped the pill on his tongue and quickly held the glass against his mouth. Obediently, his eyes never leaving her face, he forced a painful swallow, then another.

"Can you drink some more of this water?" she urged as she held the glass against his lips again, but the moment was gone. He sagged weakly against the pillows.

At least he drank some, and he didn't cough up the medicine, she thought gratefully. After she had rearranged the blankets warmly around him she picked up the bowl of ice and for more than an hour sat there, wrapped in her blanket, moving the spoon across his lips until he instinctively let the icy moisture into his mouth.

It will be morning soon, she thought tiredly when she finally decided she had done all she could for the time being. She should be going to get some rest herself. Paul had taken a good bit of ice and seemed more comfortable, his fever not too high and the coughing subsiding to occasional bursts necessary to rid his system of the bothersome phlegm. But still she sat there, hesitant to leave him.

It would be another few hours before she could consider turning his care over to the children while she took a real sleep—not until she knew if he was responding to the antibiotic. Tiredly she slipped her arm out of the blanket to rub the back of her neck. Half bending over the bed like that was an awkward position.

"How is he?" Greg's anxious whisper startled her.

Jeannie sensed that the boy had just crawled out of

the sleeping bag and stumbled straight there, so much warmth did he still emanate through his rumpled clothing. But he would soon chill.

"Your dad is no worse, Greg," she reassured him. "Go back to sleep. I'll need you to be wide awake this afternoon to take over."

His half-smile indicated he liked that, but still he did not leave, seeming to need to look at his father, even though it frightened him to see this man of strength in such a vulnerable state.

"I wish you and Dad were married," Greg blurted tactlessly in his half-asleep daze. "Who's going to take care of him when we go away to school?"

"Greg, he's going to get well. This medicine will—"

"I don't mean just when he's sick," he interrupted with a frantic whisper. "I mean . . . always. To make him eat on time and get enough rest and not be alone so much."

She was speechless with astonishment. It had never occurred to her that the Raymond children had been worried about their father in that way. The discovery confused her, upset her preconceptions.

"Go to bed, Greg," she urged gently, not wanting to think about this implication.

Long after the boy had gone she remained in her chair by Paul. The predawn light was beginning to seep in now, chasing shadows across his haggard face. Her heart tightened unbearably and she sniffed away some tears, angry at her sentimentality.

Although Paul had been resting quietly for some time, suddenly his body was racked by tight coughing. Amazingly the attack subsided as quickly as it had come, leaving him leaning weakly against the pillow with his eyes open. She placed a hand soothingly on his forehead.

"Jeannie?" he croaked painfully through his cracked lips, the blank look momentarily leaving his eyes. "What's wrong, Jeannie?"

He was struggling to get up, and she capitalized on his lucidity by holding the glass of water to his lips.

"Drink this!" she commanded.

Automatically he obeyed her, almost exhausting himself with the effort of emptying the glass. He struggled once again to get up when she moved the glass away.

"What's happening? Are you hurt?" His husky voice was alarmed.

She fell to her knees on the bed, her blanket cape tumbling around them both as she tried to hold him down.

"Shh, go back to sleep," she soothed, pressing against his chest.

"You're all right?" he asked anxiously, still fighting her efforts.

"I'm fine, I'm fine!" she reassured him harshly, angry at his question. What a height of ridiculousness, when they were all so worried about *him*! He was working his arms from under the covers, trying to reach her. Exasperatedly she allowed him to pull her to him, knowing he would not stop until he had solved his worry. Easing her awkward crouch somewhat, Jeannie managed to place her lips against his feverish cheek, then moved to his ear, clucking softly, "Shh, now, shh. Go to sleep."

His body suddenly went slack, but he still gripped her tightly.

"You're safe? That's good." He sighed, allowing his eyes to close. But almost immediately he snapped them open again, still troubled.

"The kids?"

"They're fine!" She was almost lying against him now. "Becky and Greg are asleep, as you should be." Her voice was showing its tension, and her throat ached with a curious tightness. Good Lord! She was about to cry all over him.

"And Bruce?" He still was not giving up.

That did it!

His inclusion of *her* son in his blind concern undid her. The tears poured out as she fell full length on the narrow strip between him and the edge of the bed.

"We're all fine, Paul," she sobbed, kissing him over and over—gentle, feathery, motherly kisses. He turned his face to her like a baby bird, letting the touch of a woman's lips, that method old as time itself, give him the reassurance mere words could not give. Gradually his madman's grip on her eased.

"Everyone is okay? That's good," he breathed tiredly, looking at her with one last moment of lucidity before the illness took over his mind again.

He began to tug at her hands. "You'd better get back in bed, you'll get cold," he gasped, trying to pull her closer.

She tore one hand from his grasp so she could pull his covers back over him.

"I will. You go to sleep," she kept whispering against his ear. She remained awkwardly balanced on the edge of the bed because each time she moved even slightly away he struggled to get up.

"You'll get cold," he continued to mumble fretfully. He was too weak to get his arm around her shoulders, so he settled for tucking her hand against his blanket-shrouded chest. "I'll take care of you," he mumbled distractedly.

"Shh. Go to sleep," Jeannie moaned.

"I'll take care of you..." he kept mumbling over and over again. It was a long time before he fell asleep.

Every muscle of Jeannie's body ached when she finally slipped to the floor in a heap of tangled blankets. Her hand was still held in his big work-roughened grasp as she leaned her head weakly against the bed.

Jeannie knew she was defeated, even though she looked at him pleadingly. She knew she was going to marry this man, this helpless, self-sufficient fool. No longer could she hold to her soul that once-in-a-lifetime experience of inimitable beauty they had shared together. She would have to settle for a lifetime of practical companionship, and she dreaded having that ecstatic memory changed to earthbound reality.

Nor did she want to give up her own hard-earned independence, her freedom of movement.

But somehow—she didn't quite understand why—this night she had lost control of her own destiny. Paul had won after all. He and his children. Not in their strength, but in their weakness.

It was full dawn before she summoned the energy to get up from the floor and leave him.

Chapter Fourteen

With each passing mile deeper into the southern Arizona wilderness Paul felt the desert's old power over him—the endless space was stripping from him the pressures of his artificial urban life, bringing him ease. It had always been that way for him. He wondered hopefully if Jeannie was feeling its healing power too.

Flicking his attention from the road for a brief moment, he thought her color looked better than it had last night when he had rushed her from the Phoenix airport to their hotel in Scottsdale. And she had quit twitching her fingers over her thumb in that absent-minded way she had when she was nervous.

Bad idea of his, that luxury hotel. Jeannie had been so ill, what with the natural tension of the wedding and their long plane flight, that he should have canceled his reservations and taken her to the closest airport motel. In retrospect, his dreams of a wedding-night champagne dinner on their private patio and a prebreakfast romp in their huge sunken bathtub seemed ridiculous.

The events of the night before had been ironical. Jeannie had been predicting dire results for his health if he insisted on getting married and taking a wedding trip just two weeks after his illness; yet it was she, not Paul, who had collapsed and needed care.

The rented Jeep swayed over a slight grade in the highway, and he glanced at her in concern. "I wish a four-wheel-drive vehicle wasn't necessary for us to get to my cabin,'' he apologized. "I'm afraid I'm giving you a rough ride."

"I'm not nauseated today, Paul. Not after that twelve-hour sleep." Her voice sounded as mortified as it had last night when she had moaned that never before had she suffered a sick headache.

"Good."

Paul's answer was deliberately brief. Last night, when he had been up hours placing cold cloths on her head, his sympathetic understanding had seemed only to make her more distressed. But he did understand. The rough plane ride with its unscheduled layover, and the airline providing wine and nuts, instead of a meal, had been hard even on him. And Jeannie had been tense and exhausted to begin with. Since they had decided to live temporarily in the two apartments, Jeannie had spent her evenings after work moving furniture and scrubbing. And she absolutely refused Paul's help, insisting that he needed the rest.

Personally Paul thought they could have got by with just moving an extra bed for Bruce into Greg's room. Probably he should have set his foot down and made Jeannie and the kids leave the furniture alone. Or he should have hired someone to do whatever it was Jeannie thought was so all-fired important. But she would have squawked about that; she still thought he was poor.

"I think living in the two apartments until our leases run out is going to work fine." Jeannie spoke almost as if she had picked up part of his train of thought. "When the children suggested your place for sleeping and mine for day use, I thought it was too complicated. But the furniture arrangements they came up with worked out pretty well."

"Mmm." He narrowed his eyes in apparent concentration, trying to appear engrossed in his driving. He was afraid she was going to start talking about their future again; she had already offered him her savings for a down payment on a house, and he wasn't quite up to stalling that idea yet another time. Paul's lips curled in secret satisfaction when she lapsed back into silence, apparently having assumed that he was finding the driving difficult in his present poor state of health.

At some point he was going to have to tell her about the house, about everything.

Thank God, he thought, that Lucille and Ben were taking care of things in St. Louis so he could have four days alone with Jeannie in the desert. That should do it. If they could just have a little more time together without the artificial barrier of his wealth muddling her adjustment to him.... She was so damned independent!

He'd tell her about the house soon.

The silence that deepened around them was a comfortable one. Jeannie's hands still rested easy in her lap as she drank in the passing scene. They had entered one of his favorite stretches of the desert where the giant saguaro cactus was protected by the federal government. They could look for miles in all directions and see no signs of civilization; it was a glorious wilderness, its only trees the lordly saguaros. Dozens of smaller varieties of cacti sprinkled the desert floor, breaking the sandy monotony of the arid wasteland with their color and texture.

He loved the primordial effect, loved having his woman here with him as if they were returning to their natural origins. His very intensity of feeling moved his hand toward Jeannie to reassure himself that she was sharing this experience with him. She touched him briefly but did not tear her gaze away from the desolation before her.

Paul wished he were a man of words. It was almost a curse, his coupling of a practical mind with a poetic soul. For the first time in his life he wanted someone else to understand his feelings. His heart was so committed to Jeannie that he also wanted to share with her his thoughts. And that was a problem for him.

What words could he possibly find that would tell her what the desert had given to him over the years: the physical solace when he was weary and overpressured, intellectual inspiration when his brain was stalled, healing glimpses of beauty when his spirit was sullied? Words were too meaningless.

As they drew nearer to the acreage he owned overlooking the Papago Indian Reservation, his need to share became more intense and he did begin trying to tell her of the magic he felt in this haven of his. It was awkward. He was aware that the words were coming out like a precise engineering drawing—mere dictation to a secretary—but since she was listening intently he continued to try.

He talked about the natural and scientific mysteries that could be solved by studying the desert; pointed out some of the areas he had explored himself, and described engineering ideas that had developed from his explorations; told anecdotes of the desert people he knew, hoping he could guide her perception to see beyond their eccentricities to their humanity and gentle, peaceful nature.

At first Jeannie had leaned back in relaxation, smiling slightly as he pointed out first one, then another familiar sight along their route. It was only after they turned off the highway and began to cut straight across the unmarked desert that he noticed she had stiffened, her fingers rubbing those thumbs again. Her attitude became masked, formally polite.

Perhaps, he thought, the isolation was worrying her. Maybe she felt their cabin would be too primitive, a burden instead of a pleasure. Hoping to put her at ease, he told her of the machines he had constructed to make survival in the arid desert possible not only for himself but for the two Indian ranchers to whom he leased his land.

She didn't say anything until they approached a small ranch house nestled in a low fold of the hillside.

"Is that your place?" she asked stiffly. The tone of her voice made him uneasy—it was too polite, like some stranger conversing with a computer-chosen date.

"It belongs to a neighbor. He looks after my cabin for me." Paul had answered a little too curtly, but he was concerned at the ranch's deserted appearance. What if the rancher had not turned on the generators and pump at his place, had not laid in the refrigerated provisions he had ordered? Despite his carefully made plans, Jeannie might still suffer a primitive welcome. That was all they would need.

Mercifully, his first glimpse of his own place was reassuring. The rustic little cabin high up on the hillside looked cool and inviting behind its shelter of large mesquite and saguaros. Some of the desert flowers Lucille had transplanted for him were in full bloom, lending their own vivid welcome. And—hallelujah—the power was working!

"See! The wind generator is on." He enthusiastically pointed to the tall tower behind the house as he pulled to a stop. "And look, they've brought some potted desert plants onto the porch by our bedroom. They know I like throwing open the doors and having nature right there."

"It's beautiful, Paul," she said in a hushed voice.

"You sound as if you hadn't expected it to be." He smiled at her teasingly and reached for her hand.

But she was having none of that and eased her hand away to fumble with the door handle. "I can help you unload," she said briskly, a formal little smile not quite reaching her eyes.

By the time he had turned the engine off she was pulling out the baggage stored in the rear of the Jeep. Irritated by her remote efficiency, he wanted to roar out at her, stop her ridiculous behaviour. She was behaving like a damn guest, for God's sake!

"Jeannie, I'll get all that."

"There's no reason for a man to have to carry everything for a woman. And you've been sick...." She left the rest unsaid as she struggled toward the porch with her carryall bag and a huge wobbly sack of groceries.

If you throw my sickness in my face one more time, he thought menacingly as he followed her bobbing form, *I'll swat that delectable bottom of yours.* The thought appealed to him; her rounded body looked ridiculously ill-used as a packhorse. She was marching along like a cheerleader, determined and efficient.

"I'll bet she was a Girl Scout," he muttered under his breath, wondering how on earth he was going to get her out of *this* mood. And what in hell had brought it on? It was as if they were back to the first weeks they had known each other.

The matchstick shades were still down in the house, letting in enough light to be pleasant and offer a tantalizing peek at the magnificent view, but giving a cool feel for the place. Thank God it was clean and inviting, the little efficient kitchen even having a bowl of fresh flowers on the counter top. Thanks to the rancher's wife, undoubtedly. Paul dumped the bags just inside the door, determined to do the rest of the unloading himself.

"Let me take those groceries." He reached for the wobbly sack.

Jeannie dropped the carryall with a bang and jerked past his outstretched arms. "Really, Paul! I may not understand the desert or how to use your equipment, but I can certainly find where to put the groceries by myself."

And then it hit him, what was wrong. He had goofed.

She *did* feel like a guest, a stranger. All because of his damn mouth. On the drive out he had shown her sides of his mind and talents she had not observed before. Perhaps if he had done it slowly, on her home territory with the kids and neighbors and her friends giving the revelations naturalness.... But in his own territory, strange and mysterious to her, she was disoriented; she thought she really didn't know this man she had married after all. She was back to that old saw about having no place in his needs. And it was so damned important to her independent spirit for her to be needed. How was he ever going to be able to tell her the full extent of his business success if the little bit he had talked about thus far worried her so much?

"I can get that last bag of groceries." She barely glanced at him in false cheerfulness as she brushed past him. "Why don't you rest a little? You must be tired after doing all the driving."

She was out of the door and he still couldn't figure out what to do. He wondered maliciously why she had not dusted her hands in satisfaction when she set the groceries down. The gesture would have gone well with her incredible behaviour. He had just started after her, determined to stop this nonsense before it got out of hand, when it happened.

Nature intervened. The gods were smiling on him.

She fell.

Ignominiously, gracelessly, hard on her seat. Not sprawling dangerously where you would want tender sympathy. Just feet straight out from under her, trying to walk over an obvious step she had been too efficiently busy to bother to look for. Foolishly flat on her seat with no dignity. If she had been a man, he would have laughed.

Instead he eased open the screen and walked slowly, oh, so slowly, toward her so she would have time to conquer her mortification; time for nature to halt that initial reaction to scramble up and babble apologies; time for the shock to set in.

When he eventually knelt inquiringly beside her she was drained of all tension, tractable, too dazed even to be embarrassed. She did not object when he raised her gently and led her back into the house.

"Let's see what damage you've done to yourself," he said gruffly as he halted just inside the door. She stood quietly as he ran his hands lightly over her to make certain she had not been hurt. He had not expected an injury but was still relieved to find none.

It was like a miracle, the change in her. When he straightened from his examination and laid his hands on her unresisting shoulders she was a different woman. No longer the Girl Scout, the fearless leader. She was...

His hands eased down to rest against her buttocks. "You'll be sore there tomorrow," he whispered, the vulnerability he saw in her eyes encouraging his fingers to rove over the injured area. The clinging fabric of her skirt bunched in his hands and hindered his soothing efforts.

"This is in my way," he murmured, testing the permanence of her mood. She stared at him wide-eyed and silently, her tongue moistening her lips. He half expected her to bolt, to go back for the rest of the food. But she waited there.

He realized with growing wonder that nature had done in one silly incident what it might have taken him days to accomplish: They were back on equal footing. But not the same equal footing as when they had left the hotel that morning. Not Jeannie and Paul, neighbors, parents, friends. No, it was more basic than that. Man and woman ageless in the desert. Overdramatic? Too mushy? Probably, but there it was.

Jeannie was unaware that it was *she* who arched against him and, as his body molded to hers, again moistened her lips pleadingly, a veritable Eve. Obligingly Paul leaned forward, this time moistening those lovely lips himself. She tasted good. Again he laid his mouth upon hers, moving carefully, feeling every change in the shape of her lips as they moved softly against his.

She had on a shirtwaist dress, ridiculously easy to

unbutton and toss aside. She did not help him, but then again she did not hinder him, and her eyes continued to plead. The full slip was more difficult to remove, but he enjoyed his task, lightly kissing her arms and shoulders as he worked the garment up. She was without will. Pliable clay to his ministrations. He undressed her slowly, savoring each new bare, quivering area of her body he exposed to his own fully clothed eagerness.

It was inconvenient that she had worn panty hose, but once he had disposed of them, lovely to let his hands trail slowly up her thighs as he rose. He was pleased that such a simple act had the power to make her shudder with passion.

He felt strangely excited to be fully dressed as he held her naked and eager against him, both of them uncaring of the wide-open door and the waiting audience of the sunny desert. He stood for some time just glorying in fondling her. Then, eager to explore her more fully, too anxious even to go to the bedroom, he led her past the abandoned luggage and strewn clothing to the large overstuffed couch.

How urgently beautiful she looked to him as the aroma of the plants outside and the shuttered coolness of the room cast their own tense spell of waiting. *No more,* he thought. *The waiting is over.* Turning her gently against him, his hand fully covering one throbbing breast, he sank into the soft enveloping cushions.

Instead of following his first urge to lie with her, he drew her into his lap, and it proved to be a lovely idea. How perfectly she fitted against him. He wondered incoherently if this was how the ancient kings had felt when they commanded naked women into their arms. Deliciously decadent?

She seemed as taken as he with the fascination of the contrasts in their attire, and her hands rovingly examined the rough texture of his garments against her soft flesh.

He leaned slowly down, and his mouth began to play with her hardening nipples, lifting and moistening them. She stirred in his arms, innocently arching herself even more provocatively before him, engulfing him with heat and excitement. So completely had the fall shattered her inhibitions that he was easily creating a matching frenetic excitement within her. She was fussing with his shirt buttons, her toes pushing against his feet.

Awkwardly he kicked off his shoes, not meaning to bounce her so roughly against him as he did so, but immediately enjoying the accident, driven to rubbing his tongue over her heated skin. As his questing mouth caressed her she gasped and pulled desperately at his shirt.

As they rolled back together into the cradle of cushions he fleetingly thought that his happiness would truly be complete if she had come to him voluntarily, without the inducement of emotional shock. But he quickly forgot that brief moment of regret as, tearing out of his clothes, he lost himself in the bloom of her womanhood.

Determinedly he took his time so he could help her discover many nuances of her own feelings before the urgency was so great that he could postpone no longer, both of them sighing in satisfaction that the waiting was over.

And then it began. Those great waves of delight that swept slowly, languorously over them. Their passion was beyond frenzy; they moved in glorious mutual pleasure until, in a quiet pause deep within each other, they shuddered with blessed release.

Ecstasy!

Loveliness beyond words to describe.

Paul lay against her, having no will to move. "I love you," he whispered helplessly, his mind having no control over the words.

She looked at him wonderingly, the endearment

seeming almost not to register as her eyes were still glazed with amazement at what had happened to them.

THE sounds didn't waken her. At first she couldn't even identify them, so slowly did they creep upon her hazy consciousness. They were light and airy, resurrecting childhood memories of when she and her young cousins had tentatively and daringly clinked silver spoons against the crystal goblets set out for a dinner party. And yet these tones were melodic and consistent, an ethereal tinkling, gentle as the breath of a kiss.

Wind chimes!

Lazily Jeannie turned on her side and looked past Paul's motionless body to the shaded porch on the north of the house, beyond its glass doors, which had been pushed open to the endless expanse of nature. The chimes were hanging in an irregular pattern from a pottery base mounted at the edge of the roof. The glass rectangles were hand-painted browns and pale greens of the desert, in patterns she had never seen before. They were as beautiful to look at as they were to hear. She looked at Paul in gratitude.

"I had a Papago friend do them for me." Paul's eyes scanned hers, reading her thoughts. "I had the glass pieces made in a factory in Phoenix, but he decorated and hung them for me. Each pattern has a religious meaning for the Indians. I'll explain them some-time...."

"They're beautiful! Just right for this beautiful place. They make beautiful music." She lay back deliciously, loving the way her sated body felt. "They make me feel beautiful."

He propped himself up on an elbow to better see her face. "You are beautiful," he murmured gruffly, lightly kissing her smiling lips.

She nestled against him as he lay back down, sliding her arm across his bare chest. She could hardly remember their brief shower together, or Paul toweling them both dry and carrying her to his bedroom. The light visible around the edges of the shades on the southern and western windows indicated it was still midday.

"How long have I slept?"

"Only a few minutes."

She lay contentedly beside him, thinking.

"No, that's not right." She turned on her side again and slid her hand under the thin sheet to caress his chest and waist, then tentatively and quickly down his naked thighs, then back slowly to eventually rest against his strong jaw. His look was questioning.

"I've slept a thousand years. I've never been awake before, not really." She traced his lips and watched him lazily kiss each fingertip as it passed over his mouth. "It took the kiss of a prince to waken me."

His large, hairy arm slid over her soft buttocks, then his hand roved up her back and tangled into her hair as he drew her down to him and whimsically kissed every pensive feature.

"You know what I was thinking...when I undressed you?"

She blushed, waiting for him to continue, wanting to hear and understand his inner thoughts.

"That you make me feel like a king. I'd done nothing to deserve you, but somehow you were there, at my bidding. And I didn't ever have to let you go. It was..."

He seemed frustrated with words and with a groan levered his other arm from under the delicate sheet and took her curly head reverently in his hands, kissing her thoroughly once again before tucking her against his chest and enfolding her in his arms.

Although she was not feeling drowsy anymore, she was strangely averse to getting up and dressing. She wanted to stay there forever.

They rested together in silence for some time, listening to the mysterious sounds of the gentle wind stirring the rare chimes, feeling the warm, fragrant breezes.

"I'm glad you have the chimes," she murmured at last. "Every time I hear a sound like that again, it will remind me of these moments. And my happiness today will be remembered."

She pressed her palm against his, luxuriating in the feel of his strength against hers—a pair.

"I'll have another set of wind chimes made to hang at our home." His voice was hoarse with emotion. "The pictures will cast a blessing on our marriage. But we won't need to depend on memories...."

His sentence hung unfinished as he shifted beside her, dominating her now as he restlessly lowered the sheet below her hips and buried his face in her full breasts. His mouth burned her skin, fiery dominance as he stretched her arms above her head and trailed caresses to her fingertips.

"Oh, Paul, love me!" she groaned mindlessly even as he settled his weight upon her and lowered his searching mouth to her own. It was her last conscious thought. For her own moans of ecstasy blended with his mumbled words of love.

In a honeymoon daze Jeannie kept thinking wildly, *This can't keep up. Not this... anxiety for him. I'm too old. I've just been lonely too long. It will go away.*

She had tried to put a semblance of sanity into their time together as she cooked a meal, admired his cabin, listened eagerly to his stories of the desert. But he had only to glance tenderly at her for her sanity to flee, her heart to melt, and her body to begin throbbing hungrily. She was embarrassed at her weakness and tried to hide it from him.

They had spent the remainder of that first day wandering about the hillside, then finally strolling back to the darkened cabin, not even going through the motions of eating another meal, so anxious were they to indulge once again in the wonder of each other. His touch became her manna, his lips the only well from which she could find life-giving refreshment.

The next day all the little automatic acts of living—their meals, walks over the arid countryside, simple conversations—were shaded with a private kind of magic. And the night—the moments they had been postponing, deliciously waiting for like children hoarding candy, when the magic became reality—was better than dreams. Their sleep became a lush happiness of discovering joy in each other's arms.

No sanity there, none at all.

But she had been right.

It did have to end.

In one cruel moment the honeymoon daze came to an abrupt halt. Early the third morning the neighboring rancher drove up to tell Paul that Ben was trying to reach him. The message had been radioed in from a store in the nearest village.

By late evening they were back in Jeannie's apartment watching Paul's lawyer arrange a stack of papers on the kitchen table. Never having doubted Paul's explanation that an urgent business matter required their return, Jeannie was making a pot of coffee for the two men when the lawyer seemed to disappear.

"Tell me about the Rasmussens, your in-laws," Paul said abruptly, guiding her to a chair at the table.

She looked at him in disbelief for a moment; that was the last thing she had expected to hear. But when she realized he was in deadly earnest, she drew a shaky breath and tried to compose her thoughts.

"At first, after my husband died, they pretty much ran my life. I was awfully young. I didn't know what else to do, with no home and a baby on the way. It was only after Bruce was born that I began to worry about their possessiveness. Toward my son, I mean. I ignored it for a while as I was trying to work and get my schooling, but gradually I had to begin asserting my own judgment."

He was listening patiently, obviously trying to read between the words.

"It kept becoming harder. They seemed to be mixing my Bruce up with his father, or making my son their own somehow…oh, I don't know!" Her hands brushed nervously at the table. "Why do you want to know all this?"

"They're here."

Her face went white. She looked at him bleakly, her stomach churning.

"Here?"

"That's right. They called you for some reason the evening we left. And when they learned from Bruce that you had remarried, they hotfooted it to St. Louis. Ben and Lucille have put them up at a motel."

"Oh, no! I had intended to tell them in my own time." Her face was fiery red. "I'm sorry they caused them that trouble. And the expense! I'll repay—"

"The expense is not the problem. They've been trying to take Bruce back to Hawaii with them. They appear to feel you won't want to care for him now. That's why Ben called."

She was stunned.

"They have no right!" She jumped up angrily, desperate to see her son. Paul grabbed her arm.

"He's okay. Let's not have the kids all in here, which they will be once they know we're back. We need the time to find ways to make sure this can never happen again."

"I'll never let them close to him again!" She was livid with anger. "I've tried so hard not to turn him against his grandparents no matter what difficulties I had with them. I kept thinking he needed some family besides me to love. But no more."

"Dammit, Jeannie, you've spent twelve years of your life trying to give him a sense of family. You may still be able to preserve a grandparent relationship of sorts for him if you use your head. We just have to convince them that now you have me too and that they must enjoy their grandson on *our* terms."

"I've never thought they were *bad* people," she faltered, trying to weigh his words. "It's more that they've stayed in a state of unreason since Bruce died."

"Perhaps they loved their son too well and not wisely enough?"

"That's it!" She was grateful he had found an explanation for her. "What do you think we should do?"

"I want to adopt Bruce." He didn't waste words. "I called my lawyer before we left Arizona and had him draw up the papers. I want a legal right to give Bruce my name and to care for him. If I ever lose you, I don't want to lose him too."

Tears began to blur Jeannie's vision.

"I had already signed a new will to include you and Bruce," Paul continued. "If you agree, I'd like to add a codicil specifying that if anything happens to both of us, Ben and Lucille are to be appointed guardians for all three children. They have already said they would be delighted to do so." He looked at her questioningly.

"I'd like that," she said simply.

"Let me get the lawyer out here, then, so you can be sure what we are signing."

"Paul, can't I adopt your children too?"

He strode to her, his face serious as he tilted her chin in his big hand. "Are you certain you want to?"

"Absolutely. I love them."

Paul was momentarily saddened that she could utter those simple words about his children but had never been able to say them about him. His pain did not show, however, as he leaned over and kissed her lightly. "We'll get the lawyer to arrange it."

They were both so mentally and physically exhausted by the time all the document signing was completed that they couldn't summon the energy to go to a motel for the night. Jeannie's bed was stored in Bruce's old bedroom, along with other unused furniture and boxes, so they shoved a path to it and each fell into solitary oblivion.

But not peaceful oblivion. The harsh contrasts of that honeymoon day had been almost too much: They had awakened dreamily in each other's arms in that golden desert world where no responsibilities existed; but to find themselves now in a snow-shrouded world of pain and duty to others, time zones away—it was almost too much.

LATER, looking back over the events of the next day, Jeannie marveled at the different ways men and women approach adversity. Her way of fighting her in-laws had always been to survive quietly until she could gather her son to her and completely escape—run! Ben and Paul aggressively met their adversaries head-on. But with such subtle charm.

Ben had arranged to meet the Rasmussens at a restaurant for brunch. Jeannie dreaded joining them, unsure of her own ability to keep a civil tongue. But her fears were unfounded; her new husband rarely gave her a chance to open her mouth as he carried off the occasion with a social aplomb she hadn't known he possessed.

She had only one anxious moment during the entire meal, when Bruce began to talk about Paul's dream house.

"All three of us kids are going to have a room of our own!" he told his grandparents. "There's a guest room over the garage so you can visit us! And Mom and Dad will have their own wing."

"I think it's rather bourgeois, their having a private suite," Becky teased. "Bedroom, large bath, sitting room with fireplace, private courtyard...."

"I think *you* need to look up the meaning of *bourgeois*, Miss Becky," Paul warned.

Jeannie blinked at him helplessly. She couldn't bear it if the Rasmussens started asking too many questions about Paul's precious, hopeless dream house. *Absolutely* hopeless, she only then realized, since he had taken on the added responsibility of herself and Bruce. She stared at him in wordless apology.

"Bruce loves to study blueprints"—Paul ignored her distress as he addressed the Rasmussens—"and I've let him see some I have. I've noticed he has solid skills in precision drawing, and an excellent perception of motion. Did he get that from his father?"

"Our Bruce never cared much about schoolwork," Mrs. Rasmussen stammered, taken aback at the unexpected reference to their son.

"My father was an engineer," Mr. Rasmussen ventured uncertainly.

"That explains it." Paul grinned at Jeannie. "I knew he didn't get that ability from his mother."

"Well, I'll be damned if you're going to send *both* my nephews to *your* engineering school," Ben surprised them all by interjecting. "One of them is going to a *good* school—mine. Either Greg or Bruce, but one of them." Ben's expression was shuttered, making him look so much like Paul that it was uncanny. Jeannie wondered suspiciously what he was up to.

"I absolutely refuse to have you two men ruin my lunch with that continual argument about your colleges," Lucille objected. "The only solution is for Paul to send Bruce to one school and Greg to the other, just as your father did with you two."

"I've adopted Bruce, and both my sons are going to my school," Paul told his brother, ignoring Lucille.

"The hell!" Ben argued.

"They do this every time they're together," Lucille explained to the Rasmussens. "Like little children."

There had been nothing childish, however, in the firm way Ben took charge of things when they all left the restaurant.

"Paul, I need to run over some work at the labs with you," he had said almost too casually. "We'll go on

from here and take everybody along. Lucille wants to
see the place again before we go back, and that will save
me a special trip."

Paul had looked absolutely livid. Horrified that he
would be embarrassed to have the Rasmussens see
how modest his business was, Jeannie tried to arrange
to take her in-laws home with her. But Ben had been
adamant.

The rest of the day passed in a maze of confusion
and revelations...and a total shattering of Jeannie's
perceived world.

At first her emotion was agony for her husband—
sympathy with Paul's withdrawn fury because Ben for
some unknown reason, was exposing Paul's vulnerable
dreams to strangers. Her misgivings began when they
entered a security gate into what appeared to be a nature preserve: Raymond Brothers, Inc., the sign said.
Disbelief grew as they passed a large converted farmhouse and an employee parking lot full of cars, and
then suddenly entered a large valley in which were
spread out impressive laboratories, a large office building, warehouses, and outbuildings.

Ben had dragged Paul into a private office immediately; she could hear the explosion of Paul's anger as
his secretary quickly ushered the rest of them out for a
tour. Jeannie remained in a state of shock throughout
the whirlwind visit. Explanations of solar-energy de-
vices, stream-motion studies, gasohol production, and
wind generators passed vaguely through her comprehension as her sympathy changed to mortified fury.

She did not go through the house. Lucille ran Mrs.
Rasmussen over there, but Jeannie, going along with
Bruce's wish to see some of the experimental stations
on the grounds, caught only a glimpse of its exterior
through the trees. It took her breath away—the impressive contemporary structure fitting naturally into its
wooded hillside setting, its glass-walled wings reaching
into its environment as if it grew there. Even at that

distance the house looked huge but comfortingly homey.

It was as if it were all happening to someone else, not to the Jeannie who had married that quiet man from the tacky little apartment across the way.

Had it not been for the Rasmussens she would have demanded an immediate explanation for Paul's lies. She could have supported herself indefinitely, she reasoned; she needed no one's pity. However, Jeannie could not help but sense how the Rasmussens' former attitude of barely controlled civility toward Paul had changed to shocked respect. Paul's careful handling of them in the restaurant had been a good battle. But it was Ben's blockbuster move that had provided the checkmate. And she couldn't ruin that. Bruce's future was at stake.

Eventually Paul had emerged from his office in control of his temper again, but he never looked at her directly the rest of the day.

Her in-laws had lost, and they knew it. They left that evening, thanking Paul for their visit and urging him to bring the whole family out to see them in Hawaii whenever he could. To Jeannie they said virtually nothing. That suited her fine.

She intended to have a reckoning with Paul that very night. But when he returned from driving Ben and Lucille to a motel, he went promptly to bed. Refusing to be put off, she carried the battle to him.

The bed squeaked protestingly as she crawled in beside him.

"I know you're not asleep," she said furiously.

"You'd better whisper unless you want an audience," Paul immediately responded, turning his back to her. She lay there for a few moments, agonizingly conscious of how the thin walls made every noise startlingly noticeable. She could hear Becky moving in her bedroom and Bruce thrashing about in his unfamiliar bunk in Greg's room.

"I'm not going to sleep until you talk," she finally whispered belligerently.

He remained motionless a fraction of a second before levering himself up on an elbow to face her. She returned his look unblinkingly. She was waiting for his explanations: They were due her; she expected them.

"Then you're going to be very tired tomorrow," he whispered flatly. "Good night."

His kiss caught her tightly compressed mouth and she gasped at his touch in spite of herself. Better satisfied with her open lips, he kissed her again before relaxing back against his pillow.

"Paul, why didn't you tell me?" she demanded as she bounced up on her elbow. The bed creaked with each tiny movement, but she was unmindful of the noise, or of the fact that her nightgown strap had slipped down on her shoulder and her hair had fallen into disarray. "You encouraged me to make a fool of myself over my savings, over everything! If I'd known about you—I mean the real you—I would never have—"

"Shh!" Paul put his hand warningly over her mouth, the sudden movement creating loud squawks from the bed. She stared at him in bewilderment before hearing bare feet padding toward their room.

"Mom? Dad?" Bruce's high voice announced his entrance before he pushed open the door. "Are you okay in there?"

"Hey, Bruce!" Becky and Greg called out almost in unison, both of them hitting the floor at the same time. By the time they had reached Bruce at the open door, Paul and Jeannie were sitting up in bed, staring in amazement at the three young faces. Paul's pajama shirt hung open halfway to the waist, his exposed chest thick with black and gray hairs. Self-consciously Jeannie slid her nightgown strap back up and tried to pull the covers about her more modestly.

"I heard all the noise of the bed, and I thought Dad

was sick with that fever again..." Bruce was trying to explain as Becky and Greg hastily jerked him back out of the room.

"Hey, what's wrong?" he objected sleepily as they slammed the door behind him.

"You dumbo!" Becky could be heard hissing. "Don't you know they just got married?"

"Yeah," Greg was whispering. "We guess even old folks..."

Paul had collapsed back against the pillows, shaking his head in amazement. "I don't believe it. I don't believe it," he muttered. "I live in a madhouse."

His mutterings turned to reluctant chuckles, then to full-scale laughter.

Jeannie looked at him in complete disorientation. She agreed with him. They were indeed living in a madhouse. When he tugged at her, she fell unresistingly.

"But they'll think—" she protested weakly, now painfully conscious of the noise the bed made with every slight movement.

"They already do," he said humorously, pulling her against him with tired determination. "You know what *I* think?" His voice sounded weary as he leaned his stubbly chin against her face. "I think I'm going to have to tighten all the screws in this bed tomorrow. It's either that or abstinence."

"Paul, you're trying to change the subject." She made one last desperate attempt at her threatened reckoning. "You should have told me—"

His rough fingers over her lips halted her.

"Couldn't it wait?" he asked almost sluggishly. "I admit to being worn out tonight. Your relatives have created quite an end to my honeymoon. I think I'd like this day to be over."

That simple statement was her undoing. Guilty realization of the enormity of what Paul had done for her forced her immediate silence. Involuntarily she sank against him, her resigned acceptance allowing him to shift her body until he had shaped her against him as he wanted. Once she was settled in his arms just so, Paul heaved a great sigh of satisfaction and, with one hand resting possessively on her breast, fell immediately asleep. Deeply asleep.

And she knew then that it wouldn't just wait, her reckoning; it would never occur. Because he would always defeat her one way or another.

As she lazily drifted into sleep herself, she tried to believe that someday she would find the answers she needed about this unknowable man in whose arms she was lying. Find them all by herself.

Chapter Fifteen

It was the second Thursday night since their hectic homecoming that Jeannie was to work at the hospital, and this time Paul insisted on driving her. He did not like the way her old car was running despite the repairs she'd had done, and he refused to have her out alone in it at night until his own mechanic could go over the problem.

"I will not spend another Thursday evening worrying about your safety," he had said flatly when she tried to talk him out of the day-long chauffeuring chores. And so she had given in without a fight, thinking that actually it was rather nice to look forward to a few minutes alone with him.

And that tells what it's been like around home, Jeannie mused in rare candor as she walked from her office at the center to the lot where Paul was already waiting. She would not usually admit, even to herself, that the confusion of their cramped living quarters had been more wearing than she had anticipated. Even Becky, sweet-tempered Becky, had been alarmingly moody. And the lack of privacy! You knew it was bad if a married couple looked forward to a few snatched moments alone in a car speeding down the expressway.

When she got in the Mercedes, she found Paul in excellent spirits, chuckling over Greg's indecision about whether to cook plain hot dogs or chili dogs for supper.

"Bruce is advising him that plain hot dogs would be wisest because it will save having to wash the chili pan." Paul explained the scene he had found when he stopped by the apartment to check on the family before driving to the research center.

"That figures. He's an expert at getting out of work," Jeannie laughed.

"It's uncanny how the natures of those two boys seem to complement each other," Paul commented as he pulled out into the traffic. "Have you seen those drawings they made up for a motorized go-cart?"

"No. I heard them talking about using some junk you have left over at the labs, but I didn't know they'd gone beyond that."

"They're really good drawings. As I say, it's strange how the boys fit together even in work...almost like Ben and me."

She glanced at him questioningly.

"Strangely enough, Bruce is more like me than my own son—practical, the one who will find a way to make things work. Greg, on the other hand, might have been Ben's boy. He's the theoretical scientist. You know, if those boys like the kind of work Ben and I do, and if we can keep them interested in their schooling, we're going to have a hell of a family business some-day."

"You have a hell of a family business already," she affirmed gently.

"I mean a *hell* of a family business!" He grinned widely, boyishly.

She loved it when he was in that mood—it had been a while since they had enjoyed such light gaiety. She looked forward to their ride home after her emergency-room duty.

But when Paul picked her up again that night, his mood had changed; he was curiously preoccupied, barely acknowledging her greeting as she hopped in the car. She rode along quietly, wondering guiltily if driving her had been an imposition after all, but gradually she became angry with that possibility because it had been Paul's idea to do so.

Becky was still up, running the hair dryer in her room, and the boys could be heard talking excitedly behind their closed door. Jeannie thought perhaps she would open Paul a beer and try to get him to relax. Even though she was hurt by his moodiness, she hated to see him fester inside. But before she could offer, he had picked up his briefcase and, curtly telling her to go on to bed because he had some work to do, disappeared to the study across the breezeway.

She had determined to stay awake until he returned and find out what was bothering him. But her weariness after her second job of the long day defeated her good intentions and she was sound asleep when he eventually came to bed.

It was the next evening before she found out what had upset him.

Paul had taken the boys out to the labs to begin collecting their equipment for the go-cart and Becky had stayed behind to help with the dishes. As they worked side by side in strained silence Jeannie almost wished the girl had gone also. Becky's short temper and moodiness were beginning to get on her nerves, especially now that Paul was behaving the same way.

Jeannie was just tossing around in her mind whether or not to ask point-blank what was wrong when Becky spoke out in a strained voice.

"I think maybe I need you to talk to Dad for me, Mom," she ventured hesitantly.

Jeannie glanced up in surprise, quickly seeing the troubled look on the young girl's face. But she looked back down at the sudsy work in front of her as she tried to sound casual.

"What about?"

"My dancing."

"Your dancing?" It was not at all what she might

have expected. "But, Becky, you know your father has always supported you strongly in your—"

"That's what I mean!" The girl laid aside the dish towel, unable to continue with the pretense of being helpful. "I'm beginning to wonder if I ever really wanted to be a ballerina. Dad's always encouraged it and I love performing for my own expression, but I don't feel *driven* to it."

When Jeannie didn't respond, Becky hesitantly continued her explanation.

"You must always be at your peak to be a principal dancer. And that requires concentration I don't think I'm willing to give anymore. Well, don't just think— *know* I'm not willing to give anymore."

"You talk as if the possibility of a dance career is past tense." Jeannie set the last dish in the drainer, not liking the direction of this conversation. If Becky was giving up her dancing for a new boyfriend, Paul would be furious.

"That's what I want you to talk to Dad about. I tried to tell him last night, but—"

"Last night? You mean while I was at work?"

"Yes. I decided I shouldn't put it off any longer; it's been bothering me for a month or so. Anyway, the boys were out playing football, and I thought it would be a good time to talk it out. But Dad wouldn't even listen."

"He wouldn't listen?" Jeannie was incredulous, knowing in that instant what had been wrong with Paul when he had picked her up. She was ridiculously relieved that *she* had not been the cause. How unliberated!

"Oh, he heard, but he didn't listen, if you see the difference. I tried to tell him that I want to be a doctor; that I want to specialize in athletic medicine and research; that I *do* know what I'm getting into. I've been talking with that therapist Dr. Matthews introduced me to and helping the school nurse in my free period at school. And reading—"

"You told him all that?"

"Yes! And I said dancing isn't really right for me. I love it, but not for a career. I know he feels guilty because my mother gave up her dancing career for him and later regretted it. He's afraid I'll repeat my mother's mistake. But I don't even remember my mother! Just because she—"

"Becky! I don't think you should be discussing this with me."

"But I thought you cared about me."

"I do, of course I do! But you see...well, your father has never talked about your mother with me. It isn't right that I should be hearing these things from someone else if he doesn't want me to know."

"Not even if Dad's leading me into a mistake because of her? Mom, maybe if you talked to Dad...."

Jeannie shook her head emphatically. Not this; she couldn't do it. It was the first time Paul's late wife had seriously shadowed her mind, and she was fleetingly jealous of that unknown image, then ashamed of that reaction as she tried to find a solution to the dilemma. But any way she considered it, she still concluded that this was one aspect of Paul's relationship with Becky that she had no business interfering in. Becky could read that decision in her face.

"Please, Mom," she pleaded. "I have a chance for a medical job this summer. But I was tentatively enrolled in an eight-week summer session of the New York City Ballet, and they have now accepted me. I want to turn the appointment down, but Dad refuses to let me."

"Then there isn't much more to say, is there?" Jeannie sighed fatalistically, certain that Becky would not go against Paul's wishes; the girl loved her father too much to hurt him like that.

She looked over at Becky sympathetically. What she saw stunned her. It was the first time she had ever seen the girl with that stubborn, shuttered expression so like her inscrutable father's.

"Becky?" Jeannie ventured.

But the girl turned away and resumed her work with the dishes, her fixed smile polite but remote. And Jeannie realized with foreboding that she had made a parental mistake. No longer would Becky come to her for help in this matter; she had decided to battle it out in her own way, alone.

WITHIN another couple of weeks Jeannie was beginning to feel that she was living in a jungle full of strangers. She didn't know how much more of it she could take.

It was bad enough trying to survive in the natural confusion of five of them living between two small apartments—confusion made worse because Greg and Bruce now had twenty-four hours a day together in which to indulge their natural teen-age restlessness with constant noisy poking, punching, and practical joking. Add to that the remote ill tempers of both Paul and Becky....

While Jeannie had married Paul with the belief that they would always be living in crowded, financially pressed conditions and had welcomed the opportunity of sharing his burden for the good of their children, it embarrassed her to face the reality of their present circumstances. Nerveracking chaos! Her rosy projection of the five of them struggling nobly against adversity seemed to change to a nightmare of uncontrollable disorder.

The situation was reaching epidemic proportions, in Jeannie's mind, as they approached the final few days before they could move into the new house. Realizing that they would soon have all the space and privacy they could possibly need, the children began to crack interminable jokes about the inconveniences they had endured in the weeks of living in the dual apartments. They found it hilarious once they could see the end in sight. Even Becky came out of her ill-tempered shell to add riotously noisy cracks of her own. Jeannie knew she should be pleased the girl was finding something to smile about for a change, but she wasn't. She was offended. She was tired of hearing children's laughing remarks about hearing loud snoring at night, eating off one another's elbows, tripping over furniture, always leaving in one apartment what they needed when they were in the other one, causing curiosity among the neighbors with all their comings and goings.

Paul, in his closemouthed preoccupation, seemed oblivious of it all. This made Jeannie even less willing to find any of the children's teasings funny.

What was so laughable, she wondered defensively, about independence? Independence, no matter how modest, was a trait she admired and coveted. Jeannie reasoned that she had survived for years on less luxury, was still earning her own living and could survive again in hard times if she had to. Who did these ungrateful spoiled kids, her own Bruce included, think they were with their demands for luxuries?

She blamed Paul for not stopping it all. He was the father; it was his place to implant proper values in the family. But he was so busy trying to hide his worry over Becky, masking his face in that abominable way of his and not telling his wife anything about what was raging in his mind, that he couldn't involve himself with other realities at home. He wove a barrier around himself.

He rarely even kissed her anymore. Of course there weren't many times they could be alone, but in her growing distraught state Jeannie made no allowances for that. She had expected to settle for companionship in her marriage, but now her preoccupied husband was not even giving her that. . . .

She tried to keep her growing tension and worry hidden, tried to practice patience. But as the days went by, her irritation with the whole family mounted. She was overdue for an explosion.

When Paul gave her the present, innocently setting off the fuse, her explosion was a dramatic one.

It was a Friday evening. They had eaten dinner late

because, since they were scheduled to move into the
new house on Monday, they had been packing boxes
of favorite treasures that they couldn't trust to the
movers.

Jeannie was stacking the dinner plates on the counter
preparatory to serving dessert, and wondering if it was
just imagination that the children seemed even more
wound up than usual. When she turned to set the dessert forks on the table, she noticed a tiny box with a big
yellow bow at her place.

"Open it!" the children chorused, barely giving her
time to register that she was receiving a present. Even
Becky was joining in the enthusiasm. Having just been
reflecting on how spoiled the children were and how
quickly they adapted to affluence, she was hardly in the
mood to be receiving gifts. Reluctantly she picked up
the package.

"Keys?" she queried, holding up the little set she
had discovered. It occurred to her that the children
must have thought up some joke connected with the
new house, and she believed if she heard one more
joke she would completely fall apart.

Bruce could wait no longer for her to figure out the
gift. "It's a new car. It's outside. Come see it!" Excitedly he grabbed her arm, accidently dumping the keys
on the table.

"Yeah, let's go! It's a four-wheel-drive wagon, so
you can get to work in the snow!" Greg was making for
the door.

Even Becky was watching her expectantly, a smile on
her face for the first time in weeks. "Don't worry,
Mom, it's automatic shift! And you'll just love the
color—blue. I picked it out for you."

All Jeannie could think about were the grueling
hours of pediatrics hospital duty she had struggled
through just to earn enough for her old secondhand
car, of her pride when she had come home from the
dealer's owning her very first automobile. All her re-

sentment at her sudden unearned affluence, her irritation with the children, everything, simply closed in on her.

"I have a car already."

The children paused in their headlong flight out the door, certain they had not heard her properly.

"But this one is air-conditioned!" Bruce ignored the warning signals.

"I have a car already," Jeannie repeated ungraciously, not moving from her seat. "I cannot afford a new one." She would not look at Paul.

"All right" was all he said as he stuffed the keys in his pocket and tossed the tiny box and its gay wrappings into the garbage. "Let's have dessert now."

A strained silence hung over the table as they ate, the clatter of forks against the plates and the sound of people swallowing all uncannily unpleasant. Finally, unable to stand the family's censure anymore, Jeannie mumbled an excuse and fled to the study.

She remained there with her head buried in her arms at one of the desks long after the hushed sounds of voices and washing of dishes had disappeared from the kitchen. They had all returned to Paul's apartment, but still Jeannie tarried alone. It was almost dark in the study, but she could make out the furniture, crammed in just so to make space for every desk and table. The crowded conditions depressed her.

Now that her defenses were completely swept away she had to agree that it would be a rough way to live permanently. Certainly if they couldn't afford better they would have adjusted to it. But at the price of terrible strain. Why couldn't she accept that? Why did it hurt so much to have to admit financial dependence on Paul?

Restlessly she wandered back into the kitchen, not wanting to return to the other apartment yet. She was able to admit her mistake to herself, but not yet ready to admit it to others. Jeannie could see the wrappings of the gift box caught on the edge of the garbage sack. On impulse she rescued the tiny unread gift card from on top of a sticky grape-juice lid. Cautiously she looked at Paul's firm writing:

> This is really our present to ourselves, so we won't have to worry about your safety when you are away from us.
>
> Love ...

All of them had signed it. Bruce's precise little signature had wandered up the side of the card and ended with an exclamation point. Becky had added X's and O's. Greg's writing seemed almost to match his father's.

She remained in the kitchen for a long time, feeling inept and cursing her pride.

When she finally returned to the other apartment, the three children were studying in their rooms and Paul had spread drawings out on their bed, looking extremely uncomfortable as he studied them.

Jeannie stood in the doorway and said loudly, "I want to apologize to all of you. I realize that I do need a new car, and I want to thank you for it."

It was a grudging apology at best, but the children, with the optimism of youth, accepted it willingly and called out relieved good-nights. Paul merely shrugged his shoulders and continued his work.

THE IDEA came to her the next morning when they were getting ready to take two carloads of their things out to the new house. It was most unlike her, and she felt like a teen-age girl secretly conniving to see a boyfriend. But she had to do something about the mess she was making of her marriage. So before they left she slipped across to her apartment to call Karen Matthews. Karen didn't even ask any questions as she agreed to come out to the house that afternoon and invite the children over for a long evening.

Jeannie wasn't quite clear in her mind how she was going to spend her stolen time with Paul, but she was determined she was not going to muff her opportunity to clear the air. She would apologize on her knees if she had to. Anything to get rid of this terrible tension.

The plan worked like clockwork; not too bad for one unused to subterfuge, she thought recklessly. The family had spent the day unloading the things, making some decisions on where the movers were to place the furniture the next week and testing the three fireplaces with some logs the boys picked up in the woods.

They had just finished putting out the fires in the family room and kitchen when Dick and Karen arrived. The Matthewses' breezy explanation that Dick's nieces and nephews were coming over and they wanted to give them a surprise party was so convincing Jeannie almost believed it herself.

The house seemed eerily quiet after the children had left. Paul and Jeannie walked back to their own suite to put out the third fire, their footsteps echoing musically on the lovely inlaid wood floors. As they entered their sitting room the deep carpeting muffled their movements, creating an instant welcoming hush. It was such a contrasting mood, this sudden solitude—a pensive mood heightened by the cheery little fire glowing in the open hearth that formed a semiwall between the sitting room and bedroom.

"I almost hate to put it out," Jeannie sighed spontaneously, liking the soft glow of the room contrasted with the beginnings of mysterious darkness outside. It would not be many minutes before the towering evergreens beyond the open glass wall would fade into intriguing shadows; the first star was already visible over the treetops.

"This is going to be a beautiful haven, Paul," she said sincerely. "It will be nice to start a fire early on a winter evening and still be able to enjoy it when we go to sleep."

Paul stood beside her, not answering, but also seeming to enjoy watching the way the patterns of the flickering flames on the glass contrasted with the shadowy beauty outside.

"I know what," he said suddenly. "Why don't I run back to the lab and pick up some sandwiches and sodas from the vending machines for our supper? It won't be fancy, but we could get by. And since we don't have to get home to the kids for a while we could finish putting away those books and linens."

Jeannie readily agreed to his suggestion, finding it a good solution to her dilemma of what to do next. Surely with this precious time alone in their own home she could find a suitable moment to make her apologies. Fortunately, the electricity was already connected and they were able to work companionably for some time, even after the twilight faded beyond use.

After they finished placing the books in the built-in cases in their sitting room, Jeannie unearthed an old blanket from the linen supplies and spread it in front of the fireplace.

"Now look at that!" Paul said in satisfaction as the log he added to the fire caught quickly, casting a bright glow around the room. "Just flip off that overhead light and we'll have an instant gourmet restaurant." He settled on the blanket and began laying out the sandwiches.

"I'll flip off the lights because the fire will look prettier," Jeannie laughed. "But I'm suspicious about the gourmet-restaurant bit. How long did you say those sandwiches had been in the machine?"

The food was a little dry, and the sodas had lost their chill after sitting on the hearth so long while Paul and Jeannie finished their work. But it was a pleasurable meal anyway, what with the flickering glow of the fire and the peculiar hushed sounds of the woodland setting, the night birds and crickets making a symphony all their own.

"I wasn't aware of the sounds in the woods before," Jeannie commented idly, tossing her cellophane wrapper on a glowing log, fascinated with its brief flare of startling brightness.

"You'll hear all sorts of things as summer comes on and we are staying here permanently." He leaned back on his elbow, seemingly relaxed. "It's a shame we have to get back to the apartment soon. This is nice."

Jeannie watched the play of light over the gray in Paul's dark hair. He was half lying in front of her and she wondered what he would do if she followed her inclination and traced that coloring at his temples. But she put that temptation aside, troubled that there was still this tension between them and she had not yet done anything to dispel it. She would never have a better time.

"Paul, I'm sorry I was so unreasonable about the new car," she eventually blurted, unable to think of any easy way to get started. "I really don't have any excuse except pride...." She was at a loss, struggling for words.

He turned over slowly so that he now lay on his side facing her and could study her face. Briefly he observed her hesitation.

"I'm glad you brought it out in the open, Jeannie." He spoke softly as he tried to help her. "But you really don't have to explain. I eventually realized that I had hit you with too many things too fast—my business, the house, then the car. But I was so concerned about your safety I didn't stop to think about how you would take it."

"Paul, it wasn't your fault; it was all mine. I was a real bitch." She felt like crying.

"So we're both at fault!" He grinned lopsidedly at her, not moving from his position. "Does it really matter so much anymore as long as we both keep trying to understand each other?"

She shook her head wordlessly. Satisfied, he turned

contentedly back to watch the fire. She was tempted to leave things there, but realizing she would still be upset and strained until she had talked to him about Becky, she decided she may as well get the whole mess opened up at once. And take her chances on ruining all the progress she had just made. Better to know where they stood.

"Paul, Becky has been talking to me about her dancing," she said in a small voice. "She's terribly unhappy and..."

He flipped over and rose to face her, developing anger changing his relaxed face to harshness. She shrank from him at first, then stiffened immediately and tried to strengthen herself, determined not to back down.

"And I'm worried about her," she finished firmly.

"Was it your idea, this big thing about being a doctor?" he snapped cruelly.

Hurt dominated her expression as she replied proudly, "I don't believe you mean that. You surely know better."

Although he looked a bit contrite, he merely turned his head away, not apologizing.

"I don't think she knows what she wants." His voice was hard and bitter.

"If she continued to want to be a dancer, you would think she knew what she wanted."

"Dammit, it's more than that, Jeannie! You saw her dance. Can you honestly tell me that girl is not star material?"

"I thought she was the most graceful and beautiful performer I have ever seen," she replied honestly. Her reply left him with no ammunition and he was silent, unable to continue the argument he had been planning.

"Then you can understand how I feel, surely?" he mumbled. "She's at a turning point in her life where she's questioning the discipline and commitment required to continue using her great talent."

"Is that how you see this desire to be a doctor?"

"Yes, that's how I see it," he almost shouted. "Her mother went through similar misgivings when she was four years older. And unfortunately, I happened on the scene at the time."

Jeannie's heart jumped painfully at the mention of Paul's wife, but she refused to let her own hurt stop her. "Why do you say 'unfortunately'?" she persisted.

"My God!" he exploded, grabbing her by the shoulders. "What is this, an inquisition? I finally have a chance to enjoy being with my wife in a little privacy and she deliberately starts a goddamn row."

"I'm not trying to start an argument," Jeannie objected brokenly, attempting to wriggle out of his harsh grip. "I'm worried about Becky. She is very unhappy."

"So was her mother."

He released her as if she were so much vermin. Then he stood and began gathering their supper supplies.

"Why was she unhappy?" Jeannie pressed, no longer caring if he became blisteringly angry. Better at her than at his daughter.

"Because she should have been a ballerina, that's why." He looked gigantic as he stood over her. "She was born to it and she gave it up. I'm not letting Becky make the same mistake and ruin her life. Her talent is fully as superb as LuAnne's."

"Becky is not her mother." Jeannie stood up herself in an attempt to face him on more equal ground.

Paul's anger was so overwhelming that he squinted his eyes almost shut and took deep breaths in an attempt to gain control before he answered carefully.

"I went through hell in my first marriage. I saw a beautiful loving woman waste away. And it started long before she developed the cancer; it started when she found she could not juggle her marriage with the demands of her profession. Do you think we didn't try to find a solution? I gave up my job, lived in New York, tried to adjust. She tried too. We stretched our love every way we knew, trying to work it out, but that love just degenerated."

Watching his anguish, Jeannie was beyond tears. She wanted to draw him to her breast and comfort him as she would a hurt child. But there was still Becky. She remained motionless, not touching him, saying nothing. He turned away and restlessly began to walk around the room.

"I've talked with professional dancers frequently since then, for Becky's sake as well as my own peace of mind. They tell me there comes a time in most dancers' lives when they're swamped with a realization of what they will be giving up to pursue their professional careers—just as Becky is doing now. Most of them have a wild fling for a few months and then buckle back down to work permanently. In LuAnne's case, she unfortunately fell in love during that crisis in her career, and she found that our life together wasn't easy for her to give up when she was ready to go back to dancing. So she stayed with me and was always torn between her two loves: dancing and me. Her unhappiness destroyed almost everything good about our marriage."

Then abruptly Paul snapped, "Oh, hell! Let's go on home." He practically tumbled Jeannie off the edge of the blanket as he started to snatch it up.

In desperation she grabbed the blanket herself and wouldn't let go, starting an almost ridiculous tug-of-war.

"I'm not going to let it end like this!" she almost shouted, tears blinding her, but she would not let herself cry. She pulled the blanket out of his arms and began shaping it back to the floor.

"I'm sorry about your past," she raged. "I wish I could make it better. But whatever the problem in your first marriage, my main concern right now is your daughter."

Jeannie stood flat-footed on the rumpled blanket,

throwing her head up at him defiantly, unaware that she was looking utterly wild and beautiful. He stared at her in astonishment.

"Paul, your daughter adores you. Whether dancing is right or wrong for her, you can't make it *your* decision. You can encourage her, but if you push her much harder right now, you're going to lose her. I can't bear to see that happen."

There was more she could say. And yet really nothing. Discouraged, she sank down on the blanket, utterly spent.

There was a long silence as Jeannie sat huddled there, her face in her hands, with no idea of whether her husband was still standing over her or was already gone. As a matter of fact, she did not care. All she sensed was that she had failed. Inept again. She despised her inadequacies.

Only gradually did she become aware that Paul had reseated himself on the blanket—not close to her, but at least there, staring thoughtfully into the dying flames. Well, that was something anyway. She sniffed inelegantly and scrubbed at her puffy eyes with her fists.

For a long time they silently sat there, side by side.

"Would you feel any better if I said I'll try to consider it with a more open mind?" he finally asked gruffly.

She thought about that a few moments, not really sure what was the right future for Becky or what she wanted Paul to do about it.

"I suppose so," she sniffed grudgingly. The rest, after all, was up to Becky; the girl had to know her own best interests.

Paul was still drawing great breaths, obviously trying to control his feelings. It seemed almost to hurt him to breathe. The waiting was awkward for both of them; there was, after all, nothing more to be said, and yet neither of them felt settled enough to leave it there.

Finally Paul lay back on the blanket and linked his arms under his head. Jeannie watched him sadly, wondering if she had done the right thing in stirring up his painful memories.

Seeming to read her mind, he turned his head slightly to glance at her. "I guess it's harder for me because Becky looks a great deal like LuAnne, moves like her, laughs like her. Any hint of her giving up her dancing and I panic. I feel as if disastrous history is about to repeat itself."

He reached across the blanket for Jeannie's hand and drew her closer to him. This involuntary seeking for her solace while he was thinking of his first love offended and hurt her, but she found herself unable to deny him her comfort, not even objecting when he slid his head up into her lap and closed his eyes.

Did it matter so much, she wondered as she looked at his still form, that she was second choice? She was the one who was here. Rebelliously she gave in to her urge to touch the gray at his temples. She held his head in one hand while the other explored and soothed. It fascinated her sensitive fingertips to feel the dark hair spring briskly back at her touch.

"Paul?" she finally spoke, her hand wandering slightly down to examine the stubble on his strong jaw.

"Hmm?" He turned his head to fit more comfortably against her soft hands.

"Of course I didn't know your wife"—she forced herself to say the words, even though they came out stiffly—"but from my viewpoint, Becky is her father all over again."

His eyes flickered open as he tried to gauge if she was serious.

"She looks like LuAnne," he insisted. Jeannie eased her hand away, feeling the need to withdraw, but he snatched it back. She didn't try to remove it again, not even when he absentmindedly brought her fingers upward, running them over his lips.

"But she *acts* like *you*," she insisted gently.

He gripped her hand tighter, tucking it under his chin so that his beard made her fingers tingle. She caught her breath in surprise, shocked by the sheer erotic pleasure of such a simple act.

Distracted, she waited for his reply, but it never came.

"You weren't even listening to me," she accused gently.

"You just said, 'she acts like you,'" Paul finally said, humor tinging his lazy voice, "and I was thinking that she doesn't. But then I remembered how damned closemouthed and stubborn she's been the past week, and I have to admit...." He looked up at her with a sheepish grin.

It was then, in a blinding moment of insight, in a glory of relief, that she knew it was going to be all right. What the outcome would be, she did not know. But it would be all right.

Abruptly the mundane world pressed its demands again: She became aware of the lateness of the hour, of how the chill of the April evening was beginning to invade the house, overriding the slight warmth emitted by the dying fire.

"It's probably time we were getting home," she sighed, unmoving.

"I know it," he agreed reluctantly. "I don't remember whether the kids have a key. Do you?"

"No."

She wondered how she could have overlooked such an obvious thing. Karen and Dick would have to sit in the parking lot and wait for her and Paul to get home.

But still they both hesitated, curiously reluctant to leave their bare, chilly, wondrously private little haven.

"Do you realize, Mrs. Raymond, that in just a few days we'll be living in this house?" Paul said in a pensive voice as he stirred slightly in her lap. "And that then I can actually have some moments alone with my

wife like this every single day? No more furtive fondling in the middle of the night." He grinned in satisfaction at his tongue-twister silly choice of words. "I
can lock that door over there anytime I want. I can give
my wife a loud, noisy smacky kiss and not have to
worry about three sleepy adolescents hearing me and
running in to find out what's wrong."

"I'm not sure I want a loud, noisy, smacky kiss!"
She laughed at his nonsense, enjoying his change of
mood. "It sounds unpleasant."

He laughed too and heaved himself to a sitting position.

"Now that's a challenge if ever I heard one," he
threatened as he reached for her.

"Oh, no, Paul!" She giggled like a schoolgirl as she
tried to roll away from him, hysterical at the silly, juicy,
smacking noises he was making with his lips. It was so
unlike his usual dignified nature.

But he was too fast for her, and they tumbled down
together on the blanket, laughing and shoving like kids.

"I may even shout!" He was really warming up to
his role and tried to pin her by the shoulders. "I won't
ever worry about noise again. I may yell, 'I'm going to
make love to my wife!' and if the children come
pounding on that locked door I'll just drag you into that
bedroom where they can't hear us and...."

She became suddenly still, her eyes deep pools. And
he realized that he was sprawled on top of her. The cool
of the evening surrounded them, the fire slowly flickering out, the shadows creeping in on them—all emphasized their aloneness. The humor left his eyes as the
night sounds primitively filled the room, inexorably
pressuring them into nature's ways, old as time. For a
brief moment she saw his raw desire.

"I thought you didn't want me anymore." She
couldn't stop the broken admission.

"Oh, God, Jeannie," he moaned, burying his face
against her neck.

This time the magic didn't blind them to the real world. They both were aware of the late hour, and of their duties to the children. But they still could not stop themselves. They were driven to relieve unbearable longing.

They came together frantically, clothes only partially thrown off, uncaring of the hardness of the floor beneath their rough blanket or of the cold lashing of their passion-heated bodies.

The tension built to unbearable heights and they were both angry with each other for causing this vulnerability; they tried to punish each other, but wise nature soothed them just before granting them the joy each could find only in the other.

Afterward, panting and unbelieving, they pulled the blanket around them as they lay shivering together, trying to regather their composure. There had been no beauty in it, no gentleness. It was unlike anything they had experienced before. But cleansing, enormously satisfying in its own way.

There was a light on in the apartment when they arrived home. Someone had had a key.

Chapter Sixteen

"I can't ever seem to beat you in to work," Karen Matthews complained lightly as she entered Jeannie's office. "I was sure I'd be here a few minutes before you this morning and could have everything set up for our meeting."

"I found a better shortcut," Jeannie laughed as she continued to stack files neatly around the conference table preparatory to the coming evaluation session with the center's doctors. "In the month since we've been in the house the boys average two new suggestions a week for avoiding traffic."

"Are you enjoying your new car?"

"I love it—it handles so smoothly, and yet with that four-wheel drive we can just take off over the countryside. I hate to admit it, but now I wonder how I ever got along without it. I even had the air conditioner on one warm day last week!"

"And it's only early May!" Karen laughed outright. "So you're living up to your fears and succumbing to the influence of affluence."

"If you only knew," Jeannie admitted a little ruefully. "Now that I'm not frantically saving up money for a house down payment, I've admitted to myself how wearing that extra job at the hospital is. I've turned in my notice to quit it when school is out. I'll let some of the younger nurses without families take a turn at these constant life-death situations."

"I'll bet Paul's glad to hear that."

"I haven't told him yet, but I guess he will be. I know he's been worried about my being out so late, even though he's never asked me to quit."

"Will you miss it?"

"No, I won't. For one thing, there's lots I'd like to do at home. And I get more professional satisfaction from this job at the center than I ever did from emergency care. I don't know why."

"I know I couldn't take emergency-room pressure, even if I had your skill and training," Karen observed as she began to stack her own papers on top of Jeannie's. "And besides, your husband needs you at home."

"Oh, I don't know about that," Jeannie denied modestly, unaware of the sadness creeping into her voice. "He's gotten along for years without a wife."

Karen glanced over at her, wondering how Jeannie could be unaware of Paul's great emotional dependence on her; it was so obvious to any skilled observer. But she discreetly changed the subject.

"If this new research into so-called minor aches and pains of adults is finally approved, you'll have plenty to do here for several years anyway."

"Isn't that project exciting?" Jeannie agreed. "I hear the possibility of funding looks good now. We'll have to be hiring more help if we try to run both programs."

"If they take on student workers you should involve your daughter. She seems seriously interested in physical therapy."

"Hmm," Jeannie murmured, busying herself with setting up a flip chart. She wasn't ready to talk about Becky's interest in medicine yet. It might be years before the question of her career was firmly resolved, and Jeannie was content to go from day to day, glad that at least her husband and daughter had gradually found their way back to their old affectionate relationship.

Not noticing that she had received no response,

Karen looked the preparations over approvingly, then headed for the door.

"I'm going down to get the brunch fixings we ordered," she explained.

Nodding absentmindedly at her, Jeannie finished setting up the flip chart, then settled down at her desk. The conference wouldn't begin for almost an hour, so she had time to review some of her notes.

But despite her best intentions she could not concentrate on her work. Her mind kept wandering back to Becky, remembering the evening two weeks earlier when Becky had announced to Paul that she was not going to attend the summer ballet school.

Jeannie and Paul, although undressed for bed, had been reading in their sitting room when Becky materialized at their door. Becky hadn't wasted time trying to soften the words, just lifted her chin and blurted them firmly with no question of compromise in her voice. Sensing a stormy confrontation, Jeannie had unwound her bare feet from under her robe and moved to leave, but Becky had urged her to stay.

"You both may as well know," she said, "that I've written a letter of resignation and asked that if any refund is possible they send it directly to Dad."

Helpless fury seemed to cross Paul's face briefly before he caught himself under stony control, his big hand framing the letter she handed him. He studied his daughter's writing on the crisp envelope—it was as graceful and womanly as the girl herself.

"I don't expect I'll bother to mail this," he drawled.

"I don't want to cause you to lose all your money, but that has to be up to you. It won't make any difference in my decision." Becky's chin had quivered momentarily, but she quickly masked her feelings with that shuttered look. She had never, Jeannie thought, resembled her father more than at that moment.

The two had stared at each other like combatants, expressionless.

"A group of doctors in the university medical school specializes in athletic medicine," Becky continued curtly. "They have a new research center on Lindell Boulevard in the city. I've taken a job there as an aide for the summer."

Surprise had flickered briefly in Paul's eyes.

"The job usually goes to college students. Even though it's just minimum wage, many premed students compete for it because the experience is so valuable. I'm proud I got it."

Paul had looked questioningly at Jeannie, but her stunned reaction made it obvious she was as shocked by this development as he.

"Mom didn't know anything about it." Becky had almost read her father's mind. "I knew she wouldn't let me go behind your back, so I forged her signature to excuses twice and took a bus downtown during school for interviews."

"Becky!" Jeannie had objected, shocked.

"I wouldn't think they would give you the job without my permission," Paul inserted.

"I'm sixteen now." Becky hadn't really needed to remind him since he had gone with her when she passed her driving test. "And I already had a social security number."

"You may as well give it up, Becky. I have no intention of letting you have a car to get down there to work, and I won't let Jeannie become involved in this. It's between you and me."

"No, it's not, Dad. It's between me and my own commitment. I've already thought about transportation. If you won't help me work it out, I've located a nurse's aide who lives within walking distance of the center and she would rent me her daughter's old room. There's a gym where I can continue dancing practice and workouts."

"I wouldn't want that arrangement." Jeannie couldn't stop herself.

"I don't want it either, Mom." Becky's voice had faltered only briefly. "I love you both very much and prefer to stay home. But I will move out if I have to. I'll always dance for pleasure, but one way or another I *am* going to be a doctor."

Still ignoring the papers on her desk, Jeannie remembered how she and Paul had sat up late that evening, drinking a beer and talking about the development. At first Paul had seemed in anguish, but as they talked he appeared to relax and finally mused aloud that perhaps one summer off from serious dancing would not be such a tragedy either way. It was then that Jeannie had noticed a grin spreading fleetingly across his face.

"Paul?" She couldn't comprehend his absence of anger.

"Can you imagine my little baby forging those notes to school?" He had shaken his head, a trace of admiration in his wry mirth.

She had wanted to throw her beer at him.

"Well, as I've said," she snapped, "she's her father's daughter."

"I'm not going to make it easy for her, Jeannie. I want her to be very sure."

"Then you'd let her take that room downtown?" Jeannie hadn't been able to keep the concern from her voice.

"If, as you say, she's her father's daughter, I'm sure she already knows which bus stop she wants to be taken to. I have only to give an inch and she'll present me with several suitable transportation alternatives." A certain mischief gleamed in his eye. "But I think I'll avoid giving that inch for a while."

Jeannie had held up her glass, watching the tiny bubbles rise to the top of the beer, pondering how curiously golden Paul looked through the liquid—a golden god, forever sure of himself.

"I have a feeling my role in life is going to be as a

constant neutral at a father-daughter fencing match,'' she sighed fatalistically.

"You don't have to take sides. Just be there.''

"Oh, I'll be there, all right. And I had better find both of you speaking to each other, joking, loving, just as you used to do before all this came up.''

"Yes, dearest,'' he had said meekly.

She was laughing helplessly at her desk as she recalled that meek response. He always did that to her when he wanted his own way—just acted agreeable and called her "dearest.'' It was most disconcerting.

"You look a million miles away!'' Karen came bustling back to the office efficiently wheeling a trolley with coffee and doughnuts.

"I'm not a million miles away, my husband is,'' Jeannie grumbled, jumping up to help Karen in the door.

"Paul on a business trip?''

"Yes, in Cincinnati. He's attending a five-day government seminar on world-energy projections. But after all, I'm used to being alone anyway, so it hasn't been bad.''

"Did I ask?'' Karen teased.

Jeannie flushed and bit her lip. "Well, the kids miss him, you know. He called the first night, even though we had agreed that it wasn't necessary. So they've been expecting him to call each evening after that, and he hasn't. They've been disappointed.''

"Don't you know where he's staying?''

"Of course.''

"Well, then, the children could always call him if they get too lonely.''

"I hate to let them bother him,'' Jeannie faltered, her eyes lighting up at Karen's suggestion. "He'll think they're not coping well without him.''

"I doubt that,'' Karen observed calmly, setting the refreshment trolley next to the conference table. "After all these years, Paul understands children.''

The first doctor came in just then, so Karen didn't say anything more; but she felt it unnecessary anyway. Obviously her lonely friend was now considering placing a call herself.

When on earth, Karen wondered, was Jeannie going to realize that she was desperately in love with her husband? Psychologists were taught that it was best to let people discover and admit their own emotions themselves, but sometimes Karen was greatly tempted to help the difficult process along.

ALL three children needed new shoes, and Jeannie took them out shopping for an hour after supper. But she refused their pleas to stop for a snack, saying that their father might call and wonder where they were.

The children seemed unconcerned that by bedtime there was still no call, and they cheerily disappeared into their rooms. It was only Jeannie who continued to shuffle restlessly around, listening for the phone. Finally about midnight she was unable to stand it any longer. She dialed the number Paul had given her. It was only seconds before his sleepy response sounded in her ear; she immediately horrified herself by bursting noisily into tears.

"Hello? Hello?" Paul was sounding wide awake then.

"You didn't call!" Jeannie wailed accusingly.

"Jeannie?"

"Why didn't you call?" She felt very sorry for herself, mistreated.

"I did call earlier this evening, but nobody was home," he answered patiently. "I assumed you were all out living it up, and frankly, I was so beat I went to bed early."

"Oh, Paul, you aren't taking care of yourself. You're working too hard again! I just knew something was wrong when we didn't hear from you."

"You didn't hear from me because you made it quite

clear you didn't want me bothering you with daily phone calls.''

"Well, of course it isn't necessary," she blustered. "But since you did call that first night the children have been expecting...you should have thought of *them*, Paul. They didn't even know if you were all right." She was a little incoherent in making her point, whatever it was.

"And the children are all there beside you, right? Just dying to know how their papa is?"

"Of course they're in bed now," she snapped, not finding his teasing amusing. "They have to get their rest."

"Of course. Look, Jeannie, I'll call you tomorrow and tell you how all right I am."

"What time will you call?" she insisted.

"Are you serious?"

"Of course I'm serious. I have things to do besides sit around and wait for you to decide to call." Her voice was rising in righteous indignation.

"I'll call you around nine, your time, dearest. Is that okay?"

"Okay," she snapped and slammed down the receiver. She snatched it back immediately, regretting her angry impulse, but it was too late: The connection was broken.

"Oh, damn that man, stupidly overworking himself and then calling me 'dearest'!" she sobbed illogically.

In Cincinnati, Paul replaced the phone in a thoughtful manner, a pleased expression slowly spreading over his weary countenance.

But the nine-o'clock call the next evening didn't make Jeannie happy at all.

"Three more days?" she almost wailed into the receiver. "What's happened?"

"Nothing's happened. But I've learned that an inventors' symposium is opening here Saturday; I want to check out the new men showing this year. I have a gut feeling I might find somebody I want badly to hire."

"I thought Ben had found you the accounting engineer you needed."

"He did, but I need one more assistant, and these inventors' meetings attract the kind of man I'm looking for. Also, I want more time to dicker a little with a widow here who's trying to sell her husband's machine shop. We've been negotiating some this week and—"

"Are you going to open a business in Cincinnati, Dad?" Greg excitedly burst in from an extension.

"Son, what are you doing on the phone? I'm trying to talk to Jeannie."

"I forgot to tell you, Paul," she intervened. "All three kids are at the extension wanting to talk to you."

"Yeah, Dad, when are you coming home?" Becky asked, grabbing the receiver from her brother.

"Now you three cut out that scuffling!" Paul barked harshly. "I'm talking to your mother right now. You can listen in only if you hush up." The line was immediately silent.

"Now, to answer Greg's question: No, I am not opening a new business. But if this widow's employees will agree to move to St. Louis, I want to buy her equipment and install their shop in one corner of the new solar-energy garages. They've done work for us before, so I know that these men are extremely versatile craftsmen. The six of them could take over most machine tooling we need done, and I wouldn't have to contract it out. It's a new approach for them and they might not like the idea, or their families might not want to move. But I'm hopeful."

"Certainly you must stay and negotiate with them, then," Jeannie agreed grudgingly. She felt a terrible knot in her stomach and wanted to escape to her room and cry. "Paul, I think all the children have things they want to tell you, so I'll ring off—"

"Not yet, Jeannie, I need to ask you something. I'll talk to the kids, but I want you back on this line when they're through."

"All right, I'll stay on," she mumbled disagreeably.

It took the children several minutes to babble their messages. Paul's phone bill was going to be sizeable, she thought, as she finally heard him order them off the line.

"Jeannie, I want to ask you something. Are you still there?"

"Yes, of course; I'm listening," she snapped.

"All right. Now don't you dare hang up, because I want you up here tomorrow. Karen Matthews will take you straight to the airport from work and you can pick up your ticket at the check-in desk."

"Karen?"

"I called her first because I hoped she and Dick could stay with the kids over the weekend. For some unknown reason she sounded almost excited to help us out. Anyway, I want you to come back with me late Monday afternoon, but if you can't get off work Monday I'll put you on a return flight Sunday."

"Of course I'll stay until Monday, Paul." She was flustered, certain his health was suddenly falling apart. "Do you need any medicine? Any—"

"I'm fine; I told you that! I just need you here. Now, do you understand about that flight tomorrow?"

"I understand. I'm not a moron," she sputtered indignantly. "Did you want me to help you talk to those machinists' families? Should I bring any special clothes?"

"Dammit, Jeannie, just get yourself out here!"

"I will, I will! You don't have to be so violent. Here you disappear from our lives for more than a week and then you start yelling orders at all of us. It's quite upsetting."

It was strangely quiet on the other end of the line.

"Paul?" Her weak voice was contrite.

"I'm here, dearest," he answered quietly. "Look, I'll meet your flight tomorrow evening. Okay?"

Tightness caught at her throat. It devastated her when he was gentle. "Yes, yes. Okay. I'll be there."

THE waiting was interminable. A whole day! With unexplainable anguish Jeannie alternated between grave concern for her husband's health and impatience to berate him for his workaholic foolishness. But once she finally tumbled into his arms at the Cincinnati airport, remonstrances were beyond her. She showered him with soothing kisses and urged him to take her home. Home! Lord, that was where he was, anywhere. The realization shook her into stunned silence as she rode beside him, her hand resting against his thigh in a helpless obsession to keep him from disappearing.

Reasoning was beyond her. She knew only that the tightness in her throat was gone and she was at curious peace. But an alert peace, sensitive to the needs of this exhausted fool beside her.

"Did you have anything to eat yet?" she asked, concerned at how weary Paul looked as he carried her bag into his motel room. That exhaustion had not been precipitated by the three-hour wait he'd spent in the airport while her plane was grounded in Louisville. It had been going on for days.

"I picked up a sandwich at the airport snack bar when they announced that you would be served a meal while the plane waited out the electrical storm. Did you get enough to eat? We could go to the coffee shop."

"I've had plenty to eat. But I was sensible and avoided the complimentary wine!"

He grinned at her, remembering their disastrous honeymoon flight. He was perched on the edge of a straight-backed chair, hunching his shoulders unconsciously.

"You look good," he said softly, watching her curiously as she moved behind him. When she laid her hands on his shoulders, he groaned.

"What on earth have you been doing to yourself?" she asked as her skilled hands began to knead his tightened muscles. "You look terrible." Affection took the sting out of the words.

"Staying awake too much," Paul mumbled, luxuriously stretching under her touch. "Oooh, that feels good. I didn't know how stiff I was."

"I can do a better job when we get this coat and tie off," she promised, ignoring his protests as she loosened his collar and helped him shrug out of his coat.

"Don't get me too comfortable," he warned lazily as she resumed her massage. "You'll foul up my plans to take you out for cocktails tonight."

"I don't need cocktails," she said, idly wondering why she didn't feel more tired after the trip. Instead she was almost exhilarated. But she kept her voice relaxed as she added, "We'll probably both need the rest for tomorrow's work."

If she had hoped that her comment would lead Paul to explain why he wanted her in Cincinnati, she waited in vain. He remained silent, moving only to ease his head and neck to get more benefit from her soothing hands.

Eventually he said, "If you're sure you don't need anything right now, will you think me an utter oaf if I just lie down for a few minutes? You've got me so damned relaxed. It's dark already, so it won't matter if we wait another hour or so to run out for a drink."

"No, it won't matter at all," she agreed, having no intention of going out that night, but knowing she would make no progress by insisting that he quit trying to take care of her. She was helping him ease out of his shirt, slipping off his thick leather belt almost without his being aware of it. Her old nurse's training was at work; you never forgot certain skills.

"If you lie down on your tummy, I'll give you a complete back rub. It would feel good for me to move around a little. I'm tired of sitting."

Put that way, it was an offer he could hardly refuse. And he didn't. Obediently kicking off his shoes, he flopped on the bed where she had pulled back the covers, emitting a great sigh when she began to ease his knotted back.

He looks a little more gray, she thought sadly, hoping he would be successful in finding another assistant. All the urging in the world to ease up on his work would not help if he had no one competent to delegate his responsibilities to.

"You don't want to go out right now, then?" His voice sounded slightly slurred as he mumbled into the pillow.

"No, I'd rather relax with a book now." She moved away from him. He began to sit up, until he saw her take off her shoes and curl up in the room's only lounge chair. When she pulled a paperback out of her purse, he fell against the pillow and closed his eyes.

His skin looked winter-white against the dark hair on his chest. It would be good for him to take off his shirt this summer, she thought protectively, and putter around in their sunny yard. She wanted to see him as tanned again as when they had first met.

Jeannie tried to remain motionless in her chair, but her legs began to quiver from being cramped up so long. She absolutely had to straighten them. Using a walk across the room to turn down the lights as an excuse, she could hardly keep from moaning at the agonizing relief. But he was stirring and she quickly returned to her place, grasping a little more exercise for herself by noisily pushing the chair up closer to the bed. Paul remained lying down, sleepily watching her.

When she eventually resettled with her book, she had contrived that only the small lamp on a nearby table cast a small glow in in the room. Paul shifted slightly to give her room to prop her feet up on the edge of the bed.

"It must have been hectic at home this week," he

observed, letting his eyelids droop again. "You sounded flustered on the phone."

"A little," she admitted. "But no more hectic than for you, I suspect."

"Hmm." He slid deeper into the pillows.

It occurred to her that perhaps she should have turned the heater on. It was surprisingly chilly for May. She thought he looked a little cool lying there without a shirt on, and she regretted that she had not insisted he put on his pajamas. But then, she wouldn't have had any success with that, either, she realized resentfully. Not with his being so protectively male. He wouldn't admit that he was dead on his feet.... Kept wanting to take care of her....

"Just tell me when you want to go get a drink," he said, almost on cue.

She laughed outright. "Yes, dearest, I will. But I think it won't be for some time."

She was worried about his being cold. Resolutely she tugged the blankets up around his waist.

"Will you be too hot if I pull these up?" she asked innocently. "My feet are cold." Instinctively he pulled the blankets up around his shoulders, then slid his hand out to cup her instep.

"Of course not. I'll just stay here a minute and warm you. Then we can—"

Mercifully, exhaustion had finally claimed him. He didn't even finish his sentence.

Jeannie was almost motionless for more than an hour, reluctant to do anything that might disturb his sleep. She had the strangest pleasure sitting there watching him, her foot still enclosed in his grasp. There would be time tomorrow to discover what her role here was to be. For now she was content to see that he got his rest. His beard was obvious by this late hour, blue-black, strangely not showing any gray such as sprinkled his chest and temples. She thought he had never looked more handsome.

Finally, when his breathing had deepened to the full sleep she knew would not be challenged by tiny movements, she left her vigil. He was still sleeping soundly after she took a bath and changed for bed. Satisfied, she flipped off the final lamp and slipped in next to him, drawing the blankets around herself too.

But strangely, she was unable to go to sleep.

The scent of him reached her, disturbing her. He had done physical work today, or perhaps walked a great deal; she recognized the faint sweaty odor of him. And there was something else, a nice scent, maybe a slight splash of shaving lotion. She felt a great urge to touch him, to convince herself that he was really beside her; he had been away from her so long.

At first, not wanting to disturb him, she indulged herself in just looking at him in the dim moonlight seeping through the curtains. She turned over on her side and eased the blanket back to see better the strong muscles spreading down his back. Cautiously she ran her fingertips across the broad line from his shoulder to the middle of his spine, testing how effectively her massage had eased the tense knots. Without being aware of it, she let the heel of her hand join her fingers against his skin. Her other arm moved above her head so she could reach the texture of his hair bristling against the pillow. Then absentmindedly she leaned forward to place a light good-night kiss at the base of his neck.

That was too much of a good thing. Immediately she regretted the impulse as he slowly turned over, his sleep-glazed eyes trying hard to focus.

"Shh, go back to sleep." She tried to push him back against the pillows as he faced her dreamily. At first she thought she had succeeded, but his eyes cleared and he stared at her enigmatically a moment before grabbing her so suddenly that she was rolled over full length on top of him before she knew what was happening.

"Paul, you're supposed to be asleep!" she protested,

trying unsuccessfully to squirm out of his arms, reaching toward the covers he had kicked down to their feet.

"Stop that!" he ordered, swatting her hard on the bottom. She gasped in protest, and he immediately jerked her nightgown up around her waist, contritely rubbing the area he had, in his drowsy, uncontrolled strength, made red.

And it did hurt. She wanted to be soothed. Deserved it! She lay quietly on him, accepting his ministrations, hardly aware at what point the soothing motion had changed to a warm, fluid, erotic caress. She knew only that she had become achingly aware of him. She gloried when she realized he was hardening against her and emitted a sigh of satisfaction, dropping her head weakly against his chest.

"Oh, God, I've missed you, Jeannie," he breathed brokenly, impatiently nuzzling her hair out of his way as his tongue found its target at the delicate center of her ear. She sighed at his moist probing, involuntarily rubbing her body against his. Immediately they were both filled with a great delicious heat, an inflamed obsession, and she was kicking at the harsh fabric of his clothing still separating them. She couldn't stop her own unexpected wantonness, desperate to find cool solace from this frenzy.

Her gown was hanging crazily down below one breast; she didn't know when he had done *that*. When she finally tossed away his clothing Paul reached up to caress her breast. Gasping at the uncontrollable ecstasy, she tried to stop him, but, dominated by his own frenzy, he brushed her efforts away as of no consequence. As he jerked the other side of the gown down to her waist, his lips honed to the newly exposed fullness.

"Oh, Paul! Do you know what you're doing to me?" she moaned, almost rising to her knees under the persistent sensuous glory he was creating. They were both lost in time and space as heat, sensation, ecstasy, poured over them in great convulsive swirls. It had been so long to be lonely! Days. A lifetime!

What almost unbearable beauty it was to love one other human being, one alone to wait for and belong to in this world of incredible heights. She felt him remove her gown, and then their naked bodies pressed closer together, frantic, urgent in their need to become one. Jeannie cried and clung to him as she was swept by wave after wave of the beauty. Then came the sudden convulsion of love, the shuddering, vulnerable time lapse. Suspension in a rainbow world where only he and she existed. Yet not the two of them—the one trembling unit of them. Motionless. Eternal.

Jeannie's lonely soul overflowed with Paul's love.

Perhaps they slept. Perhaps not, nor did it matter. Gradually they struggled on the slow trip back down to the valley of near reality. But even that was a lovely journey, agonizingly sensuous, the valley itself worth waiting for in its own sated way. They touched, kissed, murmured incoherent soothings, as they settled together for sleep.

"My nightgown?" she protested weakly, somehow thinking she should make an attempt at propriety. She tried to raise herself from his arms, unable to see where he had impatiently tossed her garment.

"The children can't possibly be bursting in on us," Paul reminded her as he pulled her against him and resettled the light coverings around them. It was such a safe little world in their warm nest, feeling his dear presence along the full line of her body, and Jeannie molded willingly to him.

They lay together half dozingly, clinging to each other mindlessly, rather like sleepy children who possessively clutch their dearest treasures when trying to avert oblivion a few more precious seconds.

"Paul, I love you," she sighed as she turned her head up slightly so she could rain feather kisses on his neck and chin. She didn't want to stop and mewed protestingly when he eased her away from him. His expression was hooded as he studied her face carefully, but she was no good at hiding her newly discovered feelings—all her love had finally revealed itself in her deep brown eyes.

"It's about time you said that," he finally murmured, sliding her closer to him.

She buried her lips in the rough hair on his chest for a few moments, again compelled to distribute those silly little kisses, finding favorite spots to bless.

"I never realized it before," she admitted haltingly. "I mean, not really. I thought love was for teen-agers." His arms tightened around her punishingly and she moaned in protest until he released his pressure.

"Paul, why did you marry me?" She asked the question that always plagued her.

"I've always told you that. Because I love you."

"Oh, you always say that after we've made love," she dismissed it unhesitatingly, back at work with her little kisses, "and I know what *that* means. But love itself?"

"If you know what *that* means, then use your own words. I have none. If I say 'I love you' it means everything to me." He was impatient with the conversation.

"Paul!" she tried again.

"Shh," he cautioned, his callused hands roving over her lips to still her. She was still stubbornly insistent on finding her answers and moved her head away from his grip. She would approach the question from a different route.

"Paul, why did you need me to join you here?"

"So I can get some sleep!"

"Paul!" she objected, not wanting to joke at this special moment.

"I mean it, dammit. I'm so goddamn lonely without you during the day and I can't relax when you're not beside me at night. So you will please just lie quietly in my arms so I can get some rest? Otherwise I'll never get my work done tomorrow."

She stared at him angrily, thinking he was putting her off yet again. But as he unrelentingly shifted her in his arms until he had her settled just as he wanted her, when he wearily leaned his chin against her soft hair and immediately fell into deep slumber—she finally believed him.

He loved her.

A great wave of satisfaction swept over her, almost as if they had made love again. And he needed her! It wasn't much of a need, but she would settle for it. Welcome it! Her whole body melted against his and he involuntarily drew her even closer to him, almost snoring in his deep relaxation.

"Go to sleep, dearest," she murmured unnecessarily before joining him in sweet slumber.

Epilogue

The new house was definitely a distraction to serious work.

Jeannie stood at the glass wall that gave the kitchen its breathtaking view of Paul's business complex in the valley below and sighed in satisfaction. The buildings in their old farm environment were so lovely on the warm June evening. She marveled at how little the complex disturbed the serenity of the view—one was tempted to stare for hours.

"Which you practically have done," she chided herself. With renewed determination she walked around the work island with its oak chopping block and breadboard to the counter and sink beyond. Her dishwater had grown cold and greasy, but just one saucepan rested finished in the drainer. Absentmindedly Jeannie refilled the basin and resumed her chores, only half hearing the delicate musical tinkling stirring in the breeze outside her window while she worked. She was in a strangely contented, pensive mood.

You really have no excuse, she thought, *for taking so long to finish up.* Certainly tiredness could not be blamed. When she had gotten home from work, dinner was already simmering on the stove, because it was the night for the children's weekly assignment to cook. They had even loaded the dishwasher afterward, so the only things Jeannie had left were a few pots and pans. The problem, she justified her procrastination, was that each room of the house, and especially the kitchen, had a gorgeous view from almost any direction—a glass wall here, a strategically placed window there. She sometimes wondered if she should hang shutters in the kitchen at least, and not allow herself to open them until she had finished her tasks indoors.

Disciplining herself to ignore the equally distracting setting of the deck and woods from the window over the sink, she now worked quickly. She was on the last skillet when Becky sprang excitedly from the adjoining breakfast nook where she had been reading a medical journal loaned her by her boss.

"Mom, I forgot to tell you. They've changed the bus schedule."

"Does that mean you'll have trouble getting to work?" Jeannie looked worried as she set aside her dish towel to study the timetable Becky laid on the counter.

"No! That's what's so great. They've extended the commuter line. I can pick up a direct bus right outside Dad's gate—no more transferring!"

"Your father will like that," Jeannie said in relief as she returned to the sink. "Where is he, by the way?"

"Putting up that extra cabinet for you in the laundry room, I think." Becky stuffed the bus schedule in her magazine as a page marker.

"How do you like that medical journal?" Jeannie asked curiously as she watched her.

"It's interesting, but I'm going to need your help to understand a few of the terms. When you have time...."

"I can help you right now, if you want. I'm almost done."

"I think I'm mind boggled right now," Becky admitted ruefully. "I'm going to have to take a break for thirty minutes or so. If you don't need any help, I thought I'd go pester the boys."

Jeannie laughed at her honesty. "No, this is the last of it. Incidentally, you kids did a good job on supper."

"*I* did a good job," Becky claimed dramatically. "Bruce and Greg just gave useless advice."

"That goes without saying." Jeannie smiled. "I think we need to go back to our old way in the apartments when the three of you alternated weeks as cooks. Then those boys couldn't weasel out of so much work."

"I'm just being nice to them since this is only our second week out of school. I'll give them advice the rest of the summer." Her laughing vow was thrown over a shoulder as she wandered out the sliding glass door to join her brothers on the spacious deck nestled among the evergreens and oaks at the rear of the house. Jeannie shook her head in amazement as she watched the three perch on the broad wooden railing and immediately launch into a loud, teasing argument. She was glad they were having fun together, but equally grateful they were outside and she didn't have to hear their noisy bantering.

Smiling to herself, she pulled the mixer out of its cupboard and began to get out the ingredients for a lemon icebox pie. Jeannie prepared dinner most of the time, and frequently she would line up part of her meal the evening before. She enjoyed the routine, having so few other regular chores hanging over her head since they had hired the wife of one of Paul's new machinists to come in two days a week to help with the housework.

She even hummed a little as she cooked the lemon custard, set it aside to cool, and broke the ladyfingers into the glass pan. She was concentrating on whipping the cream, not really hearing much because of the noise of the mixer, when Paul walked into the room.

"Mmmm, that looks good," he murmured in her ear as his arms slipped around her waist from behind.

She was so addicted to his touch she didn't even jump.

"Go away, you're interfering with the cook," she ordered, leaning back against him so he couldn't possibly go away.

"What are you making?" His stubbly cheek rubbed against her neck as he tried to peek over her shoulder.

"A very fattening icebox cake. To balance out B.L.T.'s tommorrow night. You can't have any till then."

"I can wait," he said, unperturbed, his hand sliding up to encircle her breast.

"Paul!" Flushing, she glanced outside to see if the children could see them. But the three had left the deck and were tramping along the edge of the woods.

Reassured, she shamelessly relaxed against him, luxuriating in the feel of his hand calmly flowing around her softness, shaping it, exploring it as if he had never known it before.

"I think I'm going to regret your hiring that inventor and those machinists from Cincinnati," she teased, her voice becoming uncontrollably husky as a familiar, warm desire stirred low within her. "You're getting positively decadent since you have all this extra help at work."

"What nonsense are you mumbling?" He reached around her to shut off the mixer.

"I said," she let him turn her in his arms, "that—"

He closed her mouth with his kiss, his lips strong and eager against hers as if he hadn't kissed her in a long time—not since before dinner. Her sigh was absorbed in his own breath as she raised her arms around his neck and hungrily kissed him back, wondering if she would ever get enough of this man, her husband.

"So you plan to keep me exhausted all the time?" His teeth played gently with her earlobe. "I can think of better ways to do it than working the old man to death."

"You would," she gasped, wondering how he had managed to slip his hand so low within the waistband of her slacks. "Paul, the children are right outside."

He sighed, letting his hand rove one last time over her smooth warmth. "They should be getting used to us together by now," he said, but nonetheless raised his hand to a less provocative spot at the waist of her shirt.

She lowered her arms to his chest and studied his face before kissing him lightly on the mouth. "Can I take a raincheck?" Her question was more wistful than she knew.

Paul glanced out at the rapidly setting sun. "In about three hours," he promised gruffly.

He stood at her elbow, watching, as she blended the custard and cream together and poured it over the cake. "Does that have to go in the refrigerator now?" he asked, dipping a little taste out of one corner with his finger.

"Yes, after I cover it." She took a spoon and smoothed over the little hole he had made.

"I'll wash these up while you do that, then." He took charge of the few dirtied mixing utensils.

Jeannie finished before he did, and she leaned against the work counter to watch him as he completed his self-assigned task.

"I don't know if I'll ever get used to how competent you are in a kitchen."

"Good. Someday I may retire from being a house-husband. Then you can wait on me hand and foot."

"I love you."

She said the words to his back, quietly, almost in a whisper.

He was motionless for a brief second before he set the last dish aside to drain and turned slowly to face her. He couldn't seem to say anything, but his love was there in his eyes and she didn't need his words. Not anymore.

They stared happily, foolishly at each other.

"Do you hear them?" he asked, leaning his head slightly toward the window behind him.

At first she thought he meant the children, but she could see through the glass doors by the breakfast nook that they were still walking in the woods. Not under-standing his question, she let her eyes follow the direc-tion he had indicated.

Then she saw the wind chimes. In the dusky light

their pale green and brown designs were barely visible above the flower box at the window.

"You put them up!" she breathed reverently.

"This afternoon. I ran home after lunch."

"They're the most special wedding gift a woman ever received from her husband," she said softly, repeating the words she had mumbled in awe when he had given her the package earlier that week. "I adore them, especially since you explained the meaning of the designs your Papago friend painted just for us."

She moved naturally into his waiting arms, her emotions so heady and confusing that she had to be near him that moment to survive. He held her gently, protectively, his cheek against hers.

"You were right, though," she finally murmured.

"Hmmm?"

"About the chimes. I've been hearing them all the time, even before they were up outside. I don't need wind chimes to remind me of our love."

Her eyes were luminous as she brushed his lips with her own, then resettled against his shoulder. "What you told me was right, so absolutely, wisely right. The reality of our life together is even better than memories."

"I love you, Jeannie," he groaned as he drew her closer against him.

They were satisfied to just hold one another, knowing they would have plenty of time, a whole lifetime together, to express their love. Jeannie was so lost in her contentment that she did not hear the boys return to the deck.

Paul saw the two glance inside, then wave frantically to their sister to join them as they tiptoed stealthily to the sliding door.

But still he said nothing.

He just cocked an amused, parental eyebrow at the three young faces pressed grinningly against the glass, then he tightened his arms around his wife.

Share the joys and sorrows of real-life love in the new *Harlequin American Romances!*™

GET THIS BOOK FREE as your introduction to Harlequin American Romances — an exciting new series of romance novels written especially for the North American woman of today.

Mail to:
Harlequin Reader Service

In the U.S.
1440 South Priest Drive
Tempe, AZ 85281

In Canada
649 Ontario Street
Stratford, Ontario N5A 6W2

YES! I want to be one of the first to discover the new **Harlequin American Romances.** Send me FREE and without obligation *Twice in a Lifetime*. If you do not hear from me after I have examined my FREE book, please send me the 4 new **Harlequin American Romances** each month as soon as they come off the presses. I understand that I will be billed only $2.25 for each book (total $9.00). There are no shipping or handling charges. There is no minimum number of books that I have to purchase. In fact, I may cancel this arrangement at any time. *Twice in a Lifetime* is mine to keep as a FREE gift, even if I do not buy any additional books.

Name _____ (please print)

Address _____ Apt. no.

City _____ State/Prov. _____ Zip/Postal Code

Signature (If under 18, parent or guardian must sign.) **AM 304**